SILVER FOX'S SECRET BABY

AN AGE GAP, BEST FRIEND'S DAD ROMANCE

AJME WILLIAMS

DESCRIPTION

My boss stabbed my heart when he shipped me across country to fix a mistake we made.
He slept with me, knowing that I was his daughter's best friend.
That jerk has no idea I've kept a secret from him for years.
He doesn't know there's a little boy whose eyes look just like his.
If only my disappearance was permanent, he would remain a secret.
But I'm back in New York.
And every breath I take reminds me of the time Henry pinned me against the wall and got me pregnant.
I must make sure that never happens again.
Especially now that I'm in a crisis, and he's the only one that can help me.
The guilt eats at me every time he comes close.
But this silver fox will soon bear the consequences he hoped to escape all those years ago.
Coming face to face with his own flesh and blood would lead to a decision that might break not two... but three hearts.

PROLOGUE

Samantha – Five years ago.

I couldn't believe this was happening. Henry Banion's lips wrapped around my nipple and sucked hard, sending electric shock waves straight to my pussy.

I wasn't a virgin, but I'd never had anyone nearly send me screaming into an orgasm simply from sucking on my nipples. Henry Banion had skills, and it surprised me.

He was the epitome of the sexy, distinguished man with his thick silver hair and his fit body. But as far as I could tell, he'd devoted his life to raising his daughter, the product of a one-night stand with a woman who didn't want to be a mother, and his business, Banion Media Corp.

But clearly, sometime, somewhere, he'd engaged in sexual encounters because he truly knew what he was doing.

The fact that he was doing them to me was a shock. Oh, sure, I'd had a crush on him for some time, but there were so many reasons I shouldn't be propped up on his desk while his fingers probed my pussy walls while his lips continued to feast on my breasts.

The first shock was that Henry found me attractive at all. Then there was the fact that I was his intern, which didn't bother me, but I knew it concerned him because he'd said so just before he kissed me.

For me, the bigger issue was that Henry was my best friend's father. In general, Victoria was a progressive and tolerant woman who wouldn't see anything wrong with my being with an older man or even my internship supervisor.

But I suspected that having sex with her father wouldn't go over very well. I could see how it would be weird.

I wondered if it would help or hurt if she knew that I'd been falling for Henry practically since the day I met him four years ago when she and I first became roommates in college. At the time, it was just an infatuation, and then during my senior year in college, I became his intern and was able to spend more time with him. And the more I did, the more the basic attraction turned to something more. He was smart and sweet and loyal and decent, although I imagine some wouldn't think so now with his daughter's friend on his desk. But the heart didn't care about any of that. I didn't care about any of that. All I cared about was Henry touching me.

"You're so wet," he murmured against my neck. "Is that for me?"

"Yes." God, I ached for him. My pussy was throbbing with need. My hips rocked, wanting more from him.

"You're a needy one, aren't you?"

Was he teasing me? Comparing me to his other conquests? I didn't like either of those ideas. I wanted to be the only woman he thought about.

"Let me take care of you." He dropped to his knees and pushed my legs open. "Heaven help me, this is wrong, but I've got to taste you, Samantha."

"Yes ... please ... now ..."

He dragged his tongue through my folds.

"Oh!" My hands gripped the edge of the desk as a flash of white-hot heat surged through me.

"Fucking hell . . . I love how you respond." He gripped my hips and then buried his face in my pussy. He licked and sucked and did what else I didn't know. All I knew was that it was beyond anything

I'd ever felt. The torture of need was more intense. The delicious build-up had me writhing.

"Oh, Henry . . ." And then I was there. I hit the pinnacle and the most forceful, yet sweetest orgasm rolled over me like a tidal wave.

He groaned as he continued to lap at my pussy. Then he rose, his hands fumbling with his pants. "I need to be in there, Samantha. Tell me I can fuck you."

His choice of words stunned me a little bit. I'd heard it in other types of conversation, of course, but not when I was intimate with someone. I found it surprisingly erotic.

"Yes."

He dropped his pants and then stopped. "Shit, I don't have a condom." He laughed at himself. "It's been awhile."

His admission served to make me want him more. Something about me had caused him to break his celibacy. And also, it was sweet of him to reveal something I imagined most men didn't like to admit.

"I'm on the pill." I pushed away my mother's voice from when I was in high school and first went on the pill to regulate my irregular periods when she told me that the pill might protect me from pregnancy, but not from other things a man might give me. But Henry wouldn't have any diseases. He took care of himself and by his own admission wasn't very sexually active now.

His blue eyes were intense with need yet restraint. "Are you sure you're okay without a condom?"

I looked down at his freed dick, and my pussy clenched tight with need. "Yes. Yes, I want this. I want you."

He shook his head, and for a moment, I thought he was going to change his mind. "I want this too, Samantha, but good God, Tori can never know."

I nodded, only feeling a little guilty that I'd be hiding something so important from her. "I understand."

He kissed me again, groaning as his hand gripped my hip and he positioned his dick at my entrance. "Good Christ, you make me needy." He sank into me, and it was the most glorious feeling in my life.

It was like what you read in romance novels but never believe. He was thick and pulsing with life inside me. And then he moved, and the friction was mind blowing. It didn't take me long to hit the edge and fly again.

"Yes . . . Fuck, your pussy is tight." His head reared back as he drove into me. Liquid heat filled me. Emotion swept through me at the knowledge of this man now being inside me, a part of me, leaving something of his behind. Perhaps I was being a silly young woman, but one can't help how they feel, right?

And that was how it started. Three months before graduation, I began an affair with my best friend's father and internship supervisor. As graduation approached, we showed no sign of ending. I'd secured a job with the company in a different department that would keep me close to him.

I had visions of becoming Mrs. Henry Banion, even though he was still adamant that no one, especially Victoria, could know about us. I believed in time, as his love for me grew, we'd find a way past this odd situation. Victoria might think it was weird, but she'd get over it, wanting her father's happiness and mine.

It was a week before graduation, and I was certain that tonight was the night Henry was going to ask me to join him in his life and business. I hadn't seen him much this week because he'd been very busy. I'd admit, for a minute, I thought he might be ignoring me. But then he invited me to his house in the Hamptons for the weekend.

Victoria was spending most of her time in the library finishing up her senior thesis, so I knew she wouldn't notice that I was gone or ask too many questions. Of course, once Henry asked me to be part of his life, we'd have to tell her, but she and Henry were so close and I felt certain she'd support us.

I determined that Henry's busyness this week wasn't just work-related, but that he'd also been planning a romantic weekend in the Hamptons. Yes, my life was about to be set in the most perfect way possible.

Henry messaged me telling me he was heading out to the house early but that he'd arranged a ride for me once I was done with class.

It was normal for us to travel separately unless our time together was work-related.

When I arrived, I entered the house, surprised that Henry wasn't at the door to grab and pin me against the wall and take me right there like he'd been dying to have me.

"Henry?" I set my overnight bag down in the foyer and made my way through the living room to the back of the house. Henry loved to sit out on the deck and look out over the beach. But as I peered through the window, I didn't see him there.

"Samantha."

I turned my head to his voice. He stood at the bar with a nearly empty glass of bourbon sitting in front of him. Both his hands were on the bar, and his shoulders were hunched with his head slightly down.

Worry gripped my belly. "What's wrong?" I rushed over to him as a multitude of thoughts filled my brain. Was he sick? Was the company going bankrupt? Had something happened to Victoria?

When I reached him, I put my hand on his forearm.

He let out a frustrated groan, and then he pulled away. "We need to talk." He opened the bottle of bourbon, pouring more into his glass. "Do you want a glass?"

I shook my head. "I want to know what's going on?" The only other times people had said "We need to talk," it wasn't good.

He picked up his glass and walked around the bar, heading out to the living room. I stood where I was with a feeling that all my hopes and dreams were about to come apart. Finally, I made my way around the bar into the living room as well, but I didn't approach him.

He took a sip of his drink and then said, "Why don't you sit down?"

I noticed that he couldn't look me directly in the eyes. Because he couldn't, I didn't want to sit down. I wanted to go to him and make him look at me. Make him see the woman he hadn't been able to get enough of for the last few months.

But I wasn't a confrontational woman. That was Victoria. She was assertive and often demanding. I wasn't shy, but neither was I outgoing, nor was I prone to assertiveness.

I sank down on the couch and attempted to shore up my strength to hear whatever Henry was going to tell me, knowing I wasn't going to like it. I stared up at him, willing him to look me in the eyes.

He took another sip and turned to look out the large window toward the ocean. "The thing is . . ."

"Look at me, Henry. I deserve the respect of having you look at me." The words shocked me, as they weren't something I'd normally say. But I couldn't stand that he was hiding from me. That he wasn't decent enough to see how his words would impact me.

His head tilted to the side as if he was trying to stretch out his neck. He took a large gulp of his drink and then turned around, looking straight at me.

He swallowed. "Fuck." He downed his drink and inhaled the deep breath. Whatever it was he had to say, it wasn't easy for him.

"This thing between us has to end. Right now."

Even knowing it was coming didn't lessen the searing pain in my heart. The tears welled in my eyes, but I did my best to sit still and listen to him.

"I'm flying to Los Angeles tonight, where I'll remain until Tori's graduation. You'll finish up your internship as normal, and after graduation, you have a week to get your things together and start a job at the Pac-News Media Group in Seattle. You will head their online media marketing. Your starting salary will be eighty thousand, but in six months, it will go up to one hundred thousand if you prove yourself, as I know you will."

I heard the words but couldn't quite understand them. "But I have a job—"

"Dammit, Samantha, I can't be around you."

I flinched, and the tears that I didn't want to fall streamed down my face.

"Fuck." His hands went to his hips, and he turned away for a moment. When he looked back at me, he said, "I'm sorry. I don't want to hurt you. Surely, you knew this had to end at some point. That point has come. We can't just end. We have to be apart."

"And I'm the one who has to go away? I have to leave my family, my friends, the city I grew up in?"

He looked down, and I supposed it was in remorse. "Yes. New York is the corporate offices of Banion MediaCorp. I can work in other offices for short periods of time, but not permanently."

I let out a humorless laugh. "You are like the rest of them, Henry. Your money and power make you believe that you can dictate other people's lives. I don't want to go."

"I set things up very nicely for you, Samantha. No other company can give you the salary and perks that I've arranged for you. You've complained about the challenges with your father. This is a good time for you to be away from all that. To make something of your own."

For a long moment, I sat, my fingers fiddling in my lap. I wondered what Victoria would do in this situation. Would she threaten to out the affair?

Surely, that was the reason he was sending me away. He didn't want anyone to know about me. I was his dirty little secret. Of all the things going on, that was what hurt the most. He was ashamed of what we'd done.

I determined that Victoria might have a few choice words, but she probably wouldn't threaten to reveal his secret. What good would it do? It might make him change his mind, but then he would resent me, and I didn't want that.

I wanted him to love me. And like an idiot, I thought he had. Now I knew he didn't, or if he did, not enough. His reputation and business were more important. Knowing all that, Victoria would stand up and walk away.

I rose, hoping my wobbly legs would hold me. I let out a breath and looked him straight in the eyes as my heart shattered. "Your secret's safe with me, Henry. Goodbye." I made my way to the door, not even sure how I was going to get home. I supposed if my ride wasn't waiting outside—which now was likely, considering Henry hadn't intended for me to stay—I could order a rideshare back to the city.

"Samantha."

I stopped at the door, looking over my shoulder at him. His expression showed a torrent of emotion. Maybe he was going to change his mind. Maybe he was going to ask me to stay after all. Hope bloomed in my heart.

"Good luck." Then he turned toward the ocean.

At that moment, I grew to hate him. I hated him for not loving me enough. I hated him for never wanting to see me again. I hated him for making me fall in love with him. And I hated him because deep down, I'd always love him.

Initially, I wasn't going to take the job in Seattle. Henry wasn't wrong in that it would be nice to get away from my father, who was never around and made life miserable when he was. But I was close to my mother. And I loved New York. I didn't know a lot about Seattle except that it rained a lot.

But then my new employer began calling and emailing me, discussing the job, and I grew excited about what they wanted me to do and the amount of leeway they were going to give me to do it.

I supposed I should have been thankful to Henry at setting up the job, but I knew he only did it to alleviate his own guilt and to make sure that I was in a position where I could be happy and support myself and therefore stay out of his way.

A week after graduation, I packed up my belongings that I could carry with me on an airplane, deciding I'd buy whatever else I needed in Seattle with the ten-thousand-dollar bonus to my stipend Henry had arranged for me to use in getting settled in Seattle.

The night before I left, I spent time with Victoria. We were weepy, drinking wine and eating ice cream, grieving that we would be apart. She didn't know that I was grieving more than that.

And then I left. I arrived in Seattle and was quickly immersed in my work. The long hours distracted me from the pain of losing Henry.

A week later, I woke up feeling sick to my stomach. At first, I put it off to stress, especially since once I got moving, my stomach settled. A few days later, still waking up to nausea, I decided I should go to the doctor and make sure there wasn't something seriously wrong. The test results came back.

I was pregnant.

I felt completely overwhelmed by this news. I needed to talk to Victoria because she always had the best advice and support, but this was her father's child. She had no idea I'd been seeing anyone, let alone Henry. She'd find it suspicious that I hadn't told her I was dating someone.

I knew what she would say. She'd tell me that the father needed to know. He had responsibilities. But then I remembered the way Henry looked at me that night in the Hamptons. I believed that he didn't want to hurt me, but I also knew that he wanted our lives separated as quickly and as permanently as possible. The last thing he'd want was me contacting him to tell him I was pregnant.

Knowing how important it was to keep our affair secret, I figured all he would do was send money. He didn't want me or this baby, and I had enough money, so he didn't need to know.

Sure, my conscience told me that the ethical thing to do would be to tell Henry. I forced myself to push away the thoughts of Henry being a father to our child and being as devoted to it as he was to Victoria. My child deserved that, but I knew Henry wouldn't provide it. So I made the decision that the baby and I would go it alone.

1

Samantha

No! No, no, no, no, no. This was impossible. "This is wrong." I looked helplessly at my mother's attorney, Lucas Thompson.

His expression was apologetic, highlighted with a shrug. "This was your mother's wish."

I shook my head. "No, it wasn't." I turned my head, looking at my father, who appeared to be doing his best to look nonchalant, but I didn't miss the subtle smirk.

"What did you do?" I demanded. I wasn't normally an aggressive or assertive person, but I'd grown up a lot in the last five years and I'd learned to speak up when it was necessary. Right now, it was beyond necessary. I'd just been told my deceased mother was giving everything she had to my father.

He turned to look at me, trying to have the same apologetic expression that Lucas had, but he wasn't fooling me. "Your mother and I were still married, Samantha. It's not unusual for the husband to be the beneficiary of their spouse's assets."

"But that's not automatic. She updated her will. I was there when she did it." I returned my gaze to Lucas. "You were there as well."

He nodded. "Yes, but then she had a change of heart. She indicated that she hoped that the relationship between you and your father would be improved this way."

I gave a humorless laugh. "That's ridiculous. That assumes that my father cared about me. That he would share what my mother had given him. But we all know that he won't. She, more than anyone, knew that he wouldn't."

My father started to pat my arm, but I jerked it away. "Now, now, Samantha, let's not get greedy and hysterical."

"If I'm greedy, I inherited it from you."

He brushed my comments away like they were a pesky gnat. "It's your mother who spoiled you."

I turned my attention back to Lucas. "I don't know what you have there in front of you, Mr. Thompson, but I assure you, it's not a legitimate will."

He raised his hands in surrender. "Everything is in order. The court is going to see it as such."

"I want to contest it."

My father scowled. "You'll just be wasting a lot of time and money. Money, I'll point out, you don't seem to have."

I wasn't a violent person. And I had never wished to hurt anyone. But at this moment, I wanted to throttle my father. "I don't know what you did, but I'll find out."

"By fighting this, you'll be going against your mother's wishes. That gives me every right to withhold the money from you. And while we're at it, I want to move back into my house again. So, you and that bastard of yours have a week to vacate."

Yes, for the first time in my life, I wanted to kill someone. But it wasn't because my father had stolen my inheritance. It was his referring to my son, Pax, as a bastard. God, if he only knew the truth. My father was one of those men who, on the outside, acted all big, but on the inside, he had an ego the size of a peanut. Because of that, he liked to schmooze with the most important people of New York to make himself feel big. And the one man he'd love to be best buddies with was Henry Banion.

Unable to help myself, I said, "My son comes from better, and richer, stock than you."

My father frowned. "What does that mean?"

"It doesn't matter." I stood up and gave Mr. Thompson a serious look. "This is wrong. And you know it is."

He flinched and opened his mouth to say something, but I had already turned away, exiting his office.

It took me a few minutes to navigate the labyrinth of the law offices Mr. Thompson worked in, but I finally reached the elevator, jamming my finger into the *Down* button. I had to wait several minutes before the elevator arrived. As the doors opened, Mr. Thompson called my name. I didn't bother waiting and instead stepped into the elevator.

He rushed toward me, slipping in just as the doors were closing. "Whew. I made it."

"I wouldn't leave your office unattended. Who knows what my father will steal?"

He leaned casually against the back wall, his hands resting on the rail behind him. "I know this is a shitty deal. I tried to talk your mother out of it. Or at the very least, to leave you and Pax something."

I narrowed my eyes at him. "Are you a party to this, Mr. Thompson?"

His eyes rounded and he straightened. "Of course not."

"You have to be. Because there's no way my mother would've done this."

He looked down for a moment. "You're right. When I saw these papers, I totally agreed with you."

"What do you mean when you saw these papers? You just suggested that she told you all about this."

He shoved his hands into his slacks, keeping his head down like a schoolboy about to get reprimanded. "I'd received a call from your mother about her will. I thought she just had questions, and I had some other pressing clients to work with."

"More pressing than a dying woman wanting to know about her will?" I wondered if my mom had seen this copy of the will and if not, where it had come from.

He sighed. "The point is, I sent one of the paralegals out to talk with her. I said I thought she just wanted the legal aspects explained, and a paralegal could do that."

I wondered if that was true. Were there limitations to what paralegals could do?

"When I realized what was there, I reached out to her, but . . ."

"But what?"

He looked up at me with regret in his expression. "She'd already died. I'm very sorry, Miss Layton. As I said, this will is completely legal."

"So, who wrote this? The paralegal?"

"Not likely, or if they did, they had another lawyer involved."

None of this made sense. I didn't remember anyone coming to see Mom, much less the two visits it would take to write it and have her sign it.

"Where were you?"

He winced. "Like I said, I was busy."

I shook my head. "I don't know what happened, but there's no way this will is legitimate. I'm going to fight it."

I turned away from him, staring at the elevator door, wondering how much longer it was going to take to reach the bottom so I could escape. But escape to what? A week ago, my world came tumbling down. It started with losing my job. I didn't blame my boss for letting me go as my work had faltered the last several weeks of my mother's life as my time was consumed with caring for her and also making sure Pax got enough love and attention. But then my mother died, and I felt like my tether to the world was lost.

And now this. I had no job, my father was evicting me, and I wasn't going to have any inheritance. Every worst nightmare that I worried about but deep down didn't think would happen had just come true.

The elevator reached the ground floor, and when the doors opened, I rushed out.

"Miss Layton." Mr. Thompson caught up to me. "If you think there's something wrong with this, I'll look into it. I'll help you."

I stopped short, looking up at him, my eyes narrowed as they scrutinized him. "How can I trust you?"

He looked at me like a sad puppy. "I screwed up. This is my chance to make it right. I won't charge you for anything. Let me look into this."

His words were a reminder that I would need legal help if I contested the will. Legal help that costs money. Money I didn't have. "Okay, then."

He smiled. "Okay. I'll draw up the necessary paperwork and start trying to figure out what happened. "

"Starting with that paralegal, right?"

He nodded. "Right."

I still wasn't sure if I could trust him, but at this moment, I didn't feel like I had much choice. I left the building, pulling my coat around me as the chilly October air bit into me. With not much money, I decided to take the subway instead of ordering a car to take me home.

As I rode the rails, I tried to work out my next move. Neither Pax nor I had much stuff, so packing up and leaving in a week wasn't going to be a problem. The problem was where was I going to go?

When I arrived home, my mother's housekeeper-slash-assistant, Marie, opened the door. "How did it go?"

I stepped in, taking my coat off, and Marie took it from me. I realized that without my inheritance, I wouldn't be able to continue to employ Marie.

"Everything is going to my father."

Marie drew back, her eyes and mouth both rounded in shock. "No. That's not what she wanted."

"I know, but that's what the will said, apparently." I cocked my head to the side. "Do you remember Mr. Thompson or someone from their office coming to visit Mom just before she died?"

Since I didn't remember it, I must have been out when it happened. I was probably picking up Pax from preschool.

Marie thought for a moment. "I don't recall that. Maybe I was out running errands."

It would've been unusual for her and me both to be out at the same time. "Maybe the hospice nurse was here?"

Marie nodded. "That would be the only thing that made sense."

I made a mental note to contact the hospice service to see the last time the nurse had been here and if he or she had let someone in.

"Is everything all right otherwise?" I asked Marie.

She nodded but continued to look at me with concern. "You said your father got everything?"

I nodded. "None of us got anything. I'm sorry. But I won't be able to keep you—"

Marie waved her arm. "Don't you worry about me. I'll be fine. But what about you and Pax?"

I shrugged. "I have a week to figure that out. Speaking of Pax, is everything all right?"

She nodded. "Yes, he's in the living room with Mrs. Sterling."

My gut clenched at hearing Pax was with Victoria, even though I'd made arrangements for Victoria to come by and watch him while I went to the attorney's office. Marie had enough to do. She didn't need to keep her eyes on a four-year-old boy.

Considering the reality that Pax was Henry's son, and Victoria was Henry's daughter, and neither of them knew that, made seeing them together difficult. Difficult because I felt guilty that she didn't know the truth, but also terrified that she would find out the truth. But since I'd returned to New York when my mother first became ill, I hadn't met anyone or gotten reacquainted with old friends, except for Victoria. And Victoria was the best of friends. I needed her now more than ever.

I entered the living room to see Victoria sitting on the couch, rubbing her belly, which was about six weeks away from giving birth. Pax was on the other side of the coffee table, and together, they were playing with plastic interlocking blocks.

"Are we having fun?" I asked.

Both Pax and Victoria looked up.

Pax's beautiful, bright smile brightened the dark places in my chest. "Look, Mommy, I made a robot."

I wasn't sure that was what I would've called the structure, but now that he told me what it was, I could see how his mind had worked to put it together. "That's fantastic."

"I'm afraid I'm stuck with building towers. I have much to learn when it comes to building blocks." Victoria laughed. Then her eyes narrowed slightly toward me. "Everything all right?"

I shook my head. "Nothing that can't be handled."

Victoria hoisted herself off the couch and made her way over to me. "Is there anything I can do?"

I shook my head. "You've already done enough by staying here with him. I appreciate it. "

"It's nothing. I should probably pay you since I'm getting practice on what it's like to care for a child. I hope mine is as cool and interesting as Pax is."

At the table, Pax continued to build, but a grin spread on his face at hearing Victoria call him cool.

"Why don't you walk me out?" Victoria said.

"I'll be right back, Pax. I'm going to walk Tori to the door."

"Okay."

"I'll see you later, Pax." Victoria waved at him.

"See you later, alligator."

I arched a brow at Victoria, and she shrugged. "I taught him a few things."

As we left the living area and approached the door, she asked, "Did the will reading not go well?"

The burning rage built in me again. "Everything is going to my father."

She looked at me like I was speaking a foreign language. "There's no way Gwen would've done that."

I found Victoria's coat in the closet and handed it to her. "I know.

The only answer is that my father somehow was able to get her will changed. Her lawyer says it's all on the up and up. But—"

"Are you going to fight it?" Victoria slipped on her coat.

"Yes, but I don't know how. My father wants Pax and me out of the house. I lost my job—"

"What? When? Why didn't you tell me?"

"There's just so much going on so fast. They let me go, and I totally get why. My work wasn't up to snuff. And then my mom died and—"

Victoria's arms came around and held me. "I know that when you're in a bad place, it's hard to reach out, but I'm here. What can I do?" She stood back but kept her hands on my arms, looking at me intently.

"At this point, I don't know. Mr. Thompson has agreed to look into it pro bono. I guess the thing I need to do is find a job and a new place to live."

"You can come stay with me and Alex."

"No, I can't. You and Alex are just married and are about to have a baby."

She looked at me, and I got the feeling she was relieved but also felt she needed to insist.

"Really. We'll figure something out."

"Will you be returning to Seattle?"

I shrugged. "I have the same problem in Seattle as I have here. Granted, it's less expensive in Seattle. But if I'm going to fight this will, I need to stick around for a while longer."

"I'm going to think about what you can do. Alex and I will help you figure something out. I promise." She gave me another hug.

I was grateful for the friendship, despite the fact that it came with guilt and terror. Right now, I had more important issues to consider as my life further devolved.

But I'd endure. I'd spent the last five years knowing that wishes and fairy tales didn't come true. Whatever was going to happen next for me and Pax wasn't going to be easy, but we would survive it. I'd become really good at surviving.

2

Henry

I intended to work as was my usual activity when I arrived home from the office. My daughter, Victoria, would tease me that I was a workaholic, but now that she was grown and living her own life, there wasn't anything else for me to do besides work. Luckily for me, I enjoyed it.

The problem I was having tonight, as I'd had most nights ever since my daughter married six months ago, was the lack of focus because Samantha Layton had once again taken up residence in my mind.

I shouldn't be surprised by the way she haunted my dreams and interrupted my days.

Despite my best efforts over the last five years, I'd never been able to completely exorcize her from my mind. The fact that I hadn't been able to completely rid her from my psyche was validation that I'd been right to send her away five years ago. I knew then, as I had rediscovered at the wedding, that I couldn't see her and not ache for her.

I'd been with many women in my life, mostly in my younger days, but none had affected me the way Samantha had. It didn't make any sense. She was so much younger than me. She'd been my daughter's best friend, for Christ's sake. And yet, when she became my intern, I got to know an intelligent, sweet, hard-working, conscientious, and loyal woman. I suppose many women were like that, but there was something about Samantha that wound its way into my heart, tethering itself there, and even after all this time apart, it had never completely let go.

I'd only seen her once in the last six months, but that was all it had taken for her to consume my thoughts again.

I had never married. I never wanted to. Well, that wasn't exactly true. Had I met the right woman, I'd have considered it. I wanted a family. I wanted Victoria to have siblings. But I never met a woman I wanted to bring into my and Victoria's life. The only one who came close was Samantha, but there was no scenario in which I could build a life with her.

That wasn't to say that not long after she moved west, I hadn't had second thoughts about sending her away. I fantasized about ways in which she and I could be together. I pretended that Victoria would be supportive if it made me and Samantha happy. But in the end, it was a good thing I didn't change my mind.

I believe Samantha loved me and that I'd hurt her deeply by sending her away, but she had gotten over it quickly. Her son was proof of that. Maybe it was simply that she found solace in the arms of another man, but I doubted that. Samantha wasn't a woman who gave her love, or her body, easily. So she had to have met someone there, grown feelings for him, and then had his child. I wondered if he had left her too. Or maybe something happened to him. Maybe she was widowed. I could easily find out, but I didn't want to know about Samantha's life with another man.

I knew the most important bit of information, which was that her feelings for me had died. Hell, I'd killed them the night I told her she had to leave.

"Dad."

I looked up from my reverie to see Victoria entering my office.

My chest swelled with emotion to see her round with child, my grandchild. It was inevitably followed by the knowledge that my friend, Alex, was the one who created that child with her. That still irked me, although as time passed, I was growing to accept the situation. As weird as it was, I had no doubt that Alex was devoted to my daughter.

I rose from my desk and went to her, wrapping my arms around her. "What are you doing here? Come, sit down. Can I get you something to drink?"

"No, I'm fine." She took my hand, and we walked to the couch in my office and sat. She let out an "ahh" sound and rubbed her belly.

"Is everything all right?"

"Yes. Here, feel." She took my hand and placed it on her belly. Inside, her child moved as if it was rolling over.

Tears filled my eyes at the wonder of it all. I hadn't had many opportunities to feel Victoria moving inside her mother's belly. Victoria had been the result of a one-night stand. Her mother had used the opportunity to get a nice payoff, and I got Victoria. I was an active participant through all the pregnancy doctor appointments and classes, but Victoria's mother and I were not a couple. By the time she was born, our arrangement had become a business deal. It was the best deal I'd ever made.

"I guess it won't be long now."

"Not soon enough. I'm ready for this little guy to come out." She looked tired but happy.

"You sure it's a boy?" I knew she and Alex had decided to keep the gender unknown to them until the birth of the child. She felt certain that it was a boy, but Alex thought maybe it was a girl. I had no idea how they determined that.

"I'm sure of it now." She handed a sonogram image to me. "His penis is as clear as day."

Once again, emotion filled me to look at the image of my grandchild. Good Lord. He was big. It occurred to me that it was late in the game to be having tests like this unless something was wrong. Not that I was an expert. When Victoria's mom was pregnant, she had two ultrasounds. Both had been early in the pregnancy. Then again, that was twenty-six years ago and maybe the treatment of pregnancies had changed.

"This was taken recently? Is everything all right?"

"I was having some pain and a little bit of spotting, so we had another one."

Alarm shot through me. "Are you all right? Is anything wrong?"

She took my hand and squeezed it. "Everything's fine, Dad. I promise."

"Should you be up and around? Maybe you should be resting."

She rolled her eyes. "This isn't the Middle Ages. Walking and moving around are good for me at this stage. The doctor said there's no reason I shouldn't continue with my normal activities, but just rest a few times throughout the day. So, I'm resting here."

"As long as you're all right."

She nodded. "My life is nearly perfect. So different from Samantha's."

Hearing Samantha's name sent pain through my chest, but I did my best to keep it from showing on my face. "I guess it's difficult losing her mother."

"Losing her mom is probably the worst of it, but today, she went to the lawyer's office for the reading of the will, and Carl Layton is getting everything."

My brow furrowed. "That doesn't sound like something Gwen would do."

"I know it. You know it. Samantha knows it. She's going to have it contested, and luckily, her lawyer's willing to help her pro bono because she was recently laid off and Carl's kicking her out of the house."

What the hell? "Carl Layton has always been a motherfucker."

"We have to help her, Dad. I've been trying to figure out who might need someone like her. Do you think Ollie Cantor would hire her? I saw that his PBS show was looking at maximizing social media more."

My gut clenched at the thought of Samantha going to work for Oliver Cantor, Playboy Extraordinaire. His television show was less about building a business and more of a hobby of a son of an ultra-wealthy billionaire. "Maybe, but I'd worry about the stability of working with him. He could change his mind and the show and everybody working on it would be gone."

Victoria cocked her head to the side as if she was thinking about that. "I guess. I'd hire her, but I just put everything in place so that I can take time off when the baby comes. I'm down to one lean, mean business machine, and I can't afford to take her on. Plus, it wouldn't be right to get rid of somebody who has been loyal to me to give her a job." Victoria scrunched up her face. "Is that bad?"

"It's not bad, honey. Besides, she could go back to Seattle."

Victoria pouted. "I don't want her to go back to Seattle. Besides, the Seattle job laid her off. Why go back?"

"Maybe she has a life there." I thought of her son's father. What was the deal with them?

"Do you think you could call him and have him hire her back? I mean, you did get her that job in the first place," Victoria asked.

I nodded, even though inside I was saying no, I wouldn't do that. The thought of Samantha leaving again wasn't sitting right with me, which didn't make any sense because the situation hadn't changed much. She wasn't my intern, but she was still my daughter's best friend. And at forty-eight years old, I was still a pervert to be lusting after the twenty-six-year-old woman. If she stayed in town, she would continue to occupy space in my head, and wouldn't it be better to make that stop? Or at least dwindle down to almost nothing like it had been before? For that to happen, she needed to leave, and yet . . .

"If I called her boss, he might want her to go back to Seattle."

"But he allowed her to work from home for a while," she said hopefully.

"Maybe he can't allow it anymore. Maybe that's why he let her go." It couldn't have possibly been for poor work, unless caring for her mother had impacted her job.

Victoria sank back on the couch, staring ahead as she idly rubbed her belly. "There must be something we can do. She's a mom. She can't be left destitute. What father would do that?"

"Carl Layton would. He'd sell his own mother."

"I was over there today. Her little boy, Pax, is such a cutie patootie. I hope little Hank here is as cool as him."

I arched a brow. "Hank?"

She grinned at me. "Yes, that was the other reason I came to talk to you. Alex and I have decided that if the baby is a boy, which the sonogram clearly shows it is, we want to name him Henry."

I shook my head. "Does Alex think this is going to change my opinion about him?"

She made a face at me. "Naming him Henry was my idea, and Alex went along with it. And maybe there was an idea that you would soften to him a little bit more than you have, but he also knows that you're a stubborn, hard-headed man, so he's not holding his breath."

"You know, I don't like to be called Hank."

"We're not calling you Hank. We're calling the baby Hank. It's cute, Dad."

I shrugged. "Whatever you say, sweetheart."

We finished our conversation, and then I helped her up from the couch and walked her to the door. She was heading home to her husband, where her life was now. That irked me about Alex too. He got so much of her time.

I returned to my desk with the intention of going through reports, but of course, Samantha was first and foremost in my mind. But now it wasn't the memory of seeing her again six months ago at Victoria's wedding that haunted me. Now was the idea that she was jobless and homeless due to that fucker, Carl Layton. Carl was one of those assholes who was always trying to rub elbows with people of my social stature. I was sure he would've liked to have been viewed as being one of us. But he was too much of a dick.

Still, maybe I could act like I was including him as a buddy, and he'd learn to look out for his daughter like I had with mine. I quickly dismissed that idea. Carl was incapable of love. Oh, sure, he was able to fake it. He'd been able to convince Gwen, a woman from one of the oldest moneyed families in the city, that he was devoted to her. But he stopped trying to fake it a long time ago, and Gwen was too proud, or maybe she actually loved him, to get rid of him.

I began racking my brain for people I knew who might need Samantha's skills. A couple who came up wouldn't be a good fit as they weren't family-friendly employers, and as a single mom, Samantha would need that.

The other problem that needed to be solved was that she needed a place to live. Even if she got a new job tomorrow, unless it had a signing bonus or she had some savings, she was going to have a difficult time finding an affordable place in Manhattan. Deposits and first-month rent were outrageous, even in tiny apartments.

"Mr. Banion."

I looked up to see Knightly, my butler and assistant, in the doorway.

"Yes, Knightly."

"Your dinner is ready. And also, Mrs. Tillis wanted to know if she should spruce up the nursery on the third floor. Her thinking is that Victoria might come and visit with the new baby more often if they had a place."

I furrowed my brow. "She and Alex have a home not too far from us. Why would she need to stay here?"

Knightly shrugged. "I think Mrs. Tillis would love to have a child in the home again, Sir."

"Mrs. Tillis wants that, eh?" I had no doubt Knightly did two. My own parents were too stiff to be warm, loving grandparents to Victoria. No, that role had been filled by Mrs. Tillis and Knightly.

Knightly's lips twitched up. "Yes, sir."

I stood and made my way toward the dining room for dinner. I was amused by Mrs. Tillis's thinking, even as I knew there was no need to have a place for Victoria and her child.

I stopped short just before the dining room.

"Is everything okay, Mr. Banion?"

"Yes, I think so. Have Mrs. Tillis prepare my mother's old room and the nursery."

Knightly nodded. "Of course."

As I entered the dining room and sat at the large, empty table, I knew I was going mad. I was about to do something that absolutely should not be done. And yet there was no stopping me.

I was going to invite Samantha and her son to stay at my house, and I was going to find her a job in my business.

Truly, it was an exercise in sadism. The woman was haunting me six months after I'd last seen her. How was it going to be to see her every day in my house?

3

Samantha

Eight thirty at night was the first time during the course of the day that I could relax and breathe. All the day's to-dos were done, from getting Pax up and off to preschool, dealing with my mother's effects, trying to figure out how my father had ended up as my mother's beneficiary, starting to pack to move, as well as looking for a new place to live and applying to jobs.

Now with Pax in bed and my brain too tired to do anything, I poured myself a glass of wine and went into my mother's sitting room. I thought I might read a book, but I wasn't sure I had the brainpower for even that.

I had just taken a seat in her chair, closing my eyes and inhaling the scent of her that lingered and offered calm, when there was a knock on my door.

So many things were going wrong in my life, so I suppose it was natural that I assumed it was my father ready to evict me. I considered ignoring it, but if it was my father, he'd become more insistent and possibly wake up Pax and scare him.

When I was growing up, we had live-in help, including a butler and a housekeeper. When my mom became ill, mom encouraged them to seek new employment. Not because she needed to save money, but because she knew their jobs with her would be coming to an end and she wanted them to find secure employment.

Only Marie had stuck around, but Marie was off in her room probably doing like I'd been doing, looking for a new job. So if the door was going to be answered, it had to be by me.

I set my wine down and rose from the chair, feeling the weight of the world on my weary bones. I went through the foyer to the door, looking through the security screen.

I gasped. What was Henry Banyan doing here? The memory of him telling me that I had to leave and that we couldn't see each other ever again flashed through my mind. With it came the raw emotion of pain, followed by anger.

I took a breath and did my best to stand up straight and hold my head high as I opened the door.

"Hello, Samantha. I'm sorry to drop by so late—"

Maybe it was from exhaustion, or maybe the inability to deal with one more hit in my life, but I'd hit my limit. "I just buried my mother and I've been staying out of your way. I tried to get out of going to Victoria's wedding, but I stayed away ever since. You don't need to come run me out of my home, Henry."

His silver brows rose to his hairline. "I'm not here to run you out."

"As soon as I deal with my mother's estate, I'll be gone." I had no idea how long that would take or where we'd go.

"Samantha, I'm not here to tell you to leave."

His words finally sank in, but my anger and frustration continued to simmer. "Then why are you here?"

"I was hoping to talk to you. It's cold out here. Can I come in?" He gave me a soft smile.

I thought about Pax upstairs in bed and of my secret. Fortunately, once Pax was asleep, he was out for the night. I wouldn't have to worry about his getting up and making an appearance. Not that Henry didn't know I had a son, because I was sure that he did.

But I worried that if he saw Pax, he might realize the truth, and I couldn't afford that.

I opened the door to let Henry in. I wanted to keep the conversation in the foyer, but I didn't want to come off as rude, so I escorted him to my mother's sitting room.

"I was just sitting down to have a glass of wine. Would you like something to drink?" Offering him a drink was the polite thing to do, and I hoped that's how he saw it. I determined he was here to give his condolences about my mother, and once that was done, he'd be gone, and once again, we'd be out of each other's lives.

"No, thank you." He took a seat on the couch across from where I sat in my mother's chair. I picked up my wine, taking a sip while inwardly gathering my control.

When I saw Henry, all the pain and hurt returned, but also the feelings of love and yearning and hope. Five years later, he was still extremely handsome. He looked the same except for now, he sported a groomed silvery beard.

He sat on the edge of the couch, his hands clasped together between his knees, and it almost seemed as if he were uncomfortable. "I was very sorry to hear about Gwen. I'm sorry for your loss, Samantha. I know that you and she were very close."

I nodded. "Thank you."

"I hope it doesn't breach confidence, but Tori told me what Carl did. There's no way your mother would have left you and your child out of her will."

Your child. I breathed a sigh of relief that he didn't have even an inkling of the truth.

"I suppose I shouldn't be surprised. My father's antics are well-known." I wondered if that would work in my favor in court because my father was well-known for his greed and my mother was well-known for her love for me.

He nodded. "The only decent thing to come from your father was you, Samantha."

His words reached out and tried to wrap around my heart, but I did my best to stop it. I couldn't afford to soften toward Henry.

"Thank you." Now that he had said all that, it seemed to me that it was time to go. "I appreciate your taking the time to come over." I started to stand.

"I understand that Carl has left you in a difficult place. That's why I'm here. I want to help."

"Like you helped five years ago? Are you going to arrange to send me away again?" The words were out before I realized it.

His eyes closed, and he shook his head. "No. Actually, I'm offering you a place to stay. It's just me in the house. There's plenty of room for you and your son. In fact, you can have an entire floor."

It was impossible that Henry was inviting me to move into his home.

"And I want to offer you a job."

I could only stare at him, wondering what he was thinking. "I don't need your pity or your charity, Henry. I'm not a naïve twenty-one-year-old anymore. I'm quite capable—"

"I know that." He looked at me with pain and regret in his eyes. "I've never felt right about how I treated you five years ago, and I'd like to make that up to you. You don't have to worry about me wanting something more. It's been five years, and we both moved on, right?"

It was strange how much it hurt to hear that he had moved on, that whatever interest he had in me five years ago was gone.

"This will give you breathing room until you figure out what you want to do next. The job and the place to stay are there for as long as you need them."

I shook my head. "That's very generous, Henry, but I don't think I can do that. And I wouldn't want to impose a young boy into your quiet life."

"I could use some excitement in my life. I know Knightly and Mrs. Tillis would enjoy it too. And Caroline would love to bake more cookies."

"That's very nice, but I have Marie to think about."

"Bring her along."

I couldn't be sure I could afford it. Henry was offering me a job, but he hadn't offered me a salary yet. And I couldn't take it anyway.

"I understand your reservations, Samantha. I really do. Please let me do this to make up for my abhorrent behavior five years ago."

I knew I'd be an idiot to turn him down. But I couldn't imagine living in the same home with him, reliving the good, the bad, and the ugly of my time with him.

Finally, he stood. "Why don't you think about it? And if you have any other concerns or issues, let me know and I will do whatever I can to alleviate them."

I stood and walked with him to the front door. "I appreciate your generosity, Henry. I will think about it."

He smiled. "Good. It was good to see you again."

I nodded but didn't say anything because I didn't quite feel the same. I didn't like the conflicting emotions warring within me at seeing him.

When he left, I shut the door, locking it behind him, leaning against it, and blowing out a breath. Then I made my way upstairs and checked on Pax.

Because of him, I really needed to say no to Henry's offer, and yet at the same time, he was the reason I should say yes.

Pax was my priority in terms of keeping him safe and secure and taken care of. Henry was offering me exactly what I needed so I could be a good mom and take on my father. But at what cost? The risks were nearly too much to fathom, the largest of which was that Henry would learn the truth about Pax.

What would he do? Would he care? Would he be angry, or would he understand why I made the decisions I had? Would he take Pax from me?

I squeezed my eyes shut at the pain that came from the idea of losing my son. Of knowing that I'd need to risk it and take Henry up on his offer in order to provide for Pax as I got our lives in order.

4

Henry

I wasn't a daring man. I wasn't one to tempt fate or take risks, at least not since I'd become my father. But as I left Samantha's home, I realized I was being reckless.

I hadn't spent much time talking to Samantha at Victoria's wedding. My memories of that day were strongly mixed with my memories of her five years ago. But tonight, sitting with her and able to focus solely on her, I realized that she wasn't the same woman I'd known five years ago.

At the same time, her pull on me was still magnetic. The need to get to know her as this new woman was maddening. I'd been driven by guilt to help her, but there was also a fierce protectiveness. It was clear she didn't need my protection, and that pleased me. The idea that she had grown into a strong, independent woman made me proud of her, even though I had no right to feel like that.

And holy hell, she was even more beautiful than I remembered. She still appeared to be soft and round in all the right places. But she exuded a maturity and strength she hadn't had before, and that made her sexier.

Yes, I was in trouble, but I would deal with it. I owed her for the way I treated her five years ago. So, I would take her into my home and find her a job at my company, and then I'd do my damnedest to stay away. She needed my roof and my employment, but she didn't need me.

The best thing that could happen was if she declined my offer, and at the same time, I hoped she didn't. I was seriously going around the bend.

When I arrived home, I went straight to my office, working to figure out where I could place Samantha in my business. I should've figured that out first, but clearly, when it came to Samantha, I did things without thinking them through, or if I did, I didn't seem to care about the ramifications.

That was how it had been five years ago when she was my intern. I remembered the first time I'd had a dirty thought about her, and it shocked me. It made me realize that I had been attracted t' her for some time. I'd always treated her with professionalism, but after that moment, I wasn't able to look at her as my intern or my daughter's friend. I saw the woman who made me want her.

I did my damnedest to hide it, but the more we worked together, the more the need for her gnawed deep in my gut. It was so strong that it slowly eroded away the reasons touching her would be wrong until one day, I was no longer her supervisor or her friend's father. I was a man who desperately wanted a woman.

We were in my office. She'd just presented me with her ideas, which to this day I didn't know what they were. She was so lovely with her hair tied back, biting her lower lip in moments of uncertainty, and then smiling when I praised her despite not knowing what the hell she was saying. I knew then that I was in danger, and yet, I didn't heed all the warning bells. I'd stood and walked around my desk, which was normal. But once there, my eyes locked with hers. My hand pushed back a stray strand of thick blonde hair, and in doing so, my fingers touched her soft cheek. Her breath hitched, and that was when I saw the same desire in her eyes that was about to consume me. I did the unthinkable. I kissed her. And then I fucked her.

It was strange how simply thinking about Samantha could make me harder than I'd ever been with any other woman. Here I was, sitting at my desk, supposedly working while my dick was trying to escape my pants. I tried to ignore it until I couldn't anymore. The truth was, I didn't want to.

I left my office and hurried upstairs to my room on the second floor. I dug into the secret drawer at the back of my dresser, pulling out the sex toy. I had discovered years ago that basic jacking off wasn't always very satisfying, but neither were one-night stands. This toy was my compromise. The silicon sleeve covered my dick and could feel like a woman's mouth or a pussy. Of course, most of the time, I was imagining Samantha's pussy or lips. Tonight was no different as I replayed the first time I sank into her body and how electrifying and exhilarating it felt.

I conjured up the memory of her sublime tits and hard nipples. I could have feasted on them forever, but then I found her pussy. She'd been so wet, and if there was any concern in my mind about what I was doing, it vanished as the need to taste her became the only thing I could think about.

It didn't take long to make her come. But I was nearing the edge myself.

I rose, my hands shaking with need as I undid my pants. "I need to be in there, Samantha. Tell me I can fuck you."

"Yes."

I was ready to pound away this crazy need when I realized I didn't have a condom. "Shit, I don't have a condom." I laughed sheepishly at my predicament. "It's been awhile."

"I'm on the pill."

God, I wanted to get inside her, but was she really sure? Was she overcome with lust like I was? "Are you sure you're okay without a condom?"

Her gaze drifted to my dick. "Yes. Yes, I want this. I want you."

So here it was. This lovely, sweet, sexier than hell woman telling me I could take what I wanted, and yet my conscience tried to prevail. "I want this too, Samantha, but good God, Tori can never know."

She nodded. "I understand."

I kissed her again and then gripped her hip as I positioned my dick against her soft, wet, pink pussy lips. "Good Christ, you make me needy." I sank into her and . . . fuck . . . it was like sinking into heaven. "Yes . . . Fuck, your pussy is tight." Desire crashed through me. I relinquished my body to it, my head rearing back as I drove into her again and again.

Her breath came in pants as her fingers gripped my shoulders, and then her pussy gripped my dick like it wouldn't let go. That was it. I thrust in, coming so hard I felt it down to the cellular level.

I slid the sleeve one last time down my cock, coming as the final images of that encounter flickered through my brain. It had been so fucking wrong and yet, for a time, I couldn't stop, and she'd paid the price.

Once the orgasmic high was gone, I carried the toy into the bathroom, rinsing it out. I figured I'd probably be using it quite a bit with Samantha in the house.

I cleaned myself up and put the toy away and climbed in under the sheets.

"You're fucking insane, Henry."

But I was going to do this. I was going to make amends and help Samantha get back on her feet.

IT WAS no surprise that I woke from a dream about Samantha and a raging hard-on. I took care of it in the shower and then dressed for the day.

When I arrived down to breakfast, I let Mrs. Tillis, Knightly, and Caroline, my cook, know that I'd invited Samantha and her son to stay here with us until she got back on her feet. I watched their faces closely, wondering if they had any hint of my carnal thoughts about Samantha.

Mrs. Tillis nodded. "What Mr. Layton did to her is just despicable.

It breaks my heart for her and Gwen, rest her soul."

Knightly nodded. "Miss Samantha definitely deserves better."

Carolyn smiled cheerfully. "That means we can bake more cookies."

Satisfied that they thought I was helping Victoria's friend, I headed to the office. As I looked through all the various positions of all the various media outlets I owned, I wasn't finding one that I could fit Samantha into. I'd figured out years ago that the Internet was going to be important, and so I had invested heavily in our online outlets and social media for all our print, radio, and online media.

Since I didn't have anything open, I was thinking of how I could create a new position when my secretary buzzed me. "Mr. Banion, Samantha Layton is here. She doesn't have an appointment—"

"Send her in." A thrill ran through me that I would be seeing Samantha again. At the same time, it was quite possible she was going to turn down my offer. That would be best for everyone all around, but God, how I hoped she'd accept my help.

The door opened and Samantha walked in. I didn't know what I was expecting, but a voluptuous woman in a charcoal pencil skirt and a powder blue silk top that I could just barely make out the lace of her bra through wasn't it. The polite thing to do would be to stand and greet her, but since my dick had gone full tilt, that wasn't going to happen.

I smiled and motioned to the chair at the front of my desk. "Samantha. How are you? Have a seat. Would you like coffee or something?"

She strode in, exuding confidence, and yet when I looked closely into her eyes, I saw nerves. "No, thank you. I'm sorry to just drop in like this, but—"

I waved her apology away. "Nonsense. You're welcome anytime. Did you have a chance to think about my proposal?"

She sat in the chair, crossing one leg over the other.

I sat up straight and attentive, clasping my hands together and resting them on my desk, giving her every ounce of my attention.

"I have. I'll be honest, Henry. It's hard to let go of the past sometimes."

My heart stuttered to a stop in my chest. She was going to tell me no. "I'm sorry for all that, Samantha. Really, I am. I wish you'd let me make it up to you."

She nodded. "If it were just me, I would decline your offer. It's very generous, but . . ."

I nodded. "I understand."

"But I have Pax to think about. I can't take on my father and raise Pax without a place to live and a steady job." She was going to say yes because it was best for her son, not because of me.

I could accept that. "You won't have to worry about a roof over your and Pax's heads or a salary. You can focus on dealing with your mother's estate and your father."

"But I do need to know the terms of the job. What will I be doing and what would my salary be?"

Good question. I sat back, using the few seconds to think of a job I could give her. "If you could have a dream job, what would it be?" Maybe if she told me what she wanted to do, I could hire her to do it.

She shrugged and let out a breath. "What I would like to do is impossible at this time."

My brow furrowed, intrigued by her comment. "Tell me what it is anyway."

"I'd like to do what Tori did. Start my own business."

"Running social media for companies?" I didn't need that in my company.

"At first, that's what I thought, but then I've been thinking about consulting. Going into large organizations and doing social media audits and assessments, training their people."

Bingo. "That is an excellent business idea, Samantha. How about this? Let me be your first client."

She cocked her head to the side, her eyes narrowing as they scrutinized me. "That makes it sound like you didn't really have a position for me."

I tried not to shift and give away the truth of her comment. "I do have a position for you, but remember, I am wallowing and groveling to make up for my misdeeds with you. So, I want to give you the job you want to do." I couldn't be sure that she accepted that.

"I don't have a business license or any of the legalities to take on a client."

"Then I'll hire you as our social media auditor and trainer, and whatever other job goes with what you want to do." The more I thought about it, the more perfect it sounded. "You will get the experience you need and the ability to set up your processes and systems using my company as your guinea pig. Then when it's time for you to move on, you will have not only my endorsement, but I'm sure many endorsements from the other heads of my various media platforms."

The energy in her changed. It was subtle and yet palpable. The slight upward tug of her lips, the way she sat up taller, and the sparkle in her eye. She was radiant. Her response told me that she thought this situation was perfect as well.

"I would love to do that, Henry." She looked down, and that energy I'd felt a moment before waned.

"Is there a problem?"

"I think your restitution is much more than I deserve based on your offense."

"Not at all, Samantha."

"You're offering me a job and place to stay at great expense to you."

I shook my head. "It's all just money, Samantha. There is no amount of money in the world that could make up for what I did to you, what I took from you. And while I'm being selfish here, I'm hoping that you will take anything and everything that I offer to help alleviate the guilt that I've been feeling all these years."

She let out a breath. "I'm going to accept this position because I am giving something in return. But I don't want you just offering things because you're taking pity on me or because of guilt, and especially because you don't think I'm capable, because I am."

Because my hard-on had finally dissipated, I rose from my chair and walked around my desk, sitting on the edge of it. "Don't think for a minute that I believe the woman sitting in front of me is incapable. I see a strong, intelligent, independent woman who has prioritized her son over her pride. I admire that, Samantha. More than you know."

She gave a single curt nod and rose from her chair. I straightened from the desk, realizing too late that it put us both in very close proximity. The sweet scent of her perfume wrapped around me, and I couldn't stop my eyes from dropping to those luscious lips of hers.

Yes, I was in serious trouble.

I took a step back and then rounded my desk to sit in my chair. "I know you need to pack up and move, so you don't need to start until next week." I realized that I wasn't sure she was taking me up on the offer to stay in my home. The truth was, I could put her in one of our corporate apartments or give her money now to find a place. But I didn't want that. I wanted her close by. Heaven help me.

"I want to get out of the house as soon as possible, but I plan for my stay at your home to be short."

"Of course. Just so you know, you're welcome as long as you need a place to stay. You, Pax, and . . ." I couldn't remember the name of the woman who had worked for Gwen.

"Marie."

"Yes. Marie too. Also, I am giving you a signing bonus."

She gave me a dissatisfied look. "I told you I don't want your charity."

"It's not charity, it's a signing bonus. If it makes you feel any better, you can pay it back through installments from your salary."

She nodded again. "Thank you, Henry."

"You're welcome."

She turned to leave my office. I wished she had that excited energy she showed moments ago. She had been absolutely radiant in that moment, and I wanted her to feel like that all the time. It wasn't lost on me that thoughts like this were what had gotten me in trouble five years ago.

I had to try harder to fight against this need and urge to immerse myself in her. An unsettled feeling grew in my gut that I was going to fail her again. If I couldn't control myself, I would likely hurt her, and I would rather die than shatter her life again.

5

Samantha

I left Henry's office feeling like I'd just agreed to step into the frying pan.

My biggest concern was my son and what Henry might do if he learned that he was Pax's father.

Henry was extremely powerful and influential. It wouldn't surprise me if he had the president of the United States on speed dial. A man like that could take my son from me.

But there was also the risk of falling for Henry's charms again. I would have thought it impossible, considering the pain he'd caused me five years ago.

But today, as I sat across from his desk, he was sweet and charming and owning up to the selfish moves he'd made to force me out five years ago. I saw glimpses of the man I had fallen for during my internship.

I would have to make sure that I remembered how cruel he could be, especially since nothing had changed. I was still Victoria's friend, and now I'd be his employee. All the reasons we couldn't be together still existed, so I'd be a fool to allow my heart to soften toward him again.

Despite my reservations, I was strangely excited. Henry was giving me a job doing exactly what I had been hoping to do.

Granted, I wanted to do it as the owner of my own business, but he was giving me a start. With his recommendation behind me, I couldn't imagine that my business would fail. He was giving me a whole lot more than he needed to pay whatever penance he felt he owed me.

I didn't want his restitution or pity. I wasn't lying to him when I said I would have refused his generous offers if it weren't for Pax.

My own feelings took a backseat to what was most important for my son, which right now was to find him a place to live and get a job so I could support him. So I agreed to walk into that frying pan and had to hope that I wouldn't get burned.

My next stop was to go to Mr. Thompson's office. I knew the will had only just been read yesterday, but how long could it possibly take for him to figure out how my mother ended up signing over everything to my father?

Just like I had at Henry's, I showed up without an appointment, fully expecting to be seen. Unlike Henry, Mr. Thompson forced me to wait. Since I still had a couple of hours before I needed to get Pax from preschool, I settled in.

Forty-five minutes later, Mr. Thompson greeted me and escorted me to his office. "I'm sorry you had to wait so long, but I was with clients. I'm sorry I won't be able to give you much time, either. I can't afford to give up too many billable hours."

"I just need to know what you found out about my father. And how long will it be before I can file something to contest the will?"

He motioned me to sit in a chair as he rounded his desk and sat behind it. "Of course, you can always file any sort of paperwork with the court, but for the judge to really consider it, we need to have strong indications that there is something wrong with your mom's will, and so far, I have not been able to find that. Everything is legal."

"It's not legal if my mother was coerced or deceived."

Mr. Thompson nodded. "That's absolutely true, but as of yet, we have no evidence of that."

"Everyone I have talked to about this has said that there's no way my mother would've given anything, much less everything, to my father. In fact, I remember your saying something similar yesterday. Surely, that points to something not on the up."

His expression was apologetic. "I agree, but that's not proof. It could support the evidence if we found it, but in and of itself, people who don't think your mother would give everything to your father doesn't mean anything. In fact, I would venture to guess most of these people don't like your father, which would give them a reason to support you instead of your father."

I took offense at his words. "These people aren't liars."

Mr. Thompson waved his hand. "Of course not. That's not what I meant. I'm just saying that in a court of law, people's opinions don't hold weight against facts. We need hard proof."

Frustration grew, but I reminded myself that Mr. Thompson was just doing his job. "What did you find out about who went to the house and saw my mother? How did this all happen, because by my reasoning, if my mother was changing her will and told you or whoever that, they would have had to leave her to draw up the paper-work and then come back another time. There hasn't been very often in the last six months that I haven't been in the house and know who was visiting, and I don't recall one lawyer visiting, much less two, just before she died."

Mr. Thompson's brows narrowed, and he nodded as if he were intently considering what I was saying. "I haven't been able to track down all of that yet. We only just found this out yesterday and—"

"How hard can it be to track down your paralegal?"

He let out a sigh and sat back. "Harder than you might think. She left earlier this week on a several month missionary trip to South America."

"Surely, they have telephone service in South America."

"Not in every area. Not apparently where she was going." He sat up, leaning forward again. "I understand that the situation is stressful for you. I promise, I am looking into this."

"But only around your billable hours," I quipped, feeling defeated and yet determined to fight it.

He let out a sigh. "I'm on track to become a partner."

I hadn't started working yet, nor received the signing bonus Henry said he was going to give me. I knew from experience that it wasn't good to spend money before you had it.

But maybe it was time for me to retain Mr. Thompson as my attorney. "How long do you think this will take, and how much would you charge me?"

His brows rose in surprise. "Yesterday, I thought your financial circumstances were tight."

"They've loosened up a little bit."

He thought for a moment. "If you pay your retainer of, say, $3,000, that'll be about ten hours of work and I would imagine that would be enough to track down how this new will came to be. It may or may not include the work to create the papers to contest it and file them in court—"

"Fine." I stood. "Will you draw me up an invoice and send it to me? The meantime, I can give you $1,000 right now, which should give me a couple of hours of work, am I right?" It would nearly deplete my bank account.

He nodded. "Ms. Layton, I meant what I said, that I would do this pro bono."

"But I can't afford to be put at the back of the line because of that." I pulled out a notepad from my purse and wrote down Henry's address. "Pax and I will be at my mother's house for the next day or so, but then we'll be staying here."

He took the paper, looking at the address, his brows rising again. "Riverside Drive."

"It's a friend of mine."

"You have important friends." He said it more to himself than me. Then he looked up. "I assure you, we'll get to the bottom of this."

"My mother trusted you, Mr. Thompson. I hope I can too."

"Please, call me Lucas." He came around his desk. "I promise you, I'll figure this out. Gwen was a lovely woman, and she was devoted to you and your son."

I left his office, getting into the elevator for the long ride down. I wasn't normally an assertive or demanding person, and when I was, I found it took a lot of energy from me. So when the elevator doors closed, I leaned against the wall, hoping I did enough to convince Mr. Thompson . . . Lucas . . . to take my case.

None of this today had been easy, but I remembered my mother once telling me that challenges were God's way of making us stronger so that we could live a more fulfilling life and meet our potential. I wasn't sure what lessons were going to be learned by taking Henry up on his offer or pushing Lucas Thompson harder to look into my case.

In fact, I wondered if maybe I should get another lawyer. Who knew what sort of screws my father was going to put on Lucas?

Then again, he'd probably do that to any lawyer I hired. If my father had put all his time and energy into legitimate work instead of scheming and manipulating, he'd be successful. Of course, it probably wouldn't be as fun for him. I'd long suspected that there was a part of my father that enjoyed hurting people. Like yesterday, I think he relished watching my reaction to learning that I wouldn't be getting anything from my mother.

I returned home and found Marie in my mother's office.

When I walked in, she jerked up and gave me an expression as if she'd been caught. "Oh, I'm sorry. I didn't realize you'd be back so soon." She shut the drawer.

Her behavior was odd, considering she'd been my mom's assistant and probably knew more about what was in this office than my mother did. "What's going on, Marie?"

She came around the desk looking forlorn. "I just can't believe your mother would have done this to you, and I was hoping that maybe there was something in her desk that would prove she hadn't."

I nodded because that made sense. "Why are you acting like you shouldn't've been doing that?" That was the part that didn't make sense.

"I didn't want to tell you because I didn't want you to get your hopes up. I thought I would just look and see if there was something we could use, but if not, well, then you wouldn't be disappointed."

"I appreciate your trying to spare my feelings. I suppose the person—probably my father—who put this in motion likely got rid of any evidence. The good news is that I have a job and a place for us to stay. It also means that I can keep you on. I'll be honest in that the job will be mostly helping with Pax, but I'm also planning on starting a business, and maybe you can help me with that too."

Marie's eyes lit up. "How did this happen? It's like a miracle."

I nodded. "The man I had interned for during my senior year in college has offered me a job. He also happens to be Victoria's father. He's allowed us a place to stay in his house."

"He must have a big house."

"It's on Riverside. It must be five or six floors."

She gave me a devilish smile. "Your father will be so jealous."

She was right. And while there could be some enjoyment in making my father jealous, I also knew that it was also the sort of emotion that made him do despicable things.

6

Henry

Samantha, her son, and Marie were due to arrive at any moment. I stood just inside my office leaning against the door, waiting with the anticipation of a teenage boy expecting to see a girl he liked. It was fucking annoying, especially since I'd never been like this as a teenager or in college. Back then, if there was a girl I liked, I let her know, and she always liked me back. I never had trouble with women.

But of course, this was different because while the attraction to Samantha was as strong as ever, all the reasons I couldn't have her continued to exist. I'd made a deal with myself that I would allow this one-time encounter to welcome her and her son and Marie into my home and get them settled, but then I'd do my damnedest to stay out of their way.

I learned five years ago not to tempt myself around her, so my safest bet was to avoid her. Perhaps it was rude, but then if she thought I was an ill-mannered pest, that would work in my favor.

The knock on the door came, and I shut my eyes as my heart picked up its pace. I listened as Knightly made his way to the front door. I pulled in a long breath, calming my nerves. I wanted to be welcoming but not appear overly eager.

"Welcome, Miss Layton. Mr. Banion has arranged for you to stay on the third floor," Knightly greeted them.

I gave them a moment to get inside the house, and when I heard the door close, I straightened from the door, took another breath, then opened it and stepped out into the foyer. "I thought I heard the door. Welcome."

Samantha smiled, but it looked forced. "Thank you for letting us stay. We'll do our best not to get in the way."

I waved her comment away. "Nonsense. Besides, this home is very large." I looked down at the child, who was hiding behind Samantha's legs. "This must be Paxton."

Samantha tensed, and I wondered what it meant. Was she worried I wouldn't like her son? Sure, I didn't like the idea that she had moved on so quickly after she left, despite the fact that I had no right to feel like that since I was the one who'd pushed her away. But I certainly wasn't going to hold that against her son.

I squatted down, holding out my hand. "It's nice to meet you."

His right hand came out, and I took it and gave it a shake.

"Everyone calls me Pax."

"That's a terrific name, Pax. Did you know that it means peace?"

Pax his eyes lifted to his mother's, as if he was uncertain how to respond.

"Welcome to my home, Pax. I hope that you and your mom and Marie will be comfortable here while you stay." I straightened and reached out my hand toward Marie. "I'm Henry Banion. It's nice to meet you."

Marie gave me a firm shake. "It's nice to meet you too, Mr. Banion. It's a wonderful thing that you are doing. And it's really nice to meet Victoria's father in person."

"How about I show you to the third floor and all the rooms that are available to you up there?" I turned to Knightly. "Can you arrange to get their things upstairs as well?"

"Yes, of course."

I led my guests toward the stairs. "We do have an elevator if you would prefer. But I find if I take the stairs, I don't need to go to the gym."

"The stairs are fine," Samantha said.

We reached the second floor, rounding the landing and heading up to the third. "What's on this floor?" Pax asked.

"Let's not be nosy, now," Samantha said to him.

"It's not nosy. The second floor is where I stay. And when Tori was growing up, she was on the floor as well. I believe you've been on this level before, Samantha."

She stared at me and blinked wide-eyed. It was only then that I realized what I had said.

Five years ago, there had been a time or two when she and I had been working together in my home office and had snuck up to my bedroom to have sex.

I swallowed. "In college, when you and Tori would come here to get away and study."

She nodded. "Yes, I came a few times." Her eyes closed and her cheeks reddened. I wasn't sure why until I considered the innuendo in her words. She had come a few times. Boy, had she ever, and each time she had, I was driven to make her come again.

I cleared my throat and continued up to the third floor. "This had been my parents' floor, but then Tori commandeered it several months ago when she moved back for a short time."

It didn't seem necessary to tell them that at the time, my and Victoria's lives were under threat by a mobster-like businessman named George Pitney who took umbrage at what my news outlets were reporting about him.

In the end, Alex had saved both myself and Victoria at significant harm to himself, which was another reason it was difficult to hold the grudge about his falling for my daughter. I knew without a doubt that he would give his life to save her, and a father couldn't want more for his daughter than for a man to love her the way Alex did.

"I was thinking that you could stay in this room, Samantha. It has a lovely window seat overlooking the back garden. It also has its own ensuite bathroom, and through this door here, you can access the nursery where young Pax can stay." I led her through the door into the nursery.

"This nursery is as large as the apartment I grew up in," Marie said as she took in the room. The room was indeed large, but it wasn't just a bedroom, it was also a playroom.

"Pax could ride a bike in here," Marie finished.

"I don't have a bike."

I smiled down at the boy. "Well, I can get you one—"

"These rooms are lovely, Henry. Thank you." The way Samantha had cut me off told me she didn't want me buying her son a bike. She was setting limits, and while they stung a little bit, I was grateful because I knew I was vulnerable to breaking the boundaries I was trying to set.

"I asked Knightly and Mrs. Tillis to bring down some boxes of toys that we had stored. I'm sorry to say that many of them are old toys from when I was a child or when Tori was a child, but hopefully, Pax will be entertained by them."

For the first time, Pax left the clutches of his mother's side and wandered through the room. He held his hands clasped behind his back, and I wondered if it was something Samantha had taught him as a way for him to keep his hands from touching things he wasn't supposed to.

He came to a shelf filled with old trucks that I had played with as a child. His eyes turned to his mother, a desire to play evident. "Can I play with these?"

"That's why they're here. For you to play with," I said.

His hands unclasped, but he still looked at Samantha, and I had to admire the impulse control of this young man that he waited for his mother's okay.

"Yes, you may play with them."

His hands shot out, grabbing the large dump truck and pulling it down onto the floor. He tilted the back up and then looked up at me. "Is there something I can dump?"

I smiled as a wave of emotion filled me at seeing a young child in this house again. "There are some blocks over on that shelf over there."

This time, he didn't wait for his mother's permission as he rushed over and grabbed an arm full of blocks and brought them to the truck.

"If you'd like, I can show you where Marie can stay."

Samantha hesitated.

"It's just right across the hall. We won't be far from him."

Samantha nodded, and she and Marie followed me across the hall to the room that had once been my father's.

When we finished, we headed back over to the nursery where Pax had found more items to use in the dump truck. He had also pulled out the backhoe truck and was scooping up blocks with it.

"You are welcome to any spot in the house. Mrs. Tillis, Knightly, and Caroline are prepared to assist you with anything that you might need."

"I don't want to intrude on your staff."

"Nonsense. They are all giddy with joy at the idea of having a child in the home again. I do believe Carolyn has baked enough cookies to feed an army. But you also have access to the kitchen and all the amenities there. We have a pool and a gym if you'd like to make use of those. And if you have a vehicle, you can park in our garage. Essentially, *mi casa es su casa*."

Again, Samantha's smile looked forced. I knew she was grateful, but I also understood that this wasn't a situation she wanted to be in.

"I generally eat at six thirty if you would like to join me for dinner. I just need to let Carolyn know to make enough for four instead of one."

Inwardly, I kicked myself because after I brought them to their rooms, I was supposed to leave them alone. I'd been planning on having Caroline serve them dinner, and I would either eat in my office or at a different time. Yet here I was, inviting them to eat with me.

"You're being very kind, Henry." Samantha's non-answer to my invitation told me she didn't want to join me. Again, I was hurt and relieved by that.

With a slight nod, I prepared to make my exit. "I will let you all settle in. And again, if you need anything, please don't hesitate to let me or Knightly or Mrs. Tillis know."

I left them in the nursery and headed downstairs, making a beeline to my office, shutting the door behind me and leaning against it.

I should've put her up in one of our corporate apartments. I should've given her a bigger signing bonus so she could find her own place. I should've done anything but have her stay in my home.

Perhaps this was my penance for how terribly I had treated her five years ago. I'd been a selfish dick, afraid that the world would find out I had been fucking my daughter's friend, who happened to be my intern. In this day and age, that sort of scandal would likely require me to resign as the CEO of my own company. Then there was the fear of Victoria's response and losing the only family I had.

Because I was a coward, I had done a despicable thing and sent Samantha away. This time around, I needed to be a man. I needed to control my heart and my dick and stay away from Samantha. I had to make right what I did wrong, and part of that was to keep my hands to myself.

Heaven help me.

7

Samantha

Coming to stay at Henry's house was difficult enough. I didn't need to mortify myself by saying things like, "I came a few times."

When Henry first mentioned my visiting his home, I hadn't thought about the times I'd visited with Victoria. I had thought about the times I had been with him. Initially, I was shocked that he had mentioned it. But then he clarified what he meant, which made me feel foolish, and then I made it worse by responding with "I came a few times." I hadn't meant it as innuendo, but the minute it escaped my mouth, that's what I heard. I could only imagine what Henry thought of that. The worst-case scenario was that he believed that I was still interested in him. For a moment I wondered what he would think about that, if it were true, which it wasn't.

I decided that the comment had unsettled him because Mrs. Tillis showed up around five asking if we would be coming to dinner at six thirty and making Henry's excuses that he wouldn't be there. When I last saw him, he'd invited us to dine with him, and now, he'd changed his mind. It had to be because he didn't want me making comments that suggested he and I had been more than friendly at one time.

I told Mrs. Tillis that we didn't want to impose on Henry or her or any of the other staff, but she waved my concern away. "We are happy to have you stay. It's nice to have new energy and life in the house. I hope you will indulge us."

That evening, we ate dinner in the dining room without Henry, and afterward, we finished unpacking and I helped settle Pax into his new room.

He'd been very excited about all the toys in the large space, but when it was dark and time to go to bed, he grew frightened of the new space. I read him stories and stayed with them until he was asleep, and then I went to my own room.

I lay awake wondering about the wisdom of taking Henry up on his offer. It was a reminder of how hard I needed to work, not only to make the money I needed to find a suitable place to live for me and Pax and Marie, but also to fight my father over my mother's will.

The next day was the weekend, and I spent as much time as I could with Pax, going to the park and other excursions. It was fun for him, and it got me out of the house and away from the possibility of running into Henry.

I wondered if Henry was avoiding me too because even though I was staying in his house, I didn't see him Saturday or Sunday. I had remembered Henry was a workaholic, but the fact that he didn't have dinner in the dining room over the weekend was a sure sign that he was avoiding me. I should have been happy about that, but in truth, it irritated me.

I lay in bed on Sunday night, unable to fall asleep. The more I thought about Henry's behavior, the more annoyed I got. Finally, I gave up, getting out of bed and putting on my robe. It was well past midnight as I crept down the stairs to the kitchen, thinking a glass of milk and a snack would help put me to sleep. Sleep that I needed since tomorrow, I would be starting my new job.

I entered the kitchen, and the moon glowing in the window lit up the room enough that I could keep the lights off. Henry had said we could help ourselves to anything, but I still felt a little bit like I was sneaking around where I shouldn't be.

I opened up the fridge and found the carton of milk. Taking it out, I set it on the island in the middle of the kitchen. Henry hadn't been joking when he said Caroline made enough cookies to feed an army, and I figured no one would notice if I snagged a couple. I opened a cupboard to pull out a glass and a small plate.

"Can't sleep?"

I jumped, letting out a small yelp. I spun around, feeling embarrassed at being caught.

Henry held up his hands to his sides. "I'm sorry. I didn't mean to startle you." He was wearing a robe, but it was loosely tied, opening in the front to reveal the fact that he wasn't wearing a shirt underneath. For a moment, I was drawn to his chest. I remembered laying my head on it and listening to his heartbeat, fooling myself into believing it beat for me.

"I'm sorry—"

"Don't be sorry. I told you the house was yours." He came around the island toward me, and I was glad to see that he was wearing lounge pants because I knew I wouldn't be able to handle seeing any more than what was already exposed.

I stepped back as he pulled out two plates and two glasses from the cupboard, setting them on the island. He poured us both some milk and brought the tray of cookies onto the island. "Do you mind if I join you?"

"I should be asking you that."

He pulled out one of the barstools from under the island, motioning for me to sit. He pulled another one out and sat and then took several cookies off the tray, setting them on his plate. "Have you all settled in?"

I sat down on the stool, taking a cookie from the tray and dunking it in my milk. "We are. Thank you."

Henry cocked his head as I pulled my cookie from my milk and took a bite. "I haven't done that since I was a kid." He dunked his cookie in his milk and took a bite. His eyes closed as if he were savoring the taste. My heart skipped a beat remembering how sweet he'd been to me years ago.

"I forgot how good that is." He smiled warmly at me, but I fought the warm, fuzzy feeling that tried to grow.

I'd rather be irritated at him. "Are you avoiding me?"

He tensed as he dunked his cookie back into his milk. "Why would you say that?"

"Because we're in your house, and I haven't seen you since the day you showed us to our rooms. It's really important to me that we don't disrupt your life. I don't want you hiding in your office or wherever it is you spend your time because we're here."

"It's not unusual for me to spend the majority of time in my office."

I studied him, wondering if he was telling me the truth. "If you're worried that I might grow attached to you or something, you don't have to worry about it. You don't have to avoid me. That comment the other day was about Tori, not you."

His jaw tightened as he looked at me. "I'm not worried that you'll grow attached to me. I know that you've moved on. Your being a mother is proof of that."

It was my turn to flinch. I should've been relieved that he believed I'd been with another man after moving away from New York. But mostly, I felt guilty.

He let out a breath, the tension releasing with it. "And speaking of that, Samantha, Pax is a beautiful little boy. I don't know how long you've been a single mom, but I can see that you're a very good mother."

It meant a lot to me for him to say that. For all his faults, Henry was an excellent parent, so he would know. "Thank you."

Our gazes held for a minute, and the air between us started to thicken and crackle. I felt the pull from my heart toward him as I had five years ago. But I wasn't that silly young girl anymore, so I turned away, picking up my milk and taking a gulp.

Once I swallowed, I said, "You haven't told me where to report for my job tomorrow."

There was a pause, but I didn't look at him to figure out why. "Come to my office. We can discuss in more detail the various platforms and figure out which we should focus on first."

"What time should I be there?"

"I know you need to deal with Pax in the morning, so after that, you can come in."

I stopped trying not to look at him and narrowed my eyes. "I don't want special favors, Henry. I can work a full schedule just like everyone else. I was doing it before I returned to New York."

Henry let out a long sigh, and I felt embarrassed at my outburst.

"We have many parents, mothers and fathers, who have flexible schedules so that they can have quality time with their kids. But beyond that, I don't know why it angers you so much that I would try to do something nice for you."

I rolled my shoulders, trying to relieve the tension. "I'm sorry. It's just important to me that I make my own way."

He studied me for a moment, and it made me uncomfortable. What was he seeing? "There was a time when you could accept help easily."

"I was younger and naïve. And I needed more help then."

He stood, and as he did so, his robe loosened more, showing the entire expanse of his chest. The man was pushing fifty, and yet he still looked like he had a chest sculpted from marble. My hands itched to press against the hard warmth of it.

He picked up his plate and glass, taking them over to the sink. "Have a good rest, Samantha." He made his way to exit the kitchen.

"Good night, Henry."

When he left, I let out a breath, feeling like an idiot. He must think I was an ungrateful brat.

I put my plate and glass in the sink and went up to my room. I lay in bed willing sleep to come, but it still eluded me. Only this time, I wasn't thinking about Henry and how he was avoiding me. I was thinking about Henry and his chest.

I was thinking about the times that I had come to his home to work with him, and once the work was finished, he would take my hand, lead me to the elevator, and take me up to his room.

An ache filled my chest as the memory of his gentle hands on my body made me believe he loved me. The way the feral need shining in his eyes made me feel I was the most desired woman in the world. The way he encouraged me to explore his body, to tap into my own desires that made me feel more like a woman than I'd ever had. I wasn't a virgin when Henry first had sex with me, but there was so much I hadn't done or experienced until him.

The memory of the first time in his bed, when he finished bringing me to climax with his mouth and he rose over me. I expected him to enter me, but instead, he rolled us both until he was on his back.

"I want to watch you ride me, Samantha. I want to see you chase pleasure."

The idea of him watching me was embarrassing, but he guided me over him, and once I sank down, filling my body with his erection, I couldn't think of anything but pleasure.

I closed my eyes and let my body take over.

"Yes, that's it, my sweet Samantha. Feel the power. Let the sensations guide you."

I rocked and then rose over him, sinking down again, moaning as the pleasure grew.

"You're so fucking beautiful."

His words added to the moment, ratcheting up my need. It coiled tight in my belly until I felt out of control. My body wasn't my own. It was completely his.

"Yes . . . Samantha . . . yes . . ." His hands gripped my hips. He rose under me, meeting me with each move. "I'm about to come, baby . . ." This thumb rubbed over my clit, and I detonated.

I cried out, my head thrown back as pleasure rocked through me.

"Fuck!" Henry bucked, his essence filling me as we rode through the storm together.

I was completely boneless as I collapsed over him. My head rested on his chest. I felt his heartbeat against my cheek and tumbled full on into love for him.

He held me, kissed the top of my head. "My sweet Samantha."

Like a fool, I'd heard those words as a confession of love.

Today, I was smarter, stronger, and oh, so much less gullible. This time, I wouldn't let Henry's kindness and generosity dupe me.

8

Henry

I didn't sleep well last night as memories and emotions collided within me. Seeing Samantha in my kitchen last night did weird things to me. When I first saw her taking the milk from the fridge and then looking for glasses, I had this feeling like the world was right. Her being in my house with me was right. When she turned toward me, the way the moonshine illuminated her made me catch my breath. She was so fucking beautiful. Then everything went downhill from there.

I couldn't blame her for being distrustful of me considering how I had treated her five years ago, and just at the same time, it was frustrating. But as I lay in bed last night, I knew that her keeping an emotional and physical distance was crucial to this arrangement's success. There was no scenario in which she and I could build a life together, so there was no sense in letting myself be drawn to her.

This morning, I was up and out of the house early and at my desk by six thirty. I didn't want to be like a sap, hanging around to see her. Besides, I had things to do to get ready for her to start her job.

Last week, I had asked the heads of all the various media platforms to pull together their online and social media data so I could have it ready for Samantha to review. This morning, I'd had my admin pull it all together into a single file and I went through it, noting the areas that I felt might need attention.

At 7:59, my admin buzzed me, letting me know Samantha had arrived. I told my admin to send her in and rose from my desk, buttoning my suit jacket and coming around my desk to greet her as she entered.

Today, she wore a form-fitting navy dress that made my mouth go dry. It was a professional dress not meant to be sexy, and yet it was.

"Good morning, Samantha. Welcome to your first day back at Banion media."

Her smile was polite, but like before, without warmth. It was a stark contrast to her first day of her internship five years ago when she was filled with enthusiasm.

I was going to ask if everything had gone okay this morning getting Pax off to preschool but decided she would find the question intrusive or feel that I was questioning her abilities. So instead, I invited her to take a seat.

"I have pulled together reports from all the media platforms for you to review and decide which could use the most attention now." I walked over to the desk, picking up the file and handing it to her. Once she sat, I returned to my seat as well.

She began thumbing through the pages. "I'll need some time to review these. It's possible that I may want more information or to talk to staff at each platform before deciding which to focus on first."

"Whatever you need, you can have it." God, how I wished I could give her so much more, and I wasn't talking about work.

She closed the folder and stood, surprising me. I thought we might sit and chat a while longer. Out of politeness, I rose from my seat.

"Where will I be working?"

Holy shit. Why hadn't I considered that? I quickly scanned my brain, trying to determine whether there was an open office I could assign to her. I remembered we had a vacant office in the marketing department, which, considering what she was doing, would be perfect.

"I will take you there myself. It will probably need a few things, but you can let me know what you will need." I opened the door to my office and then held my hand out, gesturing for her to precede me. Like the perverted old man I was, my gaze drifted down to her heart-shaped ass as she exited my office. I had a flash of memory of the first time I had taken her from behind. I'd had the sweetest, sexiest view of that ass as my hands gripped her hips and I pumped deep inside her.

Jesus, Banion. You have to stop this.

I led her down the hall toward the elevator. On my floor were all the executive offices, and the marketing department was one level down. I would've much preferred to put her in an office on my floor, but it would look strange to my staff to do that. And of course, it would be counterproductive in my attempt to keep my distance from and my hands off Samantha.

The ride in the elevator was awkwardly silent, and I thanked God that we were only riding down one floor. As I led her down to the empty office, I realized another task I'd neglected, which was telling the head of marketing that Samantha was going to be consulting and auditing online media and marketing. I decided I would get her settled first and then I would visit him and bring him to meet Samantha. She was already suspicious that I was flying by the seat of my pants on this job offer, and I also understood that it made her feel like I was giving her charity. But it wasn't charity. It was restitution.

I opened the door to the office, hoping it hadn't been turned into a storeroom or was completely devoid of office furniture.

I breathed a sigh of relief as I saw the desk and a chair. "I will make sure the tech people set you up with a computer. Would you prefer a laptop?"

She stepped into the small room, looking around, which didn't take long because there wasn't much to see. "I'd prefer a laptop. I could also use a company phone. So much of the content consumed online these days is done through phones, so I like to be able to see the content as others see it."

"Absolutely. I'll have them here within the hour."

She stepped over to the small window that overlooked Manhattan. Was she disappointed? Was she changing her mind?

"I know that it's not much, but—"

She turned, looking at me as an employee would look at her boss. "It's fine. I like the fact that it has natural light. Besides, I imagine that I'll be spending more time out at the various platforms and working with them there." She cocked her head to the side. "I'm assuming you will want me to travel to your other offices at some point as well."

I hadn't considered that, but I nodded. "Absolutely. I'm putting you in charge of all this, Samantha, so you just let me know what you need and where you need to be, and I'll make it happen."

There was a subtle shift in her expression, and for a moment, I thought I saw the woman I'd met five years ago. The one who was eager to get started on her career. But then Samantha turned away, and I couldn't be sure whether she didn't want me to see it or I had just imagined it.

"Perhaps you can give me a list of all you'll need beyond the laptop and phone," I said.

She sat at the desk, pulling out a pad of paper and a pen, writing on it. A few moments later, she handed it to me. Along with the laptop and phone, there were office items such as a printer and paper, pens, and folders.

I put the paper in my pocket. "I'll go take care of these things while you get settled." I left her, heading down to Alan Sprout's office. His secretary announced me as I entered his office.

He rose from his desk with an expression of surprise at my unannounced visit. "Mr. Banion."

"How are you doing, Alan?" I extended my hand toward him, giving it a shake.

"I'm good. What can I do for you?"

"I wanted to let you know that I have hired a consultant to do a full audit and assessment of all our online media and social media."

His brow furrowed. "Is there a problem?"

"No problem. I just like to get a pair of outside eyes to take a look at everything and let us know if there's areas that we could improve or maximize. I'd like to introduce you to her. I've put her in the office down at the end of the hall."

Alan didn't look pleased by my news, but I suppose he felt my actions suggested I was unhappy with his work.

I patted him on the shoulder, hoping to calm his nerves. "I think you'll like working with her. Come on, let me introduce you."

I walked him back down to Samantha's office, finding her at the desk, looking at her phone, and occasionally making notes. She looked up as I stepped in with Alan.

"I'm sorry to interrupt you, but I wanted to introduce you to Alan Sprout. He's the head of all marketing."

She rose and stepped around the desk, extending her hand. "It's nice to meet you. Will I be reporting to you?"

Hell no. "I'd prefer it if you reported to me," I said.

Alan tensed, likely continuing to believe this had something to do with my opinion of his work.

"If it involves marketing, I'd like to at least be in the loop," he said.

"Absolutely, Alan," I assured him.

We made small talk for a few moments, then I excused Alan.

"I think he thinks I'm checking up on him," Samantha astutely deciphered.

"In some ways, you are, but I'll let him know that it's not because I have concerns about his performance. Let me get these things for you." I left Samantha in her office. I returned to my office and asked my admin to arrange the collection and delivery of all the items on Samantha's list.

Then I went back to work, doing my damnedest to not think about Samantha—competent, strong, smart, sexy in her blue dress Samantha one floor down.

9

Samantha

Once Henry left, I sat back in the chair and let out a breath. Since the moment I got out of bed this morning, I was a bundle of nerves.

First, I was concerned about getting through breakfast and whether Henry would be here. When Marie and I finally got Pax ready for preschool and went downstairs for breakfast, Mrs. Tillis told me that Henry had left early for the office. I relaxed a bit then, knowing I wouldn't be seeing him until I went to work.

Marie took care of getting Pax to preschool, and I walked into Henry's office at eight AM sharp, my nerves all a jumble again. It was so important to me that he saw me as a professional and not as the naïve intern he had taken under his wing five years ago.

I wore a navy-blue dress that I felt looked professional, although it was a little snug, hinting at the weight I'd gained over the last few months.

I still had the feeling that Henry was flying by the seat of his pants about this job. Yes, he'd arranged for data reports, but I don't think he'd considered where I'd be working. But he found me a cozy office that had a window and natural light. I continued to have reservations about being around him, but I was grateful for the opportunity.

It was clear that his marketing director, Mr. Sprout, wasn't aware that I'd been hired until that morning, and I had concerns that it might be a problem. Especially since Henry told me I was to report to him, not to Mr. Sprout, who would've been the more obvious supervisor. After all, the majority of what I was doing was related to marketing.

But now, alone in my office, I was able to breathe a sigh of relief. Then I got to work. True to his word, within twenty minutes, Henry had arranged for everything that I needed to do my job, the laptop and phone and office supplies, to be delivered. The tech person got me set up on the company's intranet, and before long, I was going through all the data Henry had given me that morning and using the phone and computer to assess the various platforms.

I had just made the determination that Henry's newspaper in Los could use a little work when there was a knock on my door. Before I had a chance to respond, the door opened and Mr. Sprout walked in.

I was irked that he hadn't waited for me to invite him in, but I put down my work and gave him my full attention. "Is there something I can help you with, Mr. Sprout?"

He crossed his arms over his chest, the corners of his mouth tightening into a disapproving frown. "Why is Henry having an intern check up on me?"

His comment made me suspect that he'd returned to his office after our introduction and researched me.

"I'm not an intern. I'm an employee."

His shrug suggested that he still saw me as someone inferior. "I have over twenty years' experience in marketing, and I've been the director here for the last three years. I don't need someone with less experience looking over my shoulder like you know more than I do."

My jaw clenched, but I took a breath and reminded myself that I needed to be professional. "With all your experience, you shouldn't be concerned about what I might find. You don't need to feel threatened—"

His eyes flashed in anger. "I'm not threatened by you. I am the head of marketing, and everything that happens here is my business. I need to know what's going on."

"You were here when Hen—Mr. Banion told me that I needed to report to him. I'm sure that if there's something he feels you need to know, he'll make sure that you know it."

When I'd nearly slipped and referred to Henry by his name, Mr. Sprout's eyes narrowed, and he studied me in a way that made me want to squirm. I did my best not to.

"I can't help but wonder exactly what you did to convince Henry to hire you."

My gut clenched because I could see by his expression and the tone in his voice that he was hinting that my being hired was due to sexual favors to Henry.

While I wasn't sleeping with Henry now, and wasn't ever going to in the future, I was certain that this job was offered to me because Henry and I had enjoyed a relationship in the past. He'd said himself that he wanted to make restitution for how he had treated me.

But Mr. Sprout didn't need to know that. In fact, if he found out, it would probably make working with him even more difficult than it appeared it was going to be.

I crossed my arms and gave him a hard stare. "I assure you, Mr. Sprout, that I am qualified for the job."

"Come on." His voice dripped with insinuation. "A pretty girl like you and a rich bachelor like Henry? It doesn't take a genius to put two and two together."

"I hope your misogyny doesn't come through in your marketing materials."

His lip curled up into a snarl. "Watching over someone goes both ways. If you think you have found yourself a nice sugar daddy, think again. I'll be keeping an eye on you."

"You're welcome to watch and assess me as much as you'd like, Mr. Sprout. What you'll discover is that I'm a dedicated worker who will be reporting my findings to Mr. Banion."

Ready to be finished with the conversation, I turned my attention back to my work, effectively dismissing him. Only when I was sure that he had left did I look up to confirm it.

Just what I needed.

Yes, I had a dream job, but I was having to work for Henry, the man who broke my heart and was my son's father. Added to that was Mr. Sprout, who clearly wasn't happy about my being here, and I was sure this wasn't the only or last time he was going to let me know it.

I worked to push Mr. Sprout and Henry and everything out of my mind and focus on doing my job. At lunchtime, I stayed in my office, eating a granola bar that I had stashed away in my purse.

By the time four thirty came around, I had gone through all the data that Henry had given me and researched all the platforms online, ranking them from those that could use the most help to those that were doing pretty well.

I was finishing up a report I planned to send to Henry when there was another knock on my door.

When it didn't pop open right away, I called out, "Come in."

The door opened, and a head popped in. Lucas Thompson.

"Mr. Thompson."

Lucas smiled and stepped into the room. "I found you. And please call me Lucas."

I motioned toward the chair near my desk, inviting him to sit. "How did you know I was here?"

He sat down. "I stopped by the home address that you gave me and they told me you were here. I have to tell you, Samantha, for a woman who a week ago was down on her luck, you rebounded very well."

"That doesn't change my plans about contesting my mother's will."

He nodded. "Of course. That's why I'm here. I've been looking into things and might have some leads on what is going on."

Intrigued, I sat forward, eager to find out what he had learned. "Does this mean I have a case against my father?"

He hesitated, his head tilting from one side to the other. "I don't want to get your hopes up because as I said before, on the surface, everything is legal."

"Then what are these leads that you have?"

"The question here is, how did your mother come to sign these, right?"

I nodded.

"And there's essentially two different ways that could have happened. Someone brought these papers to her and convinced her to sign them—"

"My mother would've never signed anything like this. Unless, of course, she was duped." My mother had always been a sharp woman, but near the end, with the pain and fatigue and medication, her mind was muddled.

Lucas nodded. "I agree with that. But of course, the other option is that there is some sort of forgery going on. I'm leaning a bit toward the former. It's suspicious that the paralegal I sent out to see your mom is all of a sudden away on a trip and can't be reached."

I took that in. "So maybe my father paid her to do this and then got her out of the way?"

Lucas shrugged. "It's a possibility, but not one that can be proven at this time."

I continued to think through his hypothesis. "I'm still confused on how this would've worked. Unless, of course, your paralegal already had the paperwork drawn out when she went to see my mom. And how would anyone know that you would have declined to go see my mom and sent the paralegal instead?"

For a moment, Lucas just sat, and then he gave me a sheepish smile. "Those are the elements that I have yet to answer as well."

Frustration built because Lucas wasn't telling me anything that was getting me any closer to finding out how my father had duped his way into getting my mother's money.

"I promise you, Samantha. I am going to get to the bottom of this. I know it seems like I haven't brought you anything substantive, and I vacillated on whether to come see you at all because of that. But I wanted you to know that I was taking this seriously and that I'm working on it."

I sighed and sat back in my chair. "Thank you. I appreciate everything you're doing."

"Of course. I'm here to help you. I really liked your mom a lot. And I like you too."

I had a weird feeling in my stomach at his comment, not knowing if he was saying that he liked me like he liked my mother or something else. I decided to pretend that it was the former. "Thank you."

He shifted, and he gave me another sheepish smile. "Actually, I was wondering if maybe you would be interested in having dinner with me."

Okay, so maybe his interest wasn't just friendly. I wasn't quite sure what to say or do. Lucas was handsome, and like Henry, he seemed to be trying hard to fix a problem that he had caused.

"We could talk more about the case, perhaps giving me some more insight into your father that could help me."

I really wanted to get to the bottom of what my father had done, so I was leaning toward accepting his invitation, even though it also felt like a date, and I wasn't sure I wanted to do that.

I started to accept the invitation when Henry appeared in the open doorway. He had a smile on his face, but there was something in his eyes that told me he was irritated.

"Oh, excuse me. I didn't realize you had company," he said, entering my office.

Lucas stood and extended his hand. "Lucas Thompson. I'm Samantha's lawyer."

Henry's eyes narrowed as he took in Lucas, and I got the feeling he didn't like what he saw.

But he extended his hand to shake with Lucas. "Henry Banion. Samantha's boss. I hope you don't mind, but I need to meet with Ms. Layton."

It took a moment for Lucas to catch on that Henry was dismissing him.

I gave Lucas a helpless shrug. "Thank you for stopping by, Lucas. I appreciate it."

He looked from me to Henry and then back to me. "Sure. We'll talk later."

He left the office, and Henry took a seat in the chair that Lucas had just vacated. "I hope I didn't interrupt anything important."

I studied him, and I couldn't help the feeling that he'd interrupted on purpose. But why? What was Henry up to?

10

Henry

I had fought the urge to check on Samantha all damn day. Hardly a moment went by when I wasn't wondering what she was doing, where she was doing it, and with whom. Had she gone to lunch in the staff room? Was she making friends? What men who worked for me were interested in getting to know her? Fucking hell, I was a mess.

As the sun dipped, indicating the end of the workday, I couldn't help myself any longer. I made my way down to her office. It made perfect sense for me to check and see how her first day had gone. There was nothing weird about that, right?

I'd just reached her office when I heard a man inviting her to dinner. I stopped short even though I wanted to stride in and yank whoever it was out of her office. Here I was, the CEO of a multibillion-dollar company, standing outside Samantha's office, eavesdropping like I was some fucking lovesick puppy. That pissed me off, so I strode in, not giving her a chance to answer.

Several moments later, the young man, who admittedly was

handsome, and as a lawyer, was probably doing well, and closer to her age than I was, finally left. I studied her, wondering if she had an interest in him. I didn't see signs of attraction, but that didn't mean it wasn't there.

"I wanted to come by and see how your day was. I see you received everything you need." I could hear the irritation in my voice, and I took a breath to calm it.

She studied me for a moment, but then turned to her computer, pressing a few keys. "I just finished up a report for you. The two platforms that I think could really use some attention first are your news network and the print paper out in California."

She stood and went to her printer, picking up the pages and handing them to me. She turned to sit back down at her desk, and of course, the pervert in me had to watch her fine form as she moved.

By the time she sat down, I was scanning the pages. I could see that she had done a thorough assessment. I hadn't doubted that she would, but I knew that if there were questions about her abilities, I'd have some explaining to do, especially to Alan. So I was glad to see she was giving her A-game.

"The news network posts regularly on social media." Admittedly, her assessment on the news network confused me.

"That's true, but you're mostly posting on places that older demographics use. Millennials and younger people are also interested in what's going on in the world, so you should expand to the platforms they use too."

I arched a brow. "Are you saying the news anchors are going to have to do dances on TikTok?"

Her lips twitched up in a smile, and for a moment, I was mesmerized by it. She really was a beautiful woman.

"Your news people don't need to do dances on TikTok. But you can have clips of the news like you do on the other platforms on TikTok. At the same time, I have watched many of your opinion hosts, and I suspect some of them would be interested in making short snippets of news or commentary for the platform."

My father had been resistant to bringing all our media outlets onto the Internet. But I knew that the company would die if we did not adapt and adjust to all the new ways that people were looking for and consuming their news information. And while I thought that I was keeping up on top of all the trends, Samantha's assessment was a reminder that how people got their news was still changing and would likely always be changing, probably faster now than it ever had in the past.

"Of course, I'd like the opportunity to go to the news station and talk with your staff who take care of social media and online content before making a final decision."

I nodded. "Of course. I'll make the arrangements." Feeling certain that we had talked enough that Lucas the lawyer was out of the building, I rose and buttoned my coat. "It's the end of the day. I'm heading home. Why don't you ride with me since we are heading to the same place?"

Samantha didn't say anything, instead turning off her laptop. Finally, she said, "I don't know if that's a good idea."

The words felt like tiny stabs in my chest. "I don't know why not."

She shrugged. "I don't want people to think I'm getting special favors from you. Or giving them."

It took a moment for her statement to sink in. Anger brewed deep in my gut, although I couldn't be sure why. "I would never—"

"I know, but others could think it."

I frowned, wondering where she got such an idea. "Did somebody say something to you?"

She looked down, her fingers fiddling with a pen. "It's just how it might look."

I leaned over the desk toward her. "Who said something?"

She closed her eyes, clearly not wanting to tell me. "I don't want any trouble or hostility in the workplace. Besides, it's not a problem. I just don't want to look like there's something going on between us because there isn't."

"I can't imagine why anyone would think there would be anything between us." My words came out harsher than I had intended.

Samantha flinched but then gave me a curt nod.

"You are my daughter's friend. If anybody's going to think anything of this situation, it would be that. It was the same reason I gave you an internship." It felt cruel to remind her of that. I needed to pull my annoyance into check. "It's silly for us to take two different types of transportation when we're going to the same place."

She was quiet for a moment, but then she nodded. She retrieved her purse, and we left her office together. As we headed up the hall past Alan's office, I saw him talking with his secretary. He looked up, and upon seeing us, his eyes narrowed slightly. I couldn't help but wonder if perhaps he hadn't been the impetus to Samantha's concern.

"You head on down to the garage. Knightly will be there. I'll be down in a moment."

Samantha didn't say anything. She continued to the elevator.

I took a detour toward Alan and his secretary. "I like to have a word with you, Alan, if that's possible."

"You're the boss." I followed him into his office.

"I just wanted to check and see how things went today with Ms. Layton up the hall."

He stared at me for a moment, as if he was trying to read my mind. "Did she say something?"

To my mind, that was a confession. "Is there something she should've said to me?"

He shrugged. "No."

"Why do I have the feeling you have something to share with me?"

"Look, Mr. Banion. I have no right to share my opinion on how you run your business, but hiring someone like that out of the blue, and putting her in a position with much power and responsibility . . ." His pause told me he knew he was treading in hot water.

"What's on your mind, Alan?"

"I'm just saying some people might talk. They might wonder how someone like her could get such a job."

"Are you suggesting that people are going to think that Samantha is sucking my dick and that's why I gave her a job? Is that what you're thinking?"

He winced and looked away. He probably hadn't expected me to be so graphic and blunt.

"No, of course not."

"I hired Ms. Layton for the same reason I hired you. She has experience and knowledge. Her age becomes an advantage because it's her demographic that we need to attract to all our platforms. I know that you are aware of that."

His expression reminded me of when Victoria was a little girl and I was reprimanding her.

"Ms. Layton is a friend of the family, and so I won't tolerate anyone suggesting something as vile as what you hinted at. She's my daughter's friend, for Christ's sake." I was laying it on thick, and I suppose, to a certain extent, I was being a hypocrite because while I was telling him that Samantha was like a daughter to me, I definitely didn't see her as a daughter.

"I didn't mean any offense, Mr. Banion."

"I should hope not. If you happened to share these thoughts with her, I expect you to give her an apology."

He nodded.

"Have a good evening, Alan." I didn't wait for his goodbye and instead left his office and went to the elevator, heading down to the garage. Knightly had already helped Samantha into the car. I slid in next to her.

"Is everything all right?" she asked as Knightly pulled out of the garage and into Manhattan's traffic.

"It should be from now on. I'm wondering if you had a chance to read the employee handbook? There is a section that has to do with harassment and a hostile workplace. It's been updated since you were an intern. I encourage you to read it and not be afraid to let anyone know if you're having any problems."

She studied me for a moment.

"Alan shared with me some of his concerns regarding your hiring, and I imagine he expressed them to you. I don't want you to put up with that bullshit."

She bit her lower lip and nodded.

"If it does become a problem, I'll force Alan to do dances on TikTok."

Her laugh sprang forth unexpectedly. She was beautiful and bright and she stole my breath.

"I'd like to see that."

I was mesmerized by her, my gaze drifting from the sparkle in her green eyes down to her pink, plump, luscious lips. I lifted my gaze again and our eyes caught. Electricity arced between us, and if I leaned in just a few inches, I could taste the forbidden sweetness of her lips.

But I couldn't. She was my employee. She was my daughter's friend. And now she had concerns about her reputation being hurt if she was looked upon as somebody who was getting special attention from the boss.

Thankfully, the car bounced as it entered the driveway into the garage of my home, breaking the electric current holding me to her. Once inside the house, I made a beeline for my office, planning to spend the rest of the evening there.

I wondered how much longer I could endure the tug of war raging inside me. The growing desperate need to be with Samantha, fighting with the absolute knowledge that it couldn't ever happen. What would be the breaking point? And when I hit it, what would happen?

AT 6:45 THAT EVENING, Mrs. Tillis brought in a tray of food for me. "You missed dinner with your guests again." Her tone was admonishing.

"They're not my guests. This isn't a visit. They're staying here for a short time until Samantha gets her mother's estate situated."

Mrs. Tillis tsked but didn't say any more, leaving me to my work. I ate as I reviewed Samantha's report again and arranged for her to go to the network tomorrow to discuss her ideas with our online and social media department there.

A little after seven, I'd finished my meal and decided I wanted a drink. I rose from my desk, going to the bar and pouring a couple of fingers of scotch.

The sound of my door unlatching had me looking over toward it. I watched as it opened a crack but didn't see anybody. My gaze drifted down toward the doorknob where I saw a young boy's head peeking in.

His eyes and mouth rounded in an O and he took a quick intake of breath. "Sorry."

"Pax. Come in."

He stepped in, his expression full of apprehension, his fingers fidgeting as if he expected to be in trouble.

"How are you settling in?"

"Okay."

I wondered where Samantha was. "What are you doing?"

"I was exploring."

I picked up my drink and walked to the center of the room. He peered up at me, still looking uncertain.

"And what have you found on your explorations?"

He shrugged.

I wondered how I could put him at ease. "How would you like to see a secret room?"

His mouth and eyes rounded again, but this time it appeared to be in excitement. "You have a secret room?"

"I do." I led him to the area behind my bar where floor to ceiling bookcases stood. "You can't tell anybody about this. And you can't ever come in here without me knowing about it, do you understand?"

His head bobbed up and down. I reached up to a shelf, pulling out a couple of books and then pressing the button. Part of the bookcase popped open.

"Whoa." Pax stared wide-eyed.

I pulled the bookcase door open and let him into the large room. Today it was empty, but a hundred years ago, it stored a fortune in bootleg liquor.

Pax wandered around the empty room. "Is this a dungeon?"

"No. It's just a hidden room."

He looked up at me, his expression quizzical. "What do you use it for?"

"I don't use it at all. To be honest, I'm not sure what to do with it."

Pax brought his hand to his face, tapping his cheek with his forefinger as his eyes narrowed in concentration.

I bit my lip to keep from laughing. "What do you think? What should I use it for?"

Finally, he shrugged. "You can hide in here."

This time, I did laugh. "Good point." Six months ago, I could've turned it into a panic room when I was being terrorized by George Pitney.

I let Pax roam around the room and then we exited.

"Do you like adventures?" I asked as I made sure the bookcase was shut. The last thing I needed was for Pax to get himself locked in there.

"Yeah."

"Do you like them in books?" I headed over to another area of the bookshelf where I had kept the books I had read to Victoria when she was growing up. Scanning them, I pulled out an old copy of *Peter Pan*, the original version, not Disney.

"My mommy reads to me."

"How would you like to read about children who can fly and fight pirates?"

His head bobbed up and down. I led him over to the couch. I sat down, patting the cushion next to me. He climbed up and scooted in close.

I opened the book.

"Are there pictures?"

"A few, but the best pictures are the ones that you think up in your mind using your imagination."

He shrugged but sat quietly as I began to read. I had only gotten a few pages in when the door burst open and Samantha came rushing in. Her eyes scanned the room, settling on me and then Pax.

"Pax. What are you doing?" She turned her attention to me. "I'm sorry, Henry. He was supposed to be playing quietly in the playroom."

"It's not a problem, Samantha. Pax and I were doing a little exploring, weren't we?"

"We got to see a secret room."

"That's supposed to be a secret."

Both of Pax's hands covered his mouth, and I laughed. "It's all right, Pax."

"Pax, come on. It's time to get ready for bed." Samantha looked harried.

"But he's reading to me."

I closed the book, keeping my finger at the spot we'd reached in the story. "I'll save our place. We can read again tomorrow."

Samantha's face tensed, and I wondered if she didn't want me reading to Pax. More likely, she worried that he was getting in my way. The truth was, I enjoyed spending time with him.

Pax scooted off the couch and trotted over toward Samantha, who took his hand.

"Again, I'm sorry, Henry."

I rose from the couch, waving her apology away. "It was my pleasure."

Once she and Pax left, I took the book and placed it on the side table and returned to my desk.

When I learned that Victoria's mother was pregnant, I was terrified until the moment I held Victoria. At twenty-two years of age, I probably wasn't ready to be a father. I certainly wasn't smart enough to recognize what an awesome responsibility parenthood was. But I had taken to fatherhood, loving every moment of it. There was a time when I thought I might find a woman, get married, and have more children, but that never came to pass. The only woman who ever came close to making me think of forever after had been Samantha. For a moment, I let my mind imagine what our life would have been like had I been brave enough to love her. Surely, we would have had children.

I quickly shook the image from my head. Dwelling on the past never did any good. I was too old and too set in my ways now.

Sighing, I turned back to my work. This was my life now. It was a good life. At least that was what I would keep telling myself.

11

I chastised Pax all the way up the two flights of stairs as I took him to his room.

"He didn't mind, Mommy. He was nice."

"That's not the point, Pax. The point is that you snuck away and nobody knew where you were. That made me worried. Secondly, Henry is nice, but he's a busy man. He's being nice enough to let us stay here, but we have to stay out of his way." As I said those last words, guilt roiled in my gut. While it was true that I didn't want Pax to bother Henry, deep down, my motivation was selfish and cruel. I didn't want Henry spending time with Pax out of fear that he could realize who Pax really was. I'd always thought I was a good and decent person, but clearly, I wasn't. But I'd made my decision about Pax five years ago, and I needed to stick to it.

I got Pax into bed, tucking him in and making him promise not to wander off anymore. Of course, I knew that at four years old, Pax would likely forget his promise. At his age, there was very little impulse control.

Once he was in bed, I completed my nightly routine of preparing for the next day. When I finished, I decided I wanted a glass of wine and to read a little bit before I went to bed. Quietly, I made my way downstairs into the kitchen. It was dark, telling me that Knightly, Mrs. Tillis, and Caroline were done for the evening. I found the wine cooler, taking out a bottle of white and pulling a glass out from the cabinet.

"That's a good bottle of wine. Maybe you could pour me a glass too."

I closed my eyes, gathering strength to face Henry. The whole point of the wine was to relax, but with Henry here, I was a bundle of nerves.

I got another wine glass and poured two glasses. I picked them both up, and turning, I set one on the island. "I'm heading up to my room to read." I started toward the door, but Henry stepped into my path.

"I hope Pax didn't get into too much trouble. Honestly, Samantha, I enjoyed spending time with him. He's a sweet boy."

I was both warmed by his words and at the same time, they gave me an ulcer.

"He did get reprimanded because he had run off and we didn't know where he was. I appreciate your spending time with him, but I really don't want us to be in your way. You've done so much for us already, and I don't—"

Henry's index finger reached out, pressing over my lips. A zap of awareness shot through me, nearly making me groan.

"I don't know how many times I need to tell you that you have full run of the house."

I stepped back, needing to stop the urge to lean closer to him. "I don't think you're being completely honest. I think you're just saying that to be nice. I know you avoid us, having dinner in your office—"

"It's not at all unusual for me to eat in my office. What can I do to make you more comfortable in my home?"

All the hopes and wishes I'd had five years ago bubbled up. The dream of living in this home with Henry as his wife, the mother of his children . . . wishes from a silly young woman. I knew better now. And I knew that wasn't what he meant.

He took my hand, pulling it up over his chest. "Truly, Samantha. You're not in my way."

His heart beat under my hand, and it was all I could do to stop myself from pressing my palm against it or worse, leaning my head against it as I had done five years ago. I felt like I had dragged socked-feet over shaggy carpet as little sparks of static electricity snapped and crackled all around me. I looked up into Henry's eyes, wondering what he was thinking. Did he mean to do this to me? Or was he just being nice?

Our gazes held, and it reminded me of the moment in the car earlier tonight when the same energy wrapped around me. For a moment, I thought he might kiss me. For a moment, I hoped he would. How many times had I imagined what it would feel like to have his firm lips on mine again?

But no. I stepped back, extricating my hand from his. I couldn't let him lead me down this rabbit hole to heartbreak again.

I managed to smile. "Thank you for all your generosity." Then I hurried around him and up to my room. I sank down on the edge of the bed, the urgency of making enough money to get Pax and me a separate place, and to deal with my mother's estate so that we could leave New York, bearing down on me.

THE NEXT MORNING, as I fed Pax breakfast, I checked my email, noting one from Henry indicating that I had an appointment this morning at the news network. This was good news. I would be out of the office, which meant I would be away from Henry and from Alan Sprout.

Once breakfast was finished, I handed Pax off to Marie, who took him to preschool, while I headed toward the network offices. The team in charge of online and social activities were competent and creative. I explained my ideas, and they appeared open to them, even excited about them.

"To be honest, we thought about some of the things that you're saying here but worried that Mr. Banion would be concerned about the brand."

I nodded. "I understand what you're saying, but these platforms have been around long enough that they've proven that they have staying power and are popular in a demographic that we need to capture."

The meeting emboldened me, making me feel confident that I knew what I was doing. And I enjoyed it. It was exciting to work with a team who understood my recommendations and had a collaborative spirit as we brainstormed various ideas.

I returned to work just before noon and had just reached my desk when Alan Sprout came bursting into my office.

"What do you think you're doing, meeting with people at the network? Do you think usurping my authority is going to have Henry giving you my job?"

I pulled in a breath to steady my nerves. While I had learned to be more outspoken in life, I still didn't like confrontation. "Mr. Banion set up the meeting. He emailed me with the appointment, telling me that's where I needed to be this morning. If you have a problem with that, you should take it up with him."

Alan's eyes narrowed, and his jaw went so tight it was a surprise it didn't crack and fall off. "You think you're his next shiny object, don't you?"

I had no idea what that meant. Did Henry often bring in people on a whim?

"Mr. Banion hired me to do a job, and I am going to do it." Part of me wondered if I should let him know that I saw this as a short-term gig. Even Henry knew that at some point, I would be starting my own business. But Alan seemed like the type of person who would use that information against me, so I didn't say anything.

"I won't have you undermining me."

I shrugged and sat down. "Again, I would direct you to talk to Mr. Banion. Now, if you'll excuse me, I need to write up my notes and send them to him. Should I mention your concerns to him?"

Alan seethed as he shook his head at me. He stormed out of my office, slamming the door behind him. It was yet another reminder that I needed to get my life sorted. I made a mental note to begin the process of looking at how to start my own business when I got home this evening.

AT FOUR THIRTY, I shut down my laptop and sat back in my chair, stretching my arms over my head. Technically, the day wasn't done until five, but I figured I would use the last half-hour on my phone, going through the various online posts of the Banion media platforms.

A knock on the door interrupted my efforts. "Come in."

Henry walked in. "I see things went well down at the network today."

"The team there understood my assessment and my recommendations. In fact, they had already been thinking about implementing them. You have a good team there." A part of me wanted to tell him that he didn't have a good team in Alan, but I didn't want to ruin the man's career, especially since I didn't plan to be here for the long term.

He nodded. "I try to hire only the best." He sat in the chair in front of my desk. "Alan Sprout is good."

I shrugged.

"I think he's afraid that I'm setting you up to take his job. Did he say anything to you today?"

I vacillated on what to say, if anything. "You hired him to be in charge of all marketing, and so I think it's a little upsetting to him that he's left out of the loop."

Henry nodded. "It's probably disrespectful, isn't it? Alan is really good at the overall big picture and leading people."

I couldn't help it. I arched a brow in disbelief. "I haven't seen that aspect of him yet."

Henry's eyes narrowed. "Maybe it's time I redo his employee assessment. See if he's still as good as when I hired him."

I shook my head. "Whatever you do, Henry, it shouldn't be anything related to me or what I'm doing."

He nodded. "I understand." He rose from his chair. "It's a little bit before five, but I won't tell your boss if you'd like to leave early. I'm heading out now if you'd like a ride."

I remained seated. "That's okay. I can make my way home."

He tilted his head in question. "Is there a problem?"

I shook my head. "No, I just have other plans." Inwardly, I winced because I didn't like lying. My conscience disputed that considering I'd been lying to Henry for the last five years.

"Oh?"

I scanned my brain for a reason to have something else to do other than leave with Henry. "I have a meeting with Lucas."

Henry tensed and his friendly expression waned. "I see. Has he found more information about your mother's will?"

"That's what I hope to find out."

"Well, I hope it all works out." And with that, Henry left my office.

I blew out a breath, wondering how I was becoming the type of person I didn't want to be. The only way to keep me from being a liar was to call Lucas and invite him for dinner.

I'D HAVE MUCH RATHER BEEN at home with Pax than sitting in the intimate Italian restaurant across from Lucas. I knew Pax was in good hands with Marie, but since the day Pax was born, I had done my best to spend as much time with him as possible when I wasn't work-ing. I should've come up with a better excuse to avoid Henry, but because I hadn't, I was now having dinner with Lucas.

He was a nice enough man, but he seemed to want to talk about anything and everything except for my case against my father. That told me he saw this as a date. Under different circumstances, I might have been interested. Lucas was handsome and smart and dedicated to his work. But I didn't have the time or energy to put into dating. My goal now was to deal with my mother's estate and then for Pax and me to go on with our lives. I was pretty sure we would leave New York, although I wasn't sure that we'd return to Seattle. If I could get my business up and running, it was possible I could work from home, which would be ideal in caring for Pax. It would also mean we could live anywhere. Heck, we could travel.

When dinner was finished and coffee was served, I asked Lucas directly about my case. "What sort of chance do I have in taking my father to court over my mom's estate?"

Lucas smiled, but I saw a flash of irritation in his eyes. "I'll be honest, Samantha, I've been through all the documents and there isn't anything there that supports your suspicions or that a judge would take seriously."

My heart sank. "What about the paralegal? What about everyone who knew my mother and knew she would never hand everything over to my father?"

He shrugged. "Everyone who knew your mother could support your case, but it doesn't make your case. As far as the paralegal, we have no way of reaching her. And even if we could, there's no guarantee that she could help. Right now, it's just conjecture that she was a part of getting your mother to sign these documents." He gave me a sympathetic smile. "While we can see some irregularities there, there's nothing that conclusively points to fraud or coercion on your father's part."

I shook my head, reining in my frustration. I knew it hadn't been very long since I had asked for Lucas's help, but it seemed like we were no closer to finding the truth. Surely, something would've popped up by now.

"Are you sure there's nothing else we can do?" I felt like Lucas was my last hope and that it was quickly slipping away. I knew I couldn't give up, but at the same time, if I couldn't legally challenge my father, there was little I could do.

"We could file paperwork, but like I said, your father would seek to have it dismissed and it probably would be. I wish I had better news for you, Samantha." He reached across the table, taking my hand and squeezing it in reassurance. "But don't give up. I'm not giving up."

I nodded, even though I didn't feel reassured.

As we left the restaurant, Lucas took my hand in his. "I'm going to keep working on this. You believe me, don't you?"

"Sure."

He gave me an affable smile. "I'll tell you what. Why don't you come over to my office tomorrow, and we'll have lunch and go through everything again? Sometimes, going back to the beginning or reviewing everything can reveal something that was missed."

I don't know why I needed to be there to go over documents, except it appeared that maybe Lucas was trying to forge a relationship. While I wasn't interested in that, I also had to consider that perhaps if I met with him more often, he would put more time and attention toward my case. "I'd be happy to meet with you for lunch, but could we do it closer to my office?"

"Absolutely." He brought my hand to his lips, giving it a kiss. "I'll see you tomorrow."

As I made my way back to Henry's in the rideshare I'd ordered, I wondered how my life had gotten so complicated. I was living with my son's father who had no idea that he had a son. Worse, despite all my efforts to remember how Henry had callously tossed me aside, every time I was around him, I could feel the energy of attraction down to every cell in my body.

And then there was Lucas, who would be a much better suitor, but for whom there was no spark at all. Not even a little bit.

I briefly considered giving up on my mother's estate and taking Pax and going anywhere away from New York to start over. But it was because of Pax that I couldn't do that. It would be reckless to run away without having a job or a place to live. So, for now, I was going to have to walk this tightrope with Henry and hope that Lucas could find something that would prove my father had stolen my mother's inheritance. I prayed for a miracle.

12

Henry

I was proud of myself for not going out to see Samantha when she returned from her date with Lucas. I reminded myself that my restraint was a good thing. This ridiculous desire for Samantha had to stop.

But like the fool I was, the next day, I headed down to her office around lunchtime only to learn that she wasn't in. Like some crazed stalker, I hovered around the marketing department until she returned. And who was she with? Lucas. His hand rested on her lower back as he escorted her toward her office.

My chest tightened with jealousy. I was such a fucking fool. I returned to my office, pouring myself a drink. I had to get it together. I had known being around Samantha would be difficult, but I didn't realize just how challenging it would actually be. She was still the smart, sweet woman I had met five years ago, but now to see her as a mother, to see her confidence in her work, something about her pulled at me even more than it had before. I admired how tenacious she was in trying to take on her father even though I hated that the route she was using to do so was through Lucas. There was no doubt he had set his sights on her as well.

Over the next week, I did my damnedest to keep my distance from Samantha. It was for my own sanity. I tried to ignore hearing that Samantha had once again gone to dinner with Lucas or he had come to her office. But the final straw was when he showed up at my house, and the two of them met in my living room. Like a jealous ninny, I lingered outside in the shadows, eavesdropping on their conversation. Samantha continued to ask him questions about her case and what she could do to learn more about her father's activities. Lucas seemed to want to talk about anything except the case. There was something odd about that. Was there no case and he was just leading her on because he was interested in her?

I knew Samantha's father and figured she was right that he had done something unscrupulous in order to get her mother's inheritance. Her father could be conniving and manipulative, but he didn't strike me as being very smart. There had to be evidence somewhere of what he had done. As far as I could tell, Lucas hadn't found out much of anything except there had been a paralegal who had met with Samantha's mother and was now somewhere off the grid.

When it was clear that Samantha was making comments that she was ready to end their meeting, I retreated across the foyer and up the hall to my office.

I waited until I heard the door close and then I stepped into the doorway to see her in the foyer. "Samantha."

She looked up. "Henry. I hope we weren't disturbing you."

I shook my head. "How well do you trust this guy?"

Her brow furrowed and her head tilted to the side. "Why?"

I shrugged as I leaned against the door jamb to my office. "I just wonder how it is that he's not done anything to contest this will." I realized too late that I was revealing to her that I was at the very least keeping tabs on her business and at the worst, eavesdropping.

"The paperwork is apparently flawless, and so far, we haven't been able to find any proof of my father's fraud."

I was relieved that she didn't call me out on how I knew so much about her case. "What sort of investigation has he done?"

"I don't know all the details, but he has made attempts to find the paralegal who had the papers my mother signed."

"Would you like a drink?" The question came out from left field, except that I had the urge to draw her into my office so I could sit and talk with her.

Her expression was wary, and yet she let out a sigh. "I think I could use a drink."

I smiled and motioned for her to come into my office. I went over to my bar. "Is scotch okay?"

"Yes." She sank down onto the couch as if the air had gone out of her.

"Would you like anything in it? Water or—"

"No." I brought both our glasses over to the couch. I handed her a glass and sat on the couch hoping I'd given us an appropriate amount of distance.

"You seem frustrated by this process," I said.

"I am. I know the type of man my father is. I know a lot of people also know that. But I suppose he hasn't gotten away with all the things he's gotten away with by being stupid."

"I'm of the opinion that every action leaves some sort of trail. There's something out there that reveals what your father did. The question is whether or not your lawyer can find it."

She took a small sip of the scotch, closing her eyes for a moment as if she was waiting for it to burn away her problems. "Without any proof, there's very little Lucas can do."

"Except you've been relying on him to find something, right? Maybe that's the problem. Maybe you need to find someone else to look." As I said it, I realized that I could help with that.

She sighed. "I don't know what anyone else can do. Lucas was my mother's lawyer. Isn't he the best one to figure out what went wrong?"

She had a point. And yet it seemed to me that Lucas was incompetent or, for some reason, he didn't want to find the problem. "Perhaps it might be better to have someone from the outside looking in because clearly, the guy on the inside isn't being very helpful."

She nodded. "I don't know any private investigators or how to hire one, or even if I have the resources to afford one."

But I did. And I was willing to pay for it, but I wouldn't mention that. I knew Samantha had about enough of my help. "I know of someone, and if they don't do it for free, it's very likely they'll offer you a discount."

Her expression was quizzical.

"Alex Sterling. Tori's husband." While I was starting to get over the fact that my so-called best friend had slept with my daughter and was now married to her, perhaps this would be an opportunity to redeem himself if he helped Samantha.

She shook her head. "Alex and Victoria are weeks away from having a new baby. I can't ask him to get involved in this."

"Alex might be ready to be a father, but he's also the person who runs the New York office of Saint Security. Even if he can't do it, he'll have somebody in his office who could." I was certain Alex would help her because Samantha was Victoria's friend. But suggesting that somebody else would help her might alleviate Samantha's resistance and she'd agree to getting help.

"I can invite Tori and Alex to dinner tomorrow. We can discuss it then."

"I don't know. I'm beginning to think it's a lost cause. It's entirely possible that my father talked my mother into this. He'd said something about her doing this so that he and I could be close again."

"That's bullshit and you know it. There's no way Gwen would have given everything to your father. Even if she thought she could bridge the relationship between the two of you, there's no way she wouldn't have left something for you and for Pax."

Samantha rubbed her temple. "I know, but maybe I should just let it go. Who knows how long this could take, and in the end, it might just be a waste of time and money."

"Hey." I reached my hand out, giving a gentle tug on a strand of her hair. "It hasn't been that long. Right now, you're in a transitional phase, and a lot is going on, and I know that can be stressful. But I have it on good authority that your boss is pleased with your work."

Her lips twitched up, and it made my heart squeeze.

"You've been very kind to me. And I do appreciate it, Henry. When I get my first paycheck, Pax and I will be looking for a new place—"

"You don't have to do that." Panic shot through my gut. "You're welcome to stay here for as long as you need. Use your bonus and your paycheck to save for your new business."

"You've already done enough."

I shook my head. "I don't know why you're so resistant to my help. It's not a burden or hardship to have you and Pax here. I really enjoy spending time with the little guy. Really."

She gulped down her drink, setting it on the coffee table and then standing. "Thank you for all your support." She was dismissing me just as she'd dismissed Lucas.

I set my glass on the table and then stood. "Think about what I said, about seeing if Alex can help and about staying here to save money to start your business."

"Everything you say sounds so reasonable and . . ."

I smiled. "So then you should listen to what I say." I reached out, tugging her in for a hug, intending it to be one of friendship and support. But as I started to pull away and I looked down into those beautiful green eyes of hers, my heart did a loop in my chest. Like a moth drawn to a flame, I slowly leaned forward, millimeter by millimeter until finally, my lips were on her lush mouth. At any moment, she was going to push me away, completely repulsed. But until then, I soaked in the softness of her lips, the sweetness of them.

A moment later, when she hadn't pushed me away, I realized that she was kissing me back. Warmth infused my body followed by a wild heat as the feel of her against me lit me up from the inside out. I slid my arms tighter around her and contemplated pushing her back onto the couch to take what I had missed over the last five years.

Her hands slid over my chest and then gave a push. She stepped back, bringing her hand to her lips, her green eyes wide as she looked at me in shock and regret.

I closed my eyes as reality set in. I threaded my fingers through my hair. "Samantha, I'm sorry, I—"

"Don't say anything, Henry. Let's just pretend that never happened."

Internally, there was so much I wanted to say. I wanted to pull her back into my arms and make promises I knew I couldn't keep. But more importantly, I needed to respect her and her wishes. I gave a nod to let her know that I would abide by her wishes.

She turned and rushed to exit my office. "Oh . . . Tori."

I froze. Samantha stepped back, allowing Victoria to enter my office. Holy shit. If Samantha hadn't pulled away, Victoria would have walked in on me fucking her friend.

"Hey, are you okay?" Victoria asked Samantha.

"Yeah . . . just busy . . . tired. How are you? That baby will be here any day, it seems." Samantha was good. Real good. There was no way Victoria had an inkling of what had happened moments ago.

Victoria rubbed her belly. "I hope so." She looked over at me. "Hey, Dad."

"I wasn't expecting you." I winced as that was a terrible greeting.

She laughed. "Well hello to you, too. Alex had a call with the California office, so he's not getting home until a little later, so I thought I'd stop by and say hello."

"I need to go up and check on Pax." Samantha attempted to exit my office again.

"Can I come and say hello to him too?" Victoria asked.

"Yes, of course."

"I'll be down in a minute, Dad."

I nodded. "I'll be here."

When they both left my office, I picked up my drink, finishing the contents. I'd hoped it would calm my nerves, but the frustration gnawed at me. I threw the glass against the wall in frustration. Why was I so weak when it came to Samantha?

13

Samantha

As I approached the elevator with Victoria, my fingers trembled as I pressed the button for the third floor. Victoria had very nearly caught me kissing her father! Victoria chattered on beside me, oblivious to the storm raging in my mind. Flashes of Henry's kiss replayed in my head. The warmth of his lips, the strength in his embrace . . . it had felt like a dream. A dream I'd once longed for but now knew was foolish. How stupid of me to get caught up in him again.

"Seriously, Sam, I can't get enough milkshakes and corn chips. It's so bizarre!" A soft laugh escaped her lips.

I forced a smile. "For me it was root beer and barbecue chips." I worked to focus on the moment, but thoughts spun images of Henry and his kiss, and now, Victoria stood mere feet away, oblivious that I'd just been in a lip-lock with her father. She would have been shocked had she discovered us. I also felt sad because I needed to talk to someone about this crazy situation, but I had no one. My mother was gone. I couldn't confide in Marie. Victoria would be the obvious choice, but as Henry's daughter, I couldn't. I thought back to several months ago when she confided in me about Alex. She hadn't named him or told me he was Henry's friend, but she'd indicated she was pregnant and planning to keep the child a secret. My advice had been based on my own experience with Henry without revealing the truth of it. I was lying to her as well. Inwardly, I berated myself. How did I end up in this mess?

"Samantha?" Victoria's voice pulled me back to the present, her eyes full of concern. "You seem a little distracted. Is everything okay?"

"Uh, yeah, I'm fine," I lied, rubbing my temples to chase away the memories.

The elevator reached the third floor, and we exited, heading to Pax's room. I spotted him sitting amid a sea of toys, playing without a care in the world. The sight of him brought a smile to my lips. He was why I was making the choices I was making. Right or wrong, my decisions were all about protecting him.

"Hey, Pax!" Victoria called out as she approached Pax. "I've missed you!"

Pax held up a toy truck. "I'm playing cars."

"I can see that. It looks like fun."

"You can play with me. Mommy too."

Victoria laughed. "I'd love to, but if I managed to get myself down on the floor, I don't think I'd be able to get up again."

We watched Pax return to his playing, and Victoria chatted about her pregnancy and how she'd soon be a mom herself.

"I can't wait, and yet I'm terrified," she said.

I nodded. "I remember the feeling."

She looked at me with sympathy. "I don't know how you did it alone and away from your mom."

I shrugged. "You do what you've got to do."

"I'm so grateful to have Alex. And I'm so excited for my dad to become a grandfather. He's going to be so good at it. Much better than mine was."

Envy squeezed my heart. I knew Henry would be a wonderful grandfather, giving his grandchild love and support. Pax deserved that too. If Henry knew the truth, would he love Pax as much as he'd loved Victoria? Would he even believe me?

"Sometimes, I wish Dad had remarried and had more kids," she mused, a hint of sadness in her voice.

"Oh?"

"I don't remember him dating, at least not having a relationship. But now I wonder if he's lonely. That's why I'm so glad you're here. He needs energy and life in this house again."

"He's being very good to us."

"Are things going okay staying here? In the new job?"

"Yes. Like I said, Henry has been like a godsend."

"Good. Like I said, I worry about him rattling around in this house. I wish he'd do more than work. Maybe meet someone."

"Is that a possibility?"

She shrugged. "Probably not. I think there was a woman he loved a few years ago, but it didn't work out for some reason. He wouldn't give me details."

I swallowed. "Who do you think it was?"

"I don't know. But I'm sure it was someone amazing because he hasn't been with anyone and . . . there's a reverence or something when he thinks about her. I can't explain it because he won't tell me about it. I can just tell she was special, important. I wish I could find her and ask her what happened. Maybe if I knew the truth, I could help him move on."

My heart clenched at her words, wondering if I was that woman. But then I remembered how Henry had ended our relationship. He hadn't loved me. "Maybe it just wasn't meant to be," I whispered, mostly to myself.

"Maybe." She smiled at Pax as he made car sounds, pushing the vehicles along the floor. "How is the new job?"

"It's exactly what I'd like to do, although I hope to someday do it in my own business. I've actually been researching how to get started."

"Wonderful. I know you'll be successful. I'm sure my dad will be sad to lose you, but I also know he'll help you. If there's anything I can do to help as well, just let me know."

"Thank you." I'd long admired Victoria and would love to have her as a mentor in business.

"Does that mean you'll stay in New York?"

I hesitated. I wanted to stay, I realized, but I couldn't. "Right now, I'm focused on getting my life sorted and dealing with my father."

"Of course."

Pax yawned and played down on his side, his hand still pushing a car.

"Looks like someone is ready for bed," I said. "Pax, sweetie. Let's pick up the toys and get ready for bed."

"I don't want to."

"I know. But it's time."

"That's my cue to go," Victoria said. "Can you give me a hug, Pax?"

Pax dragged himself off the floor and hugged Victoria. She laughed. "Goodnight, Pax." She started toward the door. "How about we have lunch tomorrow, Samantha? I want to pick your brain about babies."

This was what my life should have been like. Spending time with my best friend, talking about babies. But the weight of my secrets made it hard to fully embrace the wonderful friendship Victoria offered me.

"I'd enjoy that."

With a final wave, Victoria disappeared down the hall, leaving me alone with Pax. "Okay, little guy, let's get this cleaned up and you into bed."

I guided Pax through our nighttime routine of brushing his teeth and wriggling into his pajamas. I tucked him into bed, sat next to him, and opened a book about sharks to read to him. I was barely through the first page when Pax's eyes closed and he was asleep.

Closing the book, I let my head fall back against the headboard, tears pricking at the corners of my eyes. Five years ago, I thought I'd made the right choice by keeping the truth about Pax from Henry. Henry had been clear that he never wanted to see me again lest our secret come out. I still stood by that decision. But now as I gazed at my son's peaceful face, I wondered if I should come clean to Henry. All the reasons he'd sent me away still existed, and yet, the attraction was still there. The kiss tonight proved it.

For a moment, I allowed myself to think that Henry would be thrilled to discover Pax was his son. That he'd tell me I was the woman he'd loved and he wanted to start again. But the moment I thought that, I was back in the living room of his Hamptons beach house as he told me he never wanted to see me again. No, I couldn't let myself fall for him, but did that mean he couldn't know about his son? My conscience warred with me, telling me Pax deserved to know his father and Henry deserved to know his son. But was I brave enough to come clean? I would be risking a lot. Henry could reject Pax. Or he could sue for custody.

I didn't know the answer, but as I stood and kissed Pax goodnight, I knew I couldn't keep running from the truth forever. Somehow, someday, I would have to face it.

Confused and with a heavy heart, I slipped from the room and returned to my own. Guilt and regret pressed down on me as I put on my pajamas and got into bed. How much longer could I live like this?

14

Henry

I swept the shards of glass from the glass I threw into the dustpan then dumped the remains of my rage into the trash. Fucking hell. What had I been thinking, kissing Samantha like that? I hadn't been thinking. I'd been yearning, aching. I could still feel the press of Samantha's lips against mine. The surge of power . . . of joy that had coursed through me when I realized she was kissing me back.

The click of the front door shook me from my regret. Victoria breezed into the room, one hand cradling her swollen belly. Seeing her reminded me of how fortunate it was that Samantha was stronger than I was and had pulled away from the kiss or Victoria would have caught us.

Victoria's smile faltered. "What's wrong?"

I forced a grin and made my way to her, giving her a hug. "Nothing, just tired. How are you feeling?"

"Pregnant."

We settled on the sofa, and Victoria launched into happy chatter about her impending motherhood.

"Little Hank here is going to be a soccer player. Maybe rugby."

I rolled my eyes. "Still planning to call him Hank?" I was beyond the moon that Victoria and Alex planned to name the baby Henry, but not so excited to know he'd be called Hank for short. I'd never liked being called Hank.

"Yes. It's cute." Then she fixed me with a probing look. "How's it been, having Samantha and her son here?"

I hesitated, my thoughts straying to our illicit kiss. Pushing it away, I said, "It's been nice. Pax is a great kid. I showed him the secret room."

She laughed. "He probably thought that was the coolest thing. I know I did."

I smiled, remembering Pax's amazement and joy.

Victoria tilted her head. "Do you ever wish you'd settled down? Had more children?"

The momentary calm burst into chaos in my gut again. Images of Samantha flooded my mind. The yearning to make a life with her and the misery from the night I'd made sure she'd never love me. "Never met the right person, I guess."

Victoria pursed her lips. "I think there was someone, once. Wasn't there?"

I squirmed internally but kept my face neutral. "It was a long time ago. It wouldn't have worked out."

She searched my eyes, and I hoped she couldn't see the truth. Finally, she sighed, seemingly accepting my answer as she let the matter drop.

"I'm very much looking forward to spoiling little Hank here." I steered the conversation back to her.

Her smile was bright. "You're going to be a wonderful grandfather."

I frowned as I realized I'd likely be the child's only grandfather. Only grandparent. Alex was estranged from his father, and his mother was dead. Victoria's mother left the moment the hospital discharged her after Victoria's birth. From the moment she found out she was pregnant, she knew she didn't want to be a mother. I'd worked out a deal in which I'd pay her a fortune to carry the child to term, and then she could leave.

"Do you ever wonder about your mother?" I asked.

"No." Her response was quick and made with ease, telling me it was the truth. "Having you was enough, and it will be enough for Hank too."

I thought about Pax being raised by a single parent. It wasn't easy, although my wealth made it easier for me than for others. Still, it seemed like a boy should have a father figure. Perhaps I could be that for young Pax, at least while he was here.

The ring of the doorbell interrupted us.

"That's probably Alex. He said he'd come get me here and then we'd go get a milkshake."

I arched a brow.

She shrugged. "Hank likes milkshakes and corn chips."

A few moments later, Knightly came in announcing Alex's arrival.

I tensed, an automatic response when Alex entered my office. I wondered if I'd ever get over my college friend, the man I'd once chased women with, having married my daughter.

If Alex noticed my moment of tension, he didn't show it. His eyes were on Victoria. The love in his eyes for her, while weird, was what kept me from kicking his ass.

Alex leaned down to kiss Victoria. "How are you and the baby?"

"Very well." Victoria brimming with happiness was another reason I didn't kick Alex's ass.

"Henry." Alex extended his hand, and I shook it. He looked back to Victoria. "Ready for milkshakes?"

"Yes." Victoria stood, with help from Alex.

"I wondered if I could talk to you about something, Alex," I said.

Both Alex and Victoria looked at me with suspicion. Like they thought I was going to say something about how much their relationship still bugged me.

"Has Tori told you about Samantha's father getting Gwen's inheritance?"

They both relaxed, and Alex nodded. "Yes. I agree that Gwen wouldn't have left Samantha out in the cold like that."

"She has a lawyer who is supposedly looking into it, but as far as I can tell, he hasn't found anything. He says the paperwork is legal and the one person who could help explain what happened is conveniently indisposed."

Alex's brow furrowed. "Indisposed how?"

I supposed being a former mercenary, Alex's mind would go to something like murder. "The story is that she's in South America, off the grid."

"How can I help? Do you want me to find her?"

"Maybe. Mostly, I'd like you to look into Layton."

Alex nodded. "He was always a motherfucker."

"Alex . . . language."

He laughed. "Sorry." He patted Victoria's belly.

"Is Samantha on board with this?" Victoria asked. "She didn't mention it when I was visiting with her."

"She and I discussed the possibility of asking Alex." That wasn't a lie.

"Is this an official investigation?"

"If that's the best way to get it done."

"More resources and manpower, but if this needs to be off the record, I can poke around."

"I want whatever will give Samantha the evidence she needs to contest the will."

"You got it."

"Thank you." I felt relieved that Alex would look into Samantha's inheritance situation. His skills and connections would surely uncover whatever shady dealings were at play. Samantha and her son deserved that money. They shouldn't be punished because of her father's greed.

"Of course." Alex clapped my shoulder. "I'll let you know what I find."

I walked them to the door. Alex wrapped a protective arm around Victoria as he escorted her out. She looked back, giving me a searching look as if she thought something was up. I smiled reassuringly and waved.

I shut the door and made my way up to the second floor to my room. Perhaps I should leave well enough alone regarding Samantha. Or at the very, least confirm that she wanted help. But I couldn't shake the desire to help her.

My thoughts drifted back to Victoria's question about why I'd never settled down and had more children. She clearly knew I'd had feelings for a woman. She seemed to suspect that I still harbored feelings for the woman. Even now, after five long years, Samantha still occupied my mind. I thought I'd moved past it, but having her back here, under this roof again . . . it stirred up feelings I thought I'd buried.

But they weren't buried. They lived just under the surface and burst forth in that damned kiss. Just thinking about the feel of Samantha's lips on mine made my pulse quicken. I shouldn't have done it, but I'd been helpless to resist with her so close. Tasting her, holding her had felt so right. Every fiber of my being had screamed *yes, finally*. I thought she felt it too before reality set in.

I groaned, scrubbing my hands over my face. I shouldn't have kissed her. It was a moment of weakness, one I deeply regretted. She had made it clear that it could never happen again. And she was right. It was far too complicated and risky.

I should apologize to her. I needed to let her know that I wouldn't kiss her again so she wouldn't feel uncomfortable around me. But she was clear that we were to act like the kiss never happened.

Entering my bedroom, I sighed knowing I needed to respect her wishes and not mention the kiss. The urge to see Samantha was still there, but I pushed it down. I had to stay away, for both our sakes. The kiss would be yet another secret between us.

It was better this way, I told myself. Easier. All I had to do was ignore the ache in my chest. The ache of loving someone I could never have.

15

Samantha

I woke up with a start. The images of a steamy dream about Henry felt all too real. Henry's hands on my body, his lips against mine. I took a deep breath, trying to shake the lingering desire coursing through me. What was I thinking? I shouldn't be having sexy dreams about him.

Avoiding Henry became my mission as I got Pax ready for preschool and myself ready for work. Thankfully, it turned out to be easier than I thought. Henry was nowhere to be seen. Had he gone to work early? Was he avoiding me too?

When Pax and I made our way to the kitchen, Marie was there with Caroline.

"I've got pancakes this morning," Caroline said in a sing-song voice.

"Yay!" Pax bounced on his toes with excitement.

"I'm going to need a new wardrobe if I keep eating like this," I said as I helped Pax to the kitchen table and then sat with him.

"Don't forget, Pax has that sleepover tonight." Marie set a cup of coffee in front of me. "I'll take him to school, but Will's mom will pick him up this afternoon."

"Oh, right." I drank a sip of the dark brew, willing it to wake me up.

"So I was hoping I could have the evening off. Maybe get together with some friends."

"Of course. Enjoy it." With Pax and Marie out for the night, that meant I'd have an evening alone without distractions or responsibilities. It would give me the chance to think, and boy, did I have a lot to consider. My life had become a tangled web of lies and desires that were threatening my sanity.

After breakfast, Marie took Pax to school, and I headed to my office. Once at my desk, I focused on online and social media marketing plans for the network news team. Specifically, updating the posting policies that offered guardrails to keep from having content that could hurt the company. For the most part, the existing policies were good, but social media had changed since they were last updated, so I worked to fill in the gaps made by new platforms and forms of content.

Once I had my draft, I needed Henry to review for approval or feedback. I composed an email to him with the draft attached. I hesitated for a moment before hitting *Send* as my mind went back to that kiss. Goodness, he was a good kisser. Then I groaned at myself and pushed the image aside.

Technically, that task was done, but I decided to send the draft to Alan too. Maybe he'd be less obnoxious if I kept him informed. The hope was slim but worth a try.

Deciding I deserved a break, I headed to the breakroom for more coffee. As I stood at the counter waiting for the coffee to brew, Alan walked in.

"Working hard or hardly working?" he joked.

I rolled my eyes. "Just needed a break."

"Yeah, this social media policy stuff seems like busy work. A waste of time. This is a prominent news network. We don't need our team dancing to the news."

Well, that was quick. I'd only just sent him the email. "I'll note that in my report to Henry." I picked up my cup and headed to exit the breakroom.

"I'll have edits back to you later today."

I stopped short, wondering if he was talking to me. Realizing he was, I nodded. "Thanks."

Back at my desk, I took a moment to enjoy my coffee. Unfortunately, when my mind wasn't busy with work, it drifted back to my complicated mess of a life. I longed for the days when it was just me and Pax. No drama. No worries beyond the usual parenting stuff. How could I have that back? The easy answer was to leave New York. As much as I wanted to fight for what was rightfully mine regarding my mother's will, I couldn't ignore the nagging doubts about my case. Winning against my father seemed like a long shot. Even Lucas didn't think I could win. He said he was still looking into it, but I had to wonder if that was just an excuse to keep seeing me.

The other issue was that staying in New York meant being around Henry, and every moment spent with him only intensified my feelings. The man hurt me and yet somehow, being around him, I forgot that. Instead, the feelings of love and desire returned.

Ugh.

My thoughts drifted to Pax. My sweet, innocent little boy deserved a stable home, not one filled with turmoil and secrets. The best way to do that would be to move on. Let my father win and take Pax and leave New York with all my secrets intact. My conscience told me it was wrong, but what Henry didn't know wouldn't hurt him, right? God, that sounded awful. But he was the one who didn't want to see me. He'd sent me away. And the reasons he'd done that still existed.

But this wasn't just about me and Henry. It was about Pax too. What would be best for him? The decision loomed over me like a dark cloud. Why couldn't life be easier?

My phone pinged with a notification. Looking at it, I'd received an email from the head of social media at the news network sending me ideas they'd brainstormed in their meeting. I let him know that I'd look it over and get back to him.

I went back to work until just before noon. Victoria would be here any minute to take me to lunch. I considered discussing my thoughts about dropping my legal fight and leaving New York. I couldn't detail all the reasons I wanted to get away, but I could at least tell her how futile my case seemed. She'd be disappointed. Ever since she and I reconnected several months ago, she'd been so gung-ho to rekindle our friendship. I was too, except that the fear of her and Henry learning the truth had made it difficult for me to fully commit to the friendship. God, I was looking worse and worse as a person by the minute.

Right on time, Victoria breezed into my office with a bright smile. "Ready for lunch?"

Before I could respond, Alex followed close behind her. I stared at him in surprise. "Alex? I didn't know you were joining us."

"It was a last-minute change of plans," Victoria explained. "I hope you don't mind."

"Not at all." I grabbed my purse and followed them out.

We made our way to a local restaurant and settled into a cozy booth by the window.

"So, Alex is actually here because of you."

I raised my eyebrows. "Me?"

"My dad asked him to look into your legal case, see if he can dig anything up on your father."

I tensed at her words, feeling both grateful and annoyed that Henry had taken it upon himself to involve Alex. "He didn't need to do that. I've got it handled."

"But do you?" Victoria pursed her lips at me.

"Yes, I do. I have a lawyer." I felt defensive and didn't like it. It reinforced my desire to leave. I felt worried and defensive all the time now.

Alex's voice was gentle but firm. "Henry just wants to help you."

"That's kind of him but really not necessary," I hedged.

Victoria reached across the table and took my hand. "Please let us help."

God. Why did she have to put it that way?

"We all know you're a strong, capable woman, but that doesn't mean you can't use help. We all can," Victoria finished.

I sighed. "I don't deny that Alex could probably help, but I don't have the funds to afford the help of Saint Security."

"Consider it gratis for now." Alex waved my concern away. "If I need to access additional resources, we'll discuss it then."

"Besides, my dad—"

"Your dad has already done so much for me."

"You do know that my father is obscenely rich and nice, right?"

I nodded, although I wondered if she knew that Henry could be cruel too. Would she believe me if I told her how he'd dumped me and sent me across the country at only twenty-two years old? Pregnant to boot, although he didn't know that.

Our server showed up, and we ordered our meals.

"Why don't you fill me in on what you know about the case so far?" Alex said once our server left to turn in our orders.

Giving in, I recounted Lucas's limited information. "Before she died, my mom called Lucas Thompson, her lawyer, with questions about her will. He sent a paralegal over to meet with her. When she passed away, that's when I found out everything was left to my father."

"Gwen wouldn't do that," Alex noted.

"Did you know my mother?"

"I'd met her a time or two. She was a lovely woman."

"Who wouldn't have given that two-timing snake of a husband anything. Nor would she have left you and Pax nothing."

I smiled at Victoria's anger on my behalf. "Exactly. I think my father is involved somehow."

"The lawyer says the paperwork is on the up and up?" Alex asked.

"That's what he said." I took a sip of my water.

"So the paperwork was redone. It sounds like it's something this paralegal would know about. Any ideas where this paralegal is now?" Alex tapped notes into his phone.

"Supposedly, she's off the grid in South America." Was that even possible? Wasn't Internet and phone access everywhere now?

"Sounds sketchy." Victoria shook her head.

"Agreed." Alex leaned over to give Victoria a kiss as he put his phone in his pocket. "I'll start looking into it right away." He scooted out of the booth.

"What about your lunch?" I asked.

"That's all for Victoria and the baby."

Victoria blushed. "The baby is really hungry these days."

I laughed. "Thank you, Alex."

"Of course. If you think of anything else important or the lawyer gives you more details, let me know."

"I will." As much as I didn't like how this came to be, I was grateful to Alex. Of course, by doing this, it meant I'd have to stick around, but in reality, I had to stay for the time being no matter what. If I wanted to start my own consulting business, I had to follow through on the job with Henry to gain the experience and referrals I'd need.

After Alex left, Victoria and I settled into an easy conversation over our lunch. We reminisced about our college years, sharing stories of late-night study sessions and wild parties as if no time had passed at all.

"Can you believe it's been eight years since we graduated?" Victoria cradled her growing belly with a smile.

"Time really does fly. And soon, you'll be a mom."

"I know." She beamed. She was the epitome of the glowing mother. I wondered if I looked like that. I doubted it. I was excited but terrified to be a mom. But Victoria, along with about to become a mom, had a man she adored in her life. Her happiness had to stem from that as well.

"I can't wait to meet this little one," Victoria finished. "And I'm excited for my dad to be a grandfather."

"Henry will be a good one." I swallowed the ever present guilt about Pax. "I guess he's okay now with you and Alex . . . I mean, Alex was his friend."

Victoria rolled her eyes. "It still bugs him. He can't stop thinking of Alex as he a horny twenty-year-old." She sighed. "I do see that it's weird, though. I'd probably have a hard time if my child slept with my friend."

What if your friend slept with your father?

"Anyway, speaking of kids, my dad has been enjoying having Pax around."

"He's very patient."

"He's good with kids. I really wish he'd let himself fall in love again and have more kids. I'd have been a great big sister."

I laughed. "True."

"I asked him again last night about the woman he'd loved all those years ago, but he was evasive as always. I wonder what the problem was?"

I felt a pang of guilt, knowing that I was keeping such a significant secret from my best friend. "Maybe he just doesn't want to talk about it."

"Maybe," she conceded, her brow furrowing in concern. "But why? What happened? Did she break his heart?"

I tensed, feeling defensive.

"He doesn't seem bitter, though. Just sad."

"Whatever the reason, it's clear that your dad's life is changing for the better. Having you, Alex, and Pax around must be good for him." I tried to steer the conversation away from dangerous territory.

"I suppose. But he's been working so much lately—too much, if you ask me. I think having us around helps him remember what's really important in life. Plus, I'm glad you and Pax are staying with him. He needs family right now more than ever."

Family. My heart ached that I'd never really be a part of the family.

"What about you? Are you seeing anyone?"

Henry's kiss flashed in my mind. "Ah . . . no. I think my lawyer is interested, though."

"Oh . . . is he nice?" Victoria's eyes glittered with intrigue.

"I suppose. I don't feel attracted to him, though."

"Have you ever been in love, Samantha?" Victoria asked, catching me off guard. Her eyes were searching mine for an answer, not real-izing the weight of her question.

"Um . . . yes," I admitted hesitantly, my mind flashing back to those stolen moments with Henry all those years ago. "But it was complicated."

"Love always is. I just hope that one day, you and my dad will find someone who makes you as happy as Alex makes me."

I wondered what she'd say if I told her the truth. That I had loved her father. Had borne his child. And even now, after what he'd done five years ago, I found myself drawn to him. Of course, she would never know.

"Anyway, how's your job going? Do you have any big projects in the works?"

I welcomed the distraction and dived into talking about my current work responsibilities.

After lunch, I returned to work, checking my email, hoping for a response from Henry about the social media policy. There was a second email from Alan, who still felt the new social media strategy for the news network was low class, but he did give a few good ideas. However, there was no email from Henry. I couldn't move forward without his input.

By the end of the day, I still hadn't heard from him. I wondered if maybe he was planning to see me at the end of the day. A part of me desperately hoped he would even as I knew it was a fool's journey to tempt myself around him.

But as the minutes ticked by, it became clear that he wasn't coming. Was he avoiding me? Or was he simply too busy? Pushing back my disappointment, I gathered my things and slipped on my coat, eager to start my quiet night alone.

ONCE BACK AT Henry's home, I stepped into the lavish foyer.

As I took off my coat, Knightly appeared in the doorway, his ever-present smile greeting me. "Miss Layton. Shall I have dinner set up for you in the dining room since young Paxton is out?"

"Is Henry around?" I asked, trying to sound casual.

"Mr. Banion is working in his office. He stayed home today."

"Thank you, Knightly." I made my way down the hall, stopping just outside Henry's office door. I hesitated for a moment before knocking softly.

"Yes?"

I opened the door, poking my head in. Henry looked up from his desk, surprised but not displeased to see me.

"Hey. I didn't hear back from you about the email I sent earlier."

"Ah, Samantha, I'm sorry." He rubbed his temples. "I've been dealing with some issues at our Los Angeles office, and . . ." He looked at his watch. "God, is it six already?"

"Yes."

"Let me look at it now." He turned his attention to his computer. "Would you mind pouring me a drink? You can get yourself something as well."

"Sure." I walked over to the bar, noting that Henry was acting like nothing happened yesterday . . . just like I'd wanted. I felt a little annoyed that he could so easily forget the kiss, and at the same time, I relaxed. This wouldn't be awkward.

I poured him a drink, remembering how I'd gotten him so many drinks five years ago when we'd work together. I brought his glass and my own over to his desk.

"I see Alan shared some ideas," Henry said as he took his glass and sipped.

"Yes. Overall, he thinks it will hurt the reputation of the network, but he did provide a few things to think about."

As we began discussing the policy proposal, I relaxed into the conversation, enjoying the easy banter and friendly rapport that came naturally between us. This was how it had been when I'd been his intern, before I'd become his lover.

Knightly and Mrs. Tillis entered the room, bringing two trays laden with steaming dishes. "You still have to eat," Mrs. Tillis insisted.

Knightly arranged a table so we could eat and work at the same time.

"Have you considered adding content guidelines for live streaming journalists in the field?" Henry pointed at a section of the document. "It could be a valuable tool for our news team."

"Good point. We should definitely address that." I made a note to review it later.

"Also, how are we going to handle issues with user-generated content?" he inquired.

"What you have in your terms of use and privacy is pretty robust, but I'll review again."

For the rest of the evening, we worked in sync, bouncing ideas off each other and refining the proposal. I had to admit, it was lovely to be with Henry like this. It didn't alleviate my guilt, but I enjoyed working with him.

The moment we finished editing the policy, a silence settled between us. Henry leaned back in his chair, rubbing his temples. I watched him for a moment, noting that he had a few more lines in his face, and yet, it made him even sexier. I quickly worked to push that thought away.

Desperate to keep things light, I blurted out the first thing that came to mind. "Hey, Pax mentioned there's a secret room in your office?"

Henry looked up, his eyes twinkling with amusement. "Oh? It's supposed to be a secret."

"Boys only, huh?" I smirked.

He laughed, shaking his head. "I'll show you, but only if you can keep it a secret."

"Deal."

Henry led me across the room and tapped something high on a bookshelf. The door swung open, revealing a small, dimly lit chamber.

"What is this?" I stepped inside, noting the room was empty.

"It used to be where booze was hidden away."

I laughed. "Really? What was it before that?" This house was older than prohibition.

He frowned. "You know, I'm not sure?" He stepped into the room, looking around as if there would be a clue to its original purpose. "Maybe I can pull the blueprints to find out."

He turned, apparently not realizing how close I was. Our bodies stood inches apart, the air around us immediately charging with electric desire.

Our eyes caught. In his I saw desire and frustration. "I know I promised to act like nothing happened yesterday, but I haven't stopped thinking about kissing you."

I should step away. I should deny that the kiss meant anything. "Me neither."

He shook his head. "We're in the same spot as before, aren't we?"

I nodded.

"We should leave."

I nodded again.

Our gazes continued to hold as the tension between us grew. The pull to him strengthened until I was powerless to move.

"Heaven help me, Samantha—"

I closed the distance between us, covering his mouth with mine, wrapping my arms around him and holding on like my life depended on it.

He groaned, his arms banding around me as he turned me and pressed me against the wall. His hands roamed my body as if they couldn't decide where to focus. Finally, his fingers found their way between my thighs, rubbing through my folds.

"You're so wet." He dropped to his knees. "I've missed tasting you . . . I have to taste you." He pulled my panties down, helping me step out. Warning bells clanged in my head, but I told them to shut up.

Henry lifted my leg, hooking it over his shoulder and opening me to him. Then his mouth was on my pussy and thought was impossible. All that existed was sensation over sensation as his tongue and lips and teeth drove me to madness.

"Henry." I gasped as I gripped his head to hold him to me to make sure he didn't stop.

"Come, Samantha. I want to drink you up." His tongue lapped

inside me as his thumb flicked over my clit. I shot off like a rocket, pleasure blasting through me. My body shuddered, my legs quivering as Henry continued to lick and suck until my bones liquified.

"Fuck . . ." He rose, undoing his pants. "I have to fuck you. Tell me I can fuck you . . ."

I was in a haze, unable to think.

"Oh, shit . . . I don't have a condom." He looked at me in delirium. "Tell me you're on the pill."

My wits slowly returned. "It doesn't always work."

He stopped short. "What? . . . Pax?"

I swallowed as I nodded.

Henry let out a shuddering breath. He stepped back, pulling his pants back into place. I was glad he understood and yet, it felt wrong to let him go unsatisfied after the orgasm he'd given me.

I reached out, stopping him from fastening his pants. I lowered to my knees as I took his hard shaft in hand.

"You don't have to, Samantha."

"I know." Then I sucked him deep into my mouth.

16

Henry

This was wrong, but heaven help me, I couldn't stop. I felt like a perverted old man taking a handout as Samantha sank to the floor in front of me and gripped my dick. She didn't really want to suck me off. She was doing it because she thought she should since I'd gotten her off. One good turn deserves another.

The moment her lips were on my dick, I was helpless to stop her. The pleasure speared fierce and deep. Sure, I'd have rather been inside her pussy, but her mouth was fucking awesome too.

"Fuck, yes . . . Samantha . . ." My fingers thread through her hair as her lips slid down my shaft and up again. Electric sensations sizzled. It was like I stuck my dick into a light socket. "God . . . I'm nearly there . . ." It was fucking embarrassing how fast I was going to come. Normally, I could hold out, draw out the pleasure for us both. But it had been awhile, not just being with Samantha, but with a woman at all. My toys, as nice as they were, were nothing like this. This . . . good God, this was fantastic.

My balls tightened and my dick twitched. "I'm coming . . . fuck, I'm coming."

Her mouth took me deep. My tip hit the back of her throat, and my eyes rolled back into my head as my orgasm blasted through me.

"Yes . . . fuck . . . yes . . ." My hips rocked back and forth as I fucked her mouth, emptying my dick until it was limp.

She finally released me and stood, her expression wary.

What the hell was wrong with me? Why did I keep fucking up? Having sex with Samantha was wrong on so many levels. It wasn't just that I was her boss or that she was Victoria's friend. No, the problem was if this continued, I'd end up hurting her again just like I did five years ago. I'd break my own heart in the process. Why was this happening again?

Because Samantha is amazing.

God, it had been lovely to work with her again. Samantha was brilliant and creative and beautiful. I remembered being amazed by her five years ago when she was my intern, and she still wowed me now.

But it was as wrong now as it had been five years ago. I knew it, and from the expression on her face, she knew it too. Based on how she reacted to the kiss last night, I knew she was trying to figure out a way for us to pretend this didn't happen. I should make it easy for her.

"I'm sorry, Samantha. I know this was a mistake." My words sounded more like a plea than a statement, but I needed to remind myself of the truth.

She flinched, and for a split second I thought I saw pain flash in her eyes. I hesitated. Was I wrong? Did she actually want something more between us?

But as quickly as that flicker appeared, it vanished, replaced by a steely determination. "Nothing has changed, Henry."

"I know." My words didn't just acknowledge the continued barriers between us. They also acknowledged that the selfish, insatiable desire I had for hadn't changed.

Her fingers shook as she hurriedly righted her clothes. "Let's just forget this happened, okay?"

My chest tightened at the sight of her trying to hold herself together. I wanted nothing more than to pull her back into my arms and tell her everything would be okay. But deep down, I knew that wasn't possible, not with the barriers that stood between us.

"Yes. Of course." I smiled, hoping she didn't see the disappointment and sadness filling my chest.

She offered me a weak smile in return, her eyes refusing to meet mine, before turning to leave the room.

With a sigh, I returned to my desk, attempting to focus on the paperwork in front of me. It was a futile effort. My thoughts kept drifting back to Samantha, to her touch, her scent, the way she had looked at me with those haunted green eyes.

"Fucking hell," I muttered under my breath, raking a hand through my hair. This situation was maddening. How was it that I'd met the perfect woman . . . kind, sweet, smart, my match in every way, and I couldn't have her? Was there any way we could overcome the barriers between us? What if I sucked it up, letting Victoria and society think what they might about my relationship with Samantha? For a moment, I let my mind imagine a life with Samantha. Her sleeping in my bed. Her ripe and round with my child. All of us, me, Samantha, Pax, our child, Victoria, Alex, and their child, together at Christmas, filling this home with love and laughter. The risk would be huge. Victoria could be pissed, although considering she was married to my friend, she'd be a hypocrite. What would the company board do? Would they vote to remove me for having an affair with an intern who was now an employee? Maybe not. Perhaps it was a risk worth taking except for one thing. Samantha might be attracted to me, but it was equally evident that she didn't want a relationship with me. She couldn't leave the room fast enough after the kiss and tonight. And who could blame her? Her life was filled with turmoil from her mother's death to her father's betrayal. I was no saint, either. I'd hurt her five years ago, and she'd be crazy to let herself feel for me again since it was possible I'd hurt her again.

. . .

THE NEXT DAY WAS SATURDAY, but as usual, I buried myself in work. The sound of small footsteps approaching my office pulled me from my reverie. The door creaked open, and Pax's bright blue eyes peeked around the corner.

I smiled. "Hello, Pax. Did you have fun at your sleepover?"

He stepped into my office. "Yep." He frowned at me. "Do you live here?"

"This is my house."

"No, in here. This room. You're always in here." He looked around. "Where do you sleep?"

I laughed, delighted by the mind of Samantha's son. He was quite astute. Victoria often told me I worked too much, but what else was there for me to do? Victoria was grown up, married, and about to have a child of her own.

"Sometimes, it feels like it, buddy," I admitted with a weary smile. "But no, I don't actually live here."

Curiosity shone in his eyes as he took in the stacks of papers and books that cluttered my workspace. "Can I sit with you?" His gaze fixed on the empty chair across from my desk.

"Of course."

"Can I work too?" He settled into the chair.

"Sure. What do you need to work?"

He shrugged. "I can help you."

My heart squeezed in my chest, surprising me. Emotion welled for this little boy. It occurred to me that he didn't have a father figure in his life. At least not that I could tell. I doubted Samantha's father was involved. She'd indicated that Pax was the result of failed birth control last night. Did that mean the boy's father had abandoned them?

Longing filled me as I considered that I could fill that role. I had a lot of problems, but I knew I'd been a good father to Victoria. Would Samantha allow me to be a father-like person in his life? Was there a way for me to stay in his life, even if I couldn't be with Samantha?

The sound of the door opening and Samantha's voice pulled me from my thoughts. "Pax, are you in here?" Her green eyes scanned the room.

"Mommy, I'm helping with work."

Samantha sent me an apologetic smile. "Sorry, Henry. I didn't mean for him to interrupt your work."

"It's no problem at all, Samantha," I assured her, trying to keep my emotions in check. "In fact, I was thinking maybe we could all go out and do something fun together." It was a crazy thought. But like all my crazy thoughts around Samantha, I couldn't seem to stop myself.

She hesitated, her expression wary. "I appreciate the offer, but I have some things to take care of this afternoon."

My heart sank. It was a testament to how much this woman and her son had infiltrated my life.

"Okay." I swallowed the disappointment. "How about I take Pax, then? Just for a few hours?"

Samantha looked uncertain, reluctance shining in her eyes.

"Please, Mommy? Can I go? Please, please?" The boy knew how to beg. He looked up at her with big blue eyes, a hopeful expression, and his hands clasped in prayer.

She wanted to say no, but she sighed. "Okay, but just for a little while."

"Yay!" Pax's hands shot up into the air in victory.

"Run up and get your coat and mittens," Samantha told him.

Pax was out of the room in a shot. The sound of his feet clopping up the stairs made me laugh.

"You don't have to do this."

Her words stole away my amusement. "I want to, but if you don't want me to, just say so, Samantha."

"He's not your responsibility." Her eyes closed after she spoke, as if the words bothered her.

I knew they bothered me. I didn't need to be reminded that Pax wasn't mine or that I was jealous of the fucker who had created Pax with her. "Where is the man who should have responsibility?"

She stared at me but said nothing.

"He's not here and I am. Whatever is or isn't between us, I care for Pax."

She swallowed and nodded but still didn't say anything.

I SAT NEXT to Pax in the car as Knightly drove us out of the garage.

"How about a museum?" I asked.

Pax made a face. "Like pictures?"

"Pictures? No." I shook my head. "We'll see dinosaurs and sharks and bugs and planets—"

Pax clapped his hands. "Yes, I want to see all that."

Up front, Knightly laughed. "I take it we're heading to the American Museum of Natural History?"

"Exactly."

Pax was a good-natured and obedient child. He did run off once, nearly giving me a heart attack. But when I told him he couldn't do that again, he took my hand and instead would tug hard when he got excited about an exhibit.

We spent hours exploring all the exhibits little boys loved. Laughter and conversation filled our time together, and I found myself marveling at the simple joy of being with Pax. The only thing missing was Samantha.

When we returned home, I carried Pax up in the elevator from the garage. The little guy was tuckered out and sleeping.

"It's been awhile since we've had a child in the home," Knightly said.

I patted Pax's back. "It has."

"I imagine little Hank will be spending lots of time here as well."

I thought of Victoria and Alex's unborn child and how I would be a grandfather soon. Here I was imagining being a father again when I was about to be a grandfather. I was ridiculous. But as I exited the elevator on the third floor to take Pax to his room, I couldn't shake the feeling that I was meant to be in his life. He deserved a father figure, someone who could guide and support him as he grew up. Perhaps, despite the challenges and heartbreak that came with loving Samantha, maybe there was a way for me to be that person for Pax.

Marie met me in the hall. "Goodness, he must have had a wonderful time."

"I think he did." I carried him to his bedroom and lay Pax in his bed.

"Thanks for taking me." Pax had to be talking in his sleep as he curled up.

I ran my hand through his hair. "Thank you for coming with me."

I left Pax, exiting his room. Marie followed me out.

"It was very nice of you to entertain him, Mr. Banion."

"The pleasure was mine." I wondered where Samantha was but didn't want to seem obvious. "You'll be up here with him now?"

She nodded. "Yes. Samantha was invited out with Mr. Thompson."

My hands fisted at the idea of Samantha with her lawyer. "I see. Well, you have a lovely evening, Marie."

"You too, Mr. Banion."

I took the elevator down to the lower floors where my gym was. What better way to work off negative energy than with a punching bag? I was such a fool to continue pining for Samantha. If she wanted to date, who was I to stop her? I had to work harder to get her out of my system. It would be the only way I could continue to stay in Pax's life and not go insane.

17

Samantha

My heart twisted with guilt as I sat in the kitchen drinking coffee and replaying watching Henry and Pax walk to the elevator to start their adventure. Regret gnawed at my insides. I should've gone with them on their outing. I wasn't worried that Henry couldn't manage Pax. I was worried that Henry would see something in Pax that told him Pax was his son. It was a terrible thought. Henry deserved to know the truth. Pax did too. But so much could go wrong. Henry was still adamant that no one could know about our affair. What if Henry rejected Pax to keep our secret? I imagined Henry would do right by us financially, but that didn't mean he'd openly accept Pax as his son. Not if he worried about his reputation or Victoria's reaction.

I had to consider the opposite as well. Would Henry be angry at my secret and retaliate by fighting for custody of Pax?

I left the kitchen, retreating to my room. I couldn't shake the feeling of doom looming over me. Whether I told the truth or not, the outcome would be disastrous.

The shrill ring of my phone pierced the silence, causing me to jump. I checked the caller ID. Lucas. For a moment I thought I'd ignore it. But I reminded myself that the sooner I dealt with my mother's estate, the sooner Pax and I could move on.

I poked the answer button. "Hello?"

"Hey, Samantha, it's Lucas. I'm calling to see if you could meet with me this evening."

My initial thought was to turn him down. But if I stayed here, I'd just ruminate over Henry and Pax. A distraction might be just what I needed.

"Sure." I tried to sound more enthusiastic than I felt. "Where do you want to meet?"

He gave me the name of an Indian restaurant near the East Village.

"Sounds good. See you then." I hung up the phone and took a deep breath, steeling myself for the evening ahead. I slipped on a simple black dress hoping I looked like I made an effort but not so much so that Lucas thought I was into him. I let Marie and Henry's staff know that I was going out and then I ordered a car to drive to the restaurant.

When I arrived, Lucas greeted me with a warm smile. "Thanks for coming out with me again." He pulled out my chair for me as I took a seat.

"Thank you for the invitation."

We made small talk over appetizers, discussing work and life in general. I really wanted to talk about my case, but I didn't want to be rude. In truth, while I wasn't attracted to Lucas, I appreciated his company. That was until I caught Lucas studying me with a furrowed brow.

"Is something wrong?" I asked.

"You tell me. Have you hired someone to look into your father's fraud?"

I hesitated for a moment but then wondered why I should feel bad about hiring Alex. What did it matter to Lucas? "Yes. Someone from Saint Security has agreed to help me look into it." Then I wondered how he knew. "How did you know?"

His jaw clenched. Annoyance flickered in his eyes. "I was visited by Alex Sterling. I couldn't tell him much—lawyer-client privilege." He paused. "I told you I'd look into it."

I felt a pang of guilt. I understood why Lucas would feel that way. My actions suggested that I didn't think he was doing a good job. Then again, unless he had news for me, nothing had changed since the day I learned of my mother's will. "Have you learned anything new?"

He shifted in his seat, avoiding my gaze. "Nothing that proves your father scammed your mother."

In my mind, that justified my hiring Alex.

"It's possible he didn't," Lucas finished. "It's possible this is all legit."

It was my turn to feel annoyed. "It's not. There is no way my mother wouldn't have left something for me and Pax."

He shrugged. "Maybe she was in a different mindset—"

"Which is another way of saying she wasn't in her right mind, which would make anything she signed null and void, right?"

"I'm just saying that it's possible there is no fraud here."

"I believe you're doing your best, Lucas, but I also know you have other clients and so your time working on this is limited. Saint Security is a top investigative firm, and since you haven't been able to find anything that would allow me to contest the will, I accepted their help. You're not being cut out. I'll still need you to file the paperwork."

He sighed heavily, rubbing the back of his neck. "I understand, Samantha. It's just . . . frustrating. I want to help you, but it seems like I'm not doing enough."

For a moment, I wondered if he was doing enough. I'd paid him, but I wasn't a high-powered client. And while he was a family lawyer, he wasn't an investigator. Maybe he didn't know how to figure out how my father had defrauded my mother.

"I appreciate all you've done so far. It can't hurt to have more help, right?"

He nodded. "Right. Will you let me know what your investigator learns?"

"Yes, of course."

As we continued our dinner, I couldn't shake the feeling that there was something more going on regarding my father and my mother's estate. I needed to find the truth, not only for my own peace of mind but also to ensure that Pax and I could truly move forward.

After dinner, I turned down Lucas's offer to go to a club and instead returned home. The house was quiet. Checking my watch, it was after nine. Surely, Henry and Pax were back by now.

I saw a light under Henry's office door and made my way over. I knocked and opened the door when I heard him call, "Come in."

I hesitated before entering, lingering near the doorway to maintain distance between us. The last thing I needed was for him to kiss me, touch me . . .

He sat behind his desk, his eyes focused on the papers in front of him, seemingly distant and preoccupied. "How was your date?"

"Fine." I deliberately didn't correct him by saying it wasn't a date. Perhaps if he thought it was, it would keep our attraction at bay. "How did your outing with Pax go?"

"Fine," he said curtly, still not looking up from his work. The coolness in his voice made me uneasy, and I wondered what had transpired during their time together.

"Is everything okay?" My gut clenched. Did he suspect the truth? Had he seen something in Pax that made him realize that he was Pax's father?

"Everything is fine, Samantha." His gaze finally lifted to me, though his tone remained even. "He's an intelligent, well-mannered young man."

"He is. Thank you for spending time with him. I'm going up to say goodnight to him."

"Goodnight, Samantha," he murmured, his eyes returning to his work as I turned away.

Climbing the stairs, I couldn't shake the feeling that something was off with Henry. Surely, he'd have said something if he suspected Pax was his son. But what else could the sudden cold shoulder mean unless he didn't like that I went out with Lucas? I considered that as I made my way to Pax's room. Was Henry jealous? We'd had several intimate moments of late, but that was just lust. Even he said we couldn't continue to indulge our attraction, so it couldn't be that he was bothered that I'd gone out.

Pax was sound asleep, so I gave him a kiss and retreated to my own room. As I lay in bed, the tension that had been building all day finally overwhelmed me. I needed an escape from the constant turmoil of being around Henry, from the secrets that threatened to consume me. But I wasn't ready to extricate myself and Pax from our current situation. Sure, I could look for a new place to live, but what I really wanted was to leave New York and start a new life and a new business elsewhere. I didn't have the money yet.

I racked my brain for a solution until I remembered that I needed to make a trip to Los Angeles to meet with Henry's newspaper about their online and social media. The more I thought about it, the more perfect the idea was. I could do my job but also bring Pax and Marie to enjoy the sights of Southern California.

The following Monday morning, I immersed myself in work, reviewing all the data about the paper's current online and social media, connecting with the proper people in the Los Angeles office, and organizing the details for my visit. I felt like I was in my element and looked forward to the day when I did this work as the CEO of my own company.

I took a breather, reviewing my list of to-dos for the trip. I still needed to make travel arrangements to get us to L.A. and lodgings for me, Pax, and Marie while there. I grew excited about the trip. Checking the weather, I saw that it was warm in California while winter was bearing down on us here in New York. Maybe we could go to the beach.

The one thing I hadn't done yet was clear this trip through Henry. With a few quick keystrokes, I composed an email to Henry, detailing my plans for the trip—the dates, objectives, and how it would ulti-mately benefit the company. Before I could second-guess myself, I hit

Send and leaned back in my chair, hoping that the time away would provide some much-needed clarity.

As lunch time approached, my phone buzzed on my desk. Glancing at the screen, I saw Alex's name flash up and felt a surge of excitement. Had he discovered something about my father?

"Hey, Alex."

"Hi, Samantha, can you meet me for coffee? I have some questions I need to ask."

"Sure. Where?"

He gave me the address of a little bistro just down the block. I grabbed my coat, left my office, and hurried to meet him.

"Thanks for coming," he said, standing up as I approached.

"Of course." I sat across from him and ordered a coffee from the server who stopped by our table. "What did you want to ask?"

"I just need a little more background into your mother's final days. If the will is legit and not forged, then someone had to have had her sign it."

I nodded. "That was my thinking too." I wondered if he was going to tell me that if she signed it, there was nothing that could be done, as Lucas seemed to hint at. But I knew deep in my heart, my mother wouldn't have willingly given my father everything upon her death.

"Who visited her? What was her schedule like?" Alex asked, cutting straight to the point.

I took a moment to search my memories of those last days. "She mostly stayed in bed. Not many people visited," I admitted, my heart aching with the memory of her frail form.

"Did anyone come by with new paperwork?" Alex pressed, his gaze never leaving mine.

"Not that I saw. Like I said, Lucas indicated that he'd sent a paralegal. I never saw them. I must have been out. Marie says she didn't see this person either."

"What about home health care or hospice staff?"

"We did have a few people come in, but I was usually there when they came. They were all kind and professional. I don't recall any of them asking her to sign anything."

"I was thinking they might have let the paralegal in."

"Oh. Right." I thought about that. "Like I said, I always tried to be there when Mom had health workers come."

"What about other staff?"

"Just Marie, Mom's assistant. She was a real gal Friday."

"Could she have been part of it?"

"Marie? No," I protested immediately. The very idea that she could be involved in something so sinister seemed ludicrous. "She loved my mother like family." But even as I spoke those words, a memory surfaced that made me pause. I remembered seeing Marie in my mother's office, flipping through a stack of documents. I hadn't thought anything of it since she was Mom's assistant, but Marie's expression had been tense and worried. Like I'd caught her doing something she wasn't supposed to be doing.

"Samantha?" Alex prompted.

"Actually, I . . . I don't know," I admitted, my voice quavering. "I saw her once, going through some papers in my mom's office. But I never thought anything of it at the time."

"You said she was your mom's assistant."

"Right. That's why I didn't think anything of it, except she seemed nervous that I found her there. I don't know." I began to second-guess myself. Marie was a godsend for my mother and now me.

"I'll keep that in mind as I continue my investigation."

"Where are you headed next?"

"I plan to visit your mother's house. Maybe there's something there we've missed."

I rolled my eyes. "Good luck with my father. He's not going to be forthcoming with information."

"Leave that to me," Alex said, a sly smile tugging at the corners of his mouth. "I can be quite persuasive when I need to be."

"Thank you, Alex. I really appreciate this, especially with Victoria ready to pop."

His smile was radiant. It made me happy for him and Victoria that they'd found each other, even as it was strange that he'd been

Henry's friend first. "It goes without saying that if she goes into labor—"

"That takes precedence. Of course it does."

"But I do have another working with me on this, so he can take over if needed."

"Thank you."

"Of course." He rose from his chair. "I'll be in touch."

I returned to work, focusing on my duties and preparing for my trip. Henry still hadn't responded to my request, but I was determined to go, so I acted as if he would approve the travel.

At the end of the day, a knock sounded on my door.

"Come in," I called, expecting Alan to question my plans for L.A.

To my surprise, Henry appeared. My heart hitched in my chest as I regarded him, an uneasy mix of desire and apprehension swirling within me. He'd been so distant and cool the other night, and I hadn't seen him since then.

"Good news." He leaned against the doorframe with a casualness that belied the intensity of his gaze. "I've approved your trip to Los Angeles."

"Thank you." Relief filled me. A week, maybe two, of respite away from Henry and all the guilt and stress being around him brought.

"I'll be joining you." He pushed away from the doorframe, entering my office. "The L.A. office could use my attention as well. We can travel together."

His words struck me like a bolt of lightning, sending shockwaves through my already frayed nerves. The idea of traveling with him, sharing close quarters, and navigating the minefield of our attraction filled me with dread.

No. I couldn't do this. "Maybe I should postpone the trip. If the LA office needs you now, I can go later. It's no trouble, really."

"There's no reason for that. We can both deal with what needs to be dealt with."

My stomach churned as I searched for any way to escape this impending disaster. "I was planning on bringing Pax and Marie with me. I thought it would be fun for them and we could enjoy the area in my downtime."

A genuine smile spread across his face. "That's a great idea. It will be fun."

My heart pounded in my chest, the anxiety churning inside me. Surely, I was growing an ulcer. This wasn't how I'd envisioned things going.

But it was clear that Henry had already decided.

"Okay."

"Good. I'll make the arrangements. They have tar pits with dinosaurs in California. I wonder if Pax will enjoy that?"

The corners of my mouth turned up in a small, hesitant smile. The image of our little makeshift family enjoying Southern California flickered in my mind's eye, a tantalizing promise of happiness and togetherness. But beneath it all, the dark undercurrent of unresolved secrets threatened.

"I'm sure he will."

"I'll send you the itinerary." Henry studied me for a moment longer before leaving. As the door closed behind him, I sank into my chair, my head in my hands. What had I gotten myself into?

18

Henry

I sat at my desk in my downtown office trying to focus on business in the Los Angeles office. I think all the fires were out, but there was some possible smoke. Unfortunately, I couldn't focus. My mind kept drifting back to seeing Samantha when she'd arrived home from her date. I'd been dismissive, even cold toward her, and the guilt gnawed at my insides. Yes, I hated the idea of her being with another man, but our situation was my own damn fault. I'd been the one to push her away five years ago. The decision haunted me even as I knew it was the right thing to do. It was the right thing today too, and yet . . .

My computer pinged with a notification. I glanced at the screen with disinterest until I realized it was an email from Samantha.

I'd like to visit the Banion Times in Los Angeles to begin work on their online and social media updates. I've attached my report on what I'd like to cover and the best times for me and the L.A. team to meet.

The words in her email taunted me with a decision I knew I shouldn't make. I was supposed to be doing all I could to avoid her and stop this incessant need for her.

Another part of me reminded myself that I was having issues in Los Angeles. Wasn't I just thinking I should travel out there instead of trying to deal with them here? If I wasn't, I would have eventually thought that.

Maybe this was the opportunity I needed to figure things out with Samantha, to explore the complicated feelings that had resurfaced between us.

Yeah, right. I scoffed at myself, knowing there was no resolution to this situation, and yet, I opened up my calendar and made plans to travel to Los Angeles with Samantha.

I was second-guessing this decision all day up until I went to her office to inform her of the plans. She'd tried to back out of the trip. I should have let her. Instead, I remained steadfast that we'd both go.

DAYS LATER, we were on a private plane heading west.

"Can I fly the plane?" Pax asked as we'd boarded and introduced him to our pilots.

"Oh, God, no," Samantha said.

I laughed. "I'm sorry, Pax, only certified pilots can fly."

"Can I get certified?" His blue eyes shone up at me.

"Someday, sure." I had an image of arranging flying lessons for him that I tried to quickly forget. Yes, I wanted to be in this young man's life, but what were the odds that would happen?

Samantha sat at the table, pulling out her laptop as Marie and Pax sat in chairs and played a game.

I sat on the couch, taking it all in. "Any plans while in California?"

"I want to go to Disney," Pax chimed in.

"A must on any list."

"I'd like to go to the beach," Samantha said, looking up briefly from her work.

"Can we build a sandcastle, Mommy?" Pax bounced in his seat.

"Of course, sweetheart."

"How would you like to see more dinosaurs?" I asked Pax.

"Real ones?"

"Well, their bones and where they once lived." I decided not to explain that most of the fossils there were animals that got stuck and died in the tar pits.

"I want to see that."

As Samantha focused on her work, I engaged in a lively discussion with Pax about all the fun things we could do during our stay. I was enchanted to listen to Pax's excited chatter. It reminded me of when Victoria was a little girl. I used to love to see and experience the world through her eyes. This trip might have been a risky decision, but moments like these made it feel worth it.

WE LANDED IN LOS ANGELES, and the car I arranged took us to our hotel outside Beverly Hills.

"Can we go swimming, Mommy?" Pax asked as we rode the elevator up to our rooms.

"Let's get settled first, okay?"

"'K." Pax turned to look up at me. "Can you come swimming too?"

I glanced at Samantha, wondering what her thoughts were about me joining in on her family time.

"I'm sure Mr. Banion is busy." Marie spoke, but I was sure Samantha was thinking it too. Hoping it.

"I love to swim," I said. "I like to cannonball into the pool."

Pax's brows rose. "Really? Can you show me?"

"Absolutely."

"Did you bring his floaties?" Samantha asked Marie.

"I don't need floaties," I said jokingly.

Samantha's lips twitched upward.

"I did," Marie said. "Or, more accurately, I brought Pax's floaties. Not Mr. Banion's."

I walked Samantha, Pax, and Marie to their suite. The hotel had a four-bedroom suite, but I worried that such close proximity to Samantha could be a problem. Yes, she was staying in my home, but it seemed like she might think it was too intimate to be in the same suite. My suite was next door.

"See you at the pool?" I asked as Samantha entered her room.

"Give us thirty minutes."

Thirty minutes later, I was poolside with a drink.

"Look at my new floaties!" Pax came running over to where I'd staked a spot on a chaise chair.

"Those are great."

"Can we cannonball?"

I laughed, setting my drink down and standing. "If it's okay with your mom."

Samantha set her bag on the chair next to mine. "It's okay with me."

"Where's Marie?" I asked.

"She's resting."

I took Pax's hand and led him to the shallowest section of the pool. I had no idea if the little guy could swim, floaties or not.

He looked up at me expectantly. "Ready?" I asked.

He nodded.

"Cannonball!" I jumped, doing my best to bring my knees up before hitting the water. It was a reminder that I was forty-eight, not eighteen. I hit the water, dropping below the surface. Because it was shallow, I reached the bottom, smacking my knees on the hard surface. I bounced back up, holding my arms up. "Ta-da!"

Pax laughed as he wiped his face where I'd splashed him. "You got me wet."

"He's not the only one."

I glanced over at Samantha, who sat in the chaise in a black bikini. My mouth went dry to see so much of her smooth, curvy flesh.

"Cannonball!" Pax yelled.

I quickly tore my gaze from Samantha to Pax as he hit the water next to me. I waited a beat to see if he popped up but was there to grab him if needed.

His head surfaced and he grinned. "Did I do it?"

"You did it great, champ."

We cannonballed a few more times, and then I helped him stand on my shoulders and he jumped from there.

"Look at me, Mommy," Pax called out when I had him standing on my shoulders again.

"Oh, my goodness, look at you. Make sure you don't hurt Henry, okay?"

"Okay." Pax jumped.

I looked over at Samantha. "Are you suggesting I'm old? Because I'm quite fit."

"Not at all." Her green eyes scanned my chest . . . or I thought they did. Maybe it was wishful thinking.

The afternoon was the most fun I'd had in some time. Being with Pax like this made me miss the days when Victoria was a child.

After swimming, we headed up to our rooms.

"Mommy, I'm hungry," Pax said as they reached their suite.

"It's about time for dinner. We'll get cleaned up and see about getting food."

I'd reached my door, and a tinge of sadness came over me. I'd be eating alone unless, of course, I could convince Samantha and Pax to eat with me.

"Can you come too?" Pax asked me.

"Ah . . . well . . ." God, I wanted to say yes, but I didn't want to invade their family time.

"If you'd like to join us, you can," Samantha said. I searched her face to determine whether she meant it or was just being nice. I couldn't tell.

"I wouldn't mind having company."

"Yay!" Pax yelled.

"I'll shower and change and be over. We can go out or order in—"

"I think it would be best to order in and start getting him settled down or he may not sleep."

Pax zoomed into the room, and I laughed. "He looks like he has enough energy for days."

I enjoyed having dinner with Samantha, Pax, and Marie. I wondered if Mrs. Tillis was right and I should have been eating with them at my house.

After the meal, I returned to my room and prepared for the next day. When I finished that, I poured a drink and took in the view from the hotel balcony. This had been a lovely day. It had been invigorating to play with Pax. Victoria was right in that I needed to get out more and work less. I hadn't felt the desire to until now. Until Samantha and Pax.

THE NEXT MORNING, I arranged a car to take Samantha and me over to the *Banion Times* offices. We were both quiet as we sipped coffee in to-go cups. I was sure she was thinking about the day ahead. Me? I was thinking about the previous day at the pool, playing with Pax and enjoying the sight of Samantha, beautiful and sexy as she lounged in the sun.

We pulled up to the building and I helped her out. "I'll take you to meet the team you'll be working with and then head off to my own business."

As I introduced Samantha to the online and social marketing team, she greeted them with a confident handshake and hello that made me proud. Not that I had any right to feel like that.

It was clear I didn't need to linger as she and the team got right to work. I made my way to the executive offices to meet with the COO and other leaders. While I think I got most of the issues of last week resolved, it didn't hurt for the CEO to show up to make sure they knew I meant business.

After several meetings, I found an empty office and worked on my other business tasks until the end of the day. I headed down to pick up Samantha, finding her and the team in some sort of brainstorming session. Everyone seemed animated and excited. For a moment, I watched Samantha as she worked. She was the expert here. I'd brought her in to assess and consult. But she wasn't pushing her own ideas. Instead, she was listening, considering, writing down all ideas and studying them. She was a true leader, and when it came time to start her business, she'd be a success. I was sure of it. I wondered if she'd let me invest in it.

When she finished, we headed down to the car to return to the hotel. I listened attentively as she shared the work she and the team had done during the day.

"They were off track a bit, but not as much as I initially thought. I think the changes we've discussed are going to be easy and very effective."

I loved watching her talk business. Enthusiasm radiated off her. It drew me in, and I wished more than anything that I could pull her in for a hug and kiss her sweet lips.

I let her know how pleased I was, all the while sitting on my hands so I didn't take action on my urges.

At the hotel, we rode the elevator up to our floor and walked down the hall to our rooms. I considered inviting her in for an after-work drink, but I knew it would only serve to torture myself.

Still, when she went into her room and me into mine, we'd be returning to separate lives. I wasn't ready to do that yet.

As Samantha used her keycard to unlock the door, it burst open and Pax burst out. "Guess what? We went to the park today and I fed the ducks! It tickled my hand." Pax held out his hand as if he were feeding the ducks.

Samantha laughed. "Oh, boy! That sounds like fun."

"Marie ordered dinner for us. She got me spaghetti."

"We should get ready to eat, then."

That was my cue to stop ogling them and enter my room. Maybe I'd go downstairs to the restaurant to eat so it didn't seem so pathetic to be eating alone.

"Are you coming?" Pax asked me.

I hesitated, torn between wanting to spend time with them and feeling like a putz, a lonely old man they were taking pity on.

"I ordered enough for Mr. Banion," Marie's voice came through.

"Please, join us. There's plenty." Samantha's invitation was warm, and I couldn't refuse.

19

Samantha

I'd felt good about the work I'd done that day. The team had been receptive and enthusiastic about my ideas, which reassured me that I was on the right path career-wise. Henry's praise didn't hurt, either. In fact, it meant a lot. Despite all the stress between us, I respected him and his opinion. It boosted my confidence that I'd be successful when I started my own business.

Now back at our rooms, we were set to part ways. My nerves preferred that I didn't spend time around Henry, but another part of me wasn't ready to say goodnight. Plus, he was alone. I couldn't very well let him eat by himself. It would've been rude not to invite him after Pax had, so I seconded the invitation.

As we sat down to dinner, I couldn't help but steal glances at Henry. I wish I understood why he tugged at me like he did. Sure, he was kind and smart and extremely handsome. I thought back to yesterday at the pool. He was fit and trim in his swim trunks. His bare chest was sculpted, and I'd nearly jumped into the water with him and Pax to cool off from the heat watching him brought. But along with the attraction came the nearly debilitating guilt. Watching him play with Pax only made my guilt grow heavier.

"This looks delicious," Henry said as he cut into his chicken. "I appreciate that you're including me."

"I ordered more thinking you might join us," Marie said.

"When can we see the dinosaur bones?" Pax asked Henry.

"Pax, honey, we're here to work and Henry—"

"Soon."

"Yay!"

"I know the boss, so playing hooky is easy." He winked at me. "It's okay, isn't it?"

"Of course." I mixed butter into my baked potato, trying to deal with the growing ulcer in my gut. Pax was growing attached to Henry. Pax had no real father figure, and perhaps Henry was filling that void for Pax. And if I were honest with myself, I knew Henry would make an incredible father to Pax if he only knew the truth.

"Will you join us?" Henry asked. "I could put in a good word with the boss."

"Who's the boss?" Pax asked.

Henry laughed. "I am."

Pax's brows drew together as if he didn't quite get what Henry was saying. "If you're the boss, then you don't have to ask."

"That's right."

I was here to do a job, not play hooky with my boss. "I'll think about it."

Henry's amused expression faltered, and I wondered if he was disappointed. "Could you pass the salt, please?"

"Here you go." The casual exchange did nothing to alleviate the tension building inside me. The answer was to come clean to Henry, but I was a coward.

THE NEXT DAY, I was pleased that the work with the team was still going well. They were coming up with great ideas, some of which I planned to share with other platforms.

"I like the idea of user-generated news shorts," I said in answer to a suggestion by a team member. "We do need to have a system to vet the shorts to avoid problematic content." We'd already gone over the new content policy I'd created, but I referred to it again, telling them to develop a plan to review user-generated content before posting on the newspaper's website or social feeds.

At lunch time, Henry appeared. "Let's grab lunch."

I studied him, noting that he didn't ask or invite me. It wasn't necessarily an order, but it was definitely expected that I would go to lunch. Since I was hungry, it was no big deal except for the usual stress that being around Henry brought me.

We walked down the street to a Mexican restaurant.

"This place has the best authentic Mexican food I've ever had," Henry said. "Whenever I'm in Southern California, I always make time to come here."

"Sounds delicious."

We ordered our food, and Henry asked me how things were going. It felt more like chatting than wanting a report, but I filled him in as his employee. He nodded along, telling me he felt good about the work the team and I were doing.

"I wanted to let you know that we're having dinner tonight with the COO, Larry Stillson."

"We?"

"I'd like you to be there to let him know the plans for the website and social media. He's not as bad as Alan, but he has some questions. But more importantly, Larry is well connected and it could help your business if you impress him as much as you've impressed me and the team at the network."

Giddiness bubbled in my belly. This would be another opportunity to prove myself and set my business up for success. "Of course. I'll be there. I just need to let Marie know."

Our lunch arrived, and I dug into the food. Henry was right. It was excellent.

"How are plans for your business coming along?" Henry asked.

"Slow but sure," I said between bites.

"If you need any feedback or guidance—"

"I was hoping Tori would mentor me."

Henry looked down. "Of course."

Oh, hell. I'd hurt his feelings. "I mean . . . you're already helping me in that department."

He nodded, but I still got the feeling I'd said the wrong thing.

WHEN I GOT BACK to the office, I contacted Marie to let her know I'd be home late and then continued to work with the team. The tech team had joined us as we discussed changes to the website.

At five, Henry appeared again. He was pleasant on the ride toward the ocean where our dinner meeting was being held. But there was still a distance that I'd created with my remark at lunch that showed a lack of appreciation toward Henry. But at least he wasn't cool like he'd been when I arrived back from my dinner with Lucas last week.

At the restaurant, Henry introduced me to Larry Stillson who was around Henry's age, and like Henry, he wore his age well. He greeted me with a firm handshake, his eyes friendly and curious.

"I've been hearing good things about you from Henry and from Tyler Hawly," Larry said as we sat. Tyler was the head of online content at the paper.

"I'm pleased they're happy with my work."

"I'll admit, I have concerns with the Internet. One wrong move and it becomes a shitshow. I'm sure Alan has been telling you the same."

I nodded and realized that as head of all marketing, Alan was a part of marketing decisions made for the paper as well. "Yes, but he's offered his two cents as well. He's cautiously onboard."

"Let's hear what you've got for us," Larry said.

"Of course. First, I want to emphasize that this isn't all me or what I've come up with. You and your team know your market and data better than I do. My job is to assess and give feedback and provide ideas or even guardrails. You have a really great team. They're creative and enthusiastic."

"Good to know."

I went on to explain the ideas that we'd developed so far and what that would mean for the website and social media platforms. I also reviewed the content policy.

"Finally, I've been working with them on leveraging data analytics beyond what they've been doing so far so they can target better across the platforms."

"Data-driven decisions. I like that. But how do you plan to balance creativity with the need for measurable results?"

I glanced at Henry who was sitting quietly. He gave me an imperceptible nod that felt like I'd just won the lottery. In that small gesture, he was telling me that I had this, that he trusted my work. I'd remembered times when I was his intern when he'd done something similar. I'd mentioned it to my mother, and she'd told me that Henry was like a surrogate father, giving me the accolades and encouragement that my father hadn't. Once I started sleeping with Henry, that analogy got creepy, but perhaps there was something to the need for acknowledgement.

"Great question. Encouraging regular brainstorming sessions is key so everyone feels heard and valued. This fosters innovation while still keeping an eye on metrics to make informed choices," I responded.

"Sounds promising. What about addressing potential negative feedback or controversial topics that might arise? Like I said, one little thing taken the wrong way can cause a lot of problems."

"Well, for one, we have the policy. Second, there is a review process. While news moves fast, editorials or opinions can be screened. Transparency and open communication are essential. We'll address any concerns head-on and learn from them, all while maintaining the brand's integrity."

I caught Henry's eye, again noticing the hint of pride in his gaze. My chest swelled with emotion. This man meant so much to me not just professionally but personally. It was agonizingly frustrating that I couldn't be with him.

"I must say, I'm impressed with your approach, Samantha." Larry turned to Henry. "You were right. It's too bad you'll be losing her."

I looked at Henry in surprise. While he'd told me Larry would be a good contact for my business, I hadn't realized that he'd told Larry that I planned to start one.

"Not if we contract with her," Henry said.

"We should probably get on her list now. I suspect she'll be in high demand."

I held up my wine glass. "I'll drink to that."

Henry and Larry clinked their glasses with mine.

AFTER DINNER, I settled into the rideshare next to Henry feeling on top of the world.

"Tonight was a triumph, Samantha. You've come so far in these last five years, and I couldn't be prouder."

I loved the praise and hated it too. Coming from Henry, it only made me feel like the worst person in the world. "Thank you. Your support means more than you know."

"I'm glad I could help."

"I was surprised you mentioned my plans to Mr. Stillman."

"As I said, he's well-connected. He'll be a good source of referrals."

I remembered how I'd dismissed him as a mentor last night. While asking him to help me wouldn't fix all the guilt I was feeling, maybe it could show him how much I appreciated his support.

"I've been working on my business plan, but there's so much to consider."

He nodded. "I know Tori will be a great resource."

"I was hoping maybe you'd take a look too."

His head cocked to the side. "I inherited a corporation. Tori started a business. She'd be a better—"

"You have a lot of experience and insight. You've praised me for how far I've come, but you're the reason I've had the success I have."

He watched me as he inhaled a breath. I got the feeling that my words made him feel appreciated. I hoped he knew that they were the truth. "I'd be happy to see what you've come up with and offer any feedback."

I was sure he was talking about some point in the future, but I had this strong urge to keep this time with him going. "I, ah . . . I have it on my laptop." I patted my bag.

Once again, he studied me. Finally, he said, "Would you like to join me for a drink in my room? We could discuss your plans further."

I'D LIKE to say that I weighed the potential complications of being alone with him, but the truth was, I wasn't ready for the night to end. "I'd appreciate it."

Once in the hotel, we went up to his suite. Henry went to the bar and poured us each a drink, and we settled onto the plush couch.

"To your success," Henry said, holding his glass up.

"I'll drink to that." I clicked my glass with his and sipped.

"So, what do you have?"

I opened my laptop and showed him my plan so far. Mostly, it was a mishmash of notes. I wished I'd taken time to organize them better, but Henry seemed to follow along.

"What will set you apart?" he asked. "Surely, there are many online media consultants."

"Well, I want to create an environment where clients feel heard and understood while providing innovative solutions to their unique challenges."

He arched a brow, and my stomach clenched as I recognized it from my intern days when he'd challenge me.

"That sounds like a lot of words that don't mean much."

I sighed as I looked down at my laptop screen.

"Samantha, what I've seen with your working with my team is that you maximize their strengths, pull them together as a team, and you help them turn boring data into creative content."

He saw all that?

"But," he continued, "as you know, marketing is best done by highlighting benefits, outcomes. What does a maximized, cohesive team mean to a CEO?"

"Money."

"Right. You have to convert all that into the bottom line."

I nodded. Funny how that was my thinking when I was working with clients, but I'd lost focus when working on my own business. I guess I was too focused on myself and not enough on the clients I wanted to help. Another great lesson from Henry.

"Thank you, Henry. Really. I needed to hear that."

"My pleasure, Samantha." Henry likely didn't mean anything when he used the word "pleasure," but my body immediately took it to mean something sensual. I looked at him, unable to help noting the curve of his lips and the intensity in his eyes.

"Your ideas are solid, and I can see how much thought you've put into this," he finished.

"Thanks. It's been a labor of love."

"Isn't that the best kind?" Henry's eyes darkened in that way that made me think he was also thinking sensual thoughts. Thank God it wasn't just me.

"Absolutely."

The moment hung heavily in the air with the weight of desire. The soft glow of the lamp cast a warm light over Henry's face, highlighting the lines etched by years of laughter and worry. His eyes held a depth of sincerity that made my heart swell with a mix of longing and fear.

"Seeing you work this week reminded me of how much I admire you, Samantha. You're smart, good at your job, and an excellent mother."

"Thank you." My chest tightened with each word.

"Looking back on how I treated you five years ago . . . I deeply regret it."

My breath hitched. He'd told me before that he regretted his actions five years ago. His offering me a place to stay and a job was his effort to make it up to me. But there was something about his words now that hit me right in the chest. Perhaps it was because before, I was still angry about his actions. Tonight, I was once again on the cusp of falling for him.

"Seeing how well you've done for yourself even after the way I treated you is a testament to who you are."

I wasn't sure what to say to that.

"Truth is, Samantha, I wish I'd handled things differently back then." His voice was tinged with remorse.

"Like what?" I pressed him even though I knew we were careening into unsafe territory.

He sighed, watching me for a moment. I wondered if he, too, was considering whether we should go down this path. "The right answer is to say I shouldn't have ever touched you, but I can't regret that."

I pressed my lips together, trying to control the torrent of emotions beginning to swirl inside me.

"But I shouldn't have hurt you the way I did." His eyes held mine, and I could see the sincerity there.

"Thank you for saying that, but I know why you did it."

His gaze shifted to the floor, as if he felt shame. "That doesn't mean I can't wish things were different."

"Sometimes, I wish that too." The confession slipped out before I could stop it, and I bit my lip, immediately regretting my honesty.

His eyes lifted to me, and the air in the room thickened and charged as if a storm were brewing. "Do you ever think about . . . what might have happened if things had been different?"

"More often than I should," I admitted and again regretted revealing so much.

"Me too." His voice was low and thick with emotion. The energy radiating between us was palpable. Only then did I realize that we'd slowly inched closer to each other.

My brain told me to disengage. "Maybe we shouldn't talk about this." I worked to regain control over my racing emotions. But even as I spoke, I knew that I didn't want to look away or break the spell that held us captive.

"Maybe not."

It felt as if the world around us had faded away, leaving just the two of us locked in this moment of shared longing.

"Nothing's changed." I was reminding myself of this, not him.

"I know."

We continued to stare at each other, caught in the moment. The longer we sat there, the more my self-control waned, replaced by a growing need.

"Samantha." His voice was barely a whisper, but it carried the weight of longing as heavy as my own.

"Henry." Decision made, I closed the distance between us, pulling him to me with an urgency that left no room for doubt. Our lips met in a searing kiss that sent an inferno of white-hot heat coursing through my blood.

"God, Samantha." He tore his mouth away from me, and I felt it like rejection. His hand pressed against my check. "I'm not strong enough to resist you—"

"So don't."

"I can't bear it when you regret it. And as you said, nothing has changed."

I nodded in understanding. If I kept up with this, I'd be in the same situation I was five years ago. The difference was that I knew that this time. Knowing the end-game, I could prepare and protect myself.

"I know. I understand."

He studied me for a long moment, as if he needed to see in my eyes that I understood. "I'm sorry it can't be different."

I was too but didn't have a chance to say it because his lips took mine. It wasn't the fiery inferno like before. No, this was slow and sweet, and it made my heart squeeze tight in my chest.

His hands pulled me closer until I was straddling his lap. His fingers brushed my skin under my blouse. "Your skin is so soft." He kissed my neck, sending shivers down my spine.

I pressed my hands to his chest, feeling his heartbeat quickening. I unbuttoned his shirt, wanting to feel the hard planes and warmth. The room was filled with soft kisses and sighs as we undressed.

He turned us, laying me back on the couch as he took the last of my clothes from my body. I lay naked, vulnerable to him.

"You're so fucking beautiful, Samantha." His hands slid down my body, stopping for a moment at my nipples where he pinched them before leaning over to suck them.

I arched into him as a shot of pleasure raced through my body.

"So fucking beautiful," he repeated as he trailed kisses down my body. He opened my legs and settled his shoulders between them. His finger ran through my folds, and he brought it to his lips, his eyes piercing as they looked at me. "And so fucking delicious." He sucked his finger into his mouth.

My pussy clenched in anticipation and I moaned.

He dipped his head between my legs. His tongue slid through my pussy, and I cried out as more pleasure built. My fingers threaded through his hair to keep him there. His mouth was magic on my pussy. My hips rocked as he used his tongue and teeth and lips to do the most delicious things to me.

"Oh, God . . ." My body was flushed with heat and tension. Power built from my core, promising an amazing release. "Please," I pleaded, my voice barely audible as I held his head tighter. I could hardly breathe. The anticipation built to a fevered pitch. His fingers slid inside me, finding that one perfect spot as his lips suckled my clit and my world came apart. My orgasm whipped through me. My entire body shuddered and shook from the intensity of it.

"God, you're amazing." He slid up my body, kissing me hard. "Tell me I can fuck you." He lifted his head. "I have a condom."

I nodded. The truth was, with or without a condom, I had to have Henry inside me. I didn't want to think too much about what that meant or what I was willing to risk. All I knew was that I needed to be connected to this man in the most intimate way possible.

20

Henry

Good Christ. I was on fire. In the back of my mind, I knew this was wrong. I was setting myself up for her regret again. Or worse, she wouldn't regret it, and I'd end up hurting her again. But heaven help me, I couldn't stop. Not when she kissed me. Not when she held my head to her sweet pussy so I could feast.

I was hard and needy, the desire to be inside Samantha overpowering any rational thought. I fumbled with my wallet, grabbing the condom I'd stored in there as I also worked to get my pants and boxer briefs off. The realization that I had one now, when I hadn't had one in my secret room, made it clear that I'd been lying to myself about trying to avoid touching Samantha.

I looked down on her, and my heart rolled in my chest. Her blonde hair lay thick and messy on the cushion of the couch. Her skin was rosy with a light sheen of perspiration. Her nipples were taut like they wanted sucking.

I rolled the condom on and then sat, pulling her until she straddled me. "I decided you should fuck me."

Her hands rested on my shoulders. "If you insist." She rubbed her pussy over my aching dick.

I grinned up at her. This was what I'd missed. Five years ago, sex with her had been fun and playful. "Take me, baby. Ride me hard."

She sank down on me, and I hissed out a breath as pleasure rocked through me.

"Fuck . . . so good." I leaned forward and sucked her nipple, her pussy clenching around me in response.

She rose and sank down again, and again. Like the last time, my orgasm quickly neared the edge. I did my best to hold it off, wanting to feel her come around me and take me over with her.

She picked up the pace, her passion wild and unrestrained and glorious to witness. Her nails dug into my shoulders, the sensation only heightening my pleasure.

"Yes . . . baby . . . yes . . . fuck me . . ."

"Oh, God . . . Henry!"

Hearing my name on her lips as passion consumed her did something to me. Yes, this was a physical act. It was supposed to just be a physical act. But emotion welled inside me. I'd fallen for her again. Or more actually, I'd never stopped loving her. That was what made this whole situation so tragic. But it was a tragedy of my own making. I could change it, right? I could take a chance that Victoria wouldn't feel betrayed or that my board wouldn't fire me for the scandal of fucking my intern-turned-employee.

Her head flew back, and her body went taut. Watching her come was the most beautiful vision I could imagine. But it was short-lived as my body responded to her gripping my cock hard. I bucked up and yelled out as my release consumed me. We moved together, as we had in the past, as if we'd been made for each other.

The storm subsided, and Samantha fell against me. Her eyes were closed, her chest heaving as she caught her breath. I banded my arms around her, not wanting her to make an escape. I wanted to tell her then all that was in my heart, to confess my love and ask her to stay. But I was a fucking coward. Fear held me back. Not just the same old concerns about Victoria and my business, but fears of Samantha's rejection. She might have fucked me, but that didn't mean she loved me. Why would she after what I'd done to her five years ago? She wouldn't allow herself to be hurt again. This was just sex for her.

She sighed and sat back. We looked at each other, and in the aftermath of lust lay awkwardness.

"I guess I should go back to my room."

"I guess." God, I wanted her to stay.

"Right . . ." Slowly, she untangled herself from my embrace and started dressing. Watching her dress felt like a dagger through my heart. I fought the urge to beg her to stay the night, to live out the fantasies I'd held onto for far too long.

She started toward the door.

A desperate idea formed in my mind, a last-ditch effort to keep Samantha close. "Samantha?"

She paused, turning slightly to face me.

"Tomorrow . . . Why don't we take the day off? We can take Pax to the Tar Pits."

Her hesitation was palpable. She wasn't going to outright regret the sex or reject me, but she also wasn't going to go full-throttle into this connection between us.

"I don't know."

"PLEASE." I hated how desperate I felt. "I want to spend time with you and Pax, get to know him better."

She flinched, and I began to wonder if her hesitation wasn't so much because of this difficult situation between us but because she didn't want me growing close to Pax.

"I have work—"

"Then let me take him. I know that you and me . . . well . . ." I couldn't say the words that would dismiss what was in my heart. "I care about Pax. I'd like to be his friend."

She looked away, and again, I wondered what that was about. Then she sighed. "Yes, okay. We'll spend the day with you."

I didn't feel as happy about that as I'd have liked, mostly because I could tell she would have preferred to say no. Still, I accepted it.

"Great. I'll pick you and Pax up tomorrow. We'll go to breakfast and then to the Tar Pits. Maybe to the beach too."

She smiled, but it didn't reach her eyes. "We'll be ready."

When she left, I blew out a breath. What fuck was wrong with me? I was a decisive businessman. So why couldn't I be like that with Samantha? Why couldn't I just let her go and move on? Why wasn't I brave enough to deal with the potential fallout from loving her?

For a moment, I resented her for making me like this, but then I chastised myself for it. It wasn't her fault I was a coward.

THE NEXT MORNING, after coffee, a shower, and dressing, I headed over to Samantha's suite, knocking on the door.

"Yay, he's here!" Pax's voice echoed through the door. I smiled, pleased that someone was happy to see me.

The door opened, and while Samantha smiled, it was like last night, lacking in enthusiasm.

"Ready for our day off?" I asked.

"Absolutely." She turned back inside. "Marie, we're leaving. Enjoy your day."

"Will do."

"Hey, buddy, want to see some dinosaurs today?" I asked Pax as we made our way through the hotel lobby.

"Yay, dinosaurs!" His excitement was contagious, and I couldn't help but smile.

"How do you feel about pancakes first?"

"Can I have chocolate chips in mine?"

"I don't see why not." I glanced at Samantha, wondering if I should defer to her first. After all, breakfast shouldn't be a dessert.

Samantha gave me the same smile. I shrugged, determined to make this a great day for the both of them.

Breakfast was an adventure with Pax. The kid buried his pancakes in syrup, and I suspected he'd be bouncing off the walls before long. Good thing there was an outdoor section to the Tar Pits.

As we walked through the park, I kept my eye on Pax, enjoying the way his eyes lit up at each exhibit we passed. Children had a wonder about them that adults lacked. I suppose life snuffed it out of us with its hard lessons and responsibilities.

"That looks like an elephant." Pointed toward the towering model in a tar pit.

"It's a mammoth. And over there is a saber-tooth," I pointed toward the extinct cat.

Pax studied the animals and then looked at me. "Where are the dinosaurs?"

I ruffled his blond hair. "Let's go inside."

We spent hours exploring the park and indoor exhibits. The longer we were together, the greater the sense of attachment I had toward the boy grew. It felt like outings I'd enjoyed with Victoria when she was a child. Like we were a family. For a moment, I nearly took Samantha's hand as we strolled and watched Pax take in the sights. The yearning for this to be real was startling and scary.

At lunch time, we grabbed deli sandwiches and headed to a nearby park for a picnic. Pax ate about three bites before he was off playing on the playground.

"He's a busy kid."

"Hmm . . ." Samantha watched Pax. Her smile this time was genuine.

I found myself wondering why she was raising him alone. "It's not easy being a single parent."

"You'd know," she said.

"Yes, well, I had help." My parents weren't the most involved in Victoria's care. Knightly and Mrs. Tillis were more like grandparents than my parents were. "Has anyone helped you? Pax's father, maybe?"

Samantha tensed, and I swore I could feel her draw away.

"Sorry, I didn't mean to pry. It doesn't matter." I backtracked, not wanting to push her away.

She appeared to be thinking, but before she said anything, Pax rushed up to us. "There's ice cream. Can we get some?"

"Absolutely," Samantha said with some relief in her tone.

I rose from our table and gathered our trash to toss. "Let's get ice cream."

By the time we arrived back at the hotel that evening, all the sugar and excitement were drained from Pax. The kid was practically asleep as he entered the hotel room.

"Thank you for a lovely day, Henry," Samantha said.

I stood like a lovesick puppy at her door, not wanting the day to end. "Thank you, Samantha. I really enjoyed it."

"Well . . . goodnight."

"Goodnight." The door clicked shut, and that was it. I was alone.

I returned to my room, wondering how much longer I was going to be such a doofus. Would I grow balls and take what I wanted, or would I let her go when the time came for her to move on? And what would I do in the meantime?

I ordered room service and poured myself a drink. I pulled out my laptop, checking in with work to make sure there were no emergencies. I had an email from Alan with concerns about the user-generated content and wondering if Samantha was leading us down a path that would lead to being canceled or sued. I ignored it, figuring I'd deal with it when I returned to New York.

When I finished my meal and checked my work, I turned on the TV. I skipped the news and reality TV. I settled in to watch a spy movie.

When the credits rolled, there was a knock on my door. Checking my watch, it was nearly nine. I looked through the peephole. Samantha.

I opened the door. "Is everything okay?"

"Can we talk?"

Something about her demeanor made me want to say no. Like she had bad news for me. "Of course. Come in."

She stepped in. "You asked about Pax's father and I didn't—"

"It's none of my business, Samantha." The truth was, I didn't want to know. I didn't want to think about another man having been with her, sharing in the creation of the beautiful little boy who'd captured my heart.

"BUT IT IS—"

I pressed my finger to her lips. "I don't need to know." My heart clenched at the feel of her soft lips. "God, Samantha, how you make me want you. You drive me mad with it."

Her eyes were soft, and I wondered if she was taking pity on me. "This is important."

I shook my head, desperation bubbling up. "I see you and all I want to do is kiss you, touch you. I know all the reasons we can't, but right now, we're away from it. It's just us here and now. While we're here, can we give in to it?"

She looked at me, and I was sure she was going to say no. "Is that what you really want?"

"Yes." I wanted a moment in time where we could be all that we could be to each other without the outside world butting in.

"Okay."

In an instant, my lips were on hers and I'd pressed her against the door. Need gnawed at me, but it wasn't just lust. It was a need to make her mine. I knew it wouldn't happen. At least not in the long run. But she could be mine here and now. I let myself get lost in her, the rest of the world dissipating.

I swept her up in my arms, carrying her to my bed. "Give me all of you tonight, Samantha. Don't hold back."

I looked down on her as I laid her on the bed, wanting her to surrender to this thing between us if only for this moment.

She nodded and reached up to me. Relief flooded me, followed by a complete opening of my heart. Words of love lingered on the tip of my tongue, but I held them back. I would love her, but only through my touch.

I undressed her, savoring every inch of her body, searing it into my mind so that I'd never forget. The more I let myself drown in her, the more I realized that I'd never get beyond her. She was a part of me, would always be a part of me.

21

Samantha

How many times had I told myself I couldn't get caught up in Henry, only to find myself in his arms? Too many times. And here I was again, not just caught up but actively seeking him. He'd asked for this moment in time to give in to this pull between us, and I'd agreed even as my conscience told me it was wrong on so many levels. The only reason I'd come to Henry's room tonight was to tell him the truth about Pax.

The day had been beyond perfect. The laughter we shared and the way Pax's eyes lit up with excitement when he saw something new . . . it all felt like a beautiful dream that I knew couldn't last. My chest tightened as I recalled Henry asking about Pax's father, his sharp blue eyes filled with curiosity. My heart had raced with dread at that moment. I'd been relieved when he'd backed off from the question, but after today, there was no way I couldn't tell Henry the truth. He was amazing with Pax, and Pax clearly adored him. So I'd come over to confess and hoped to God that Henry would understand why I made the choice I had and that somehow, we could work something out.

But he wouldn't listen and I gave up trying. Instead, I was in his bed as his lips and hands revered my body. Electricity surged through my body at his touch. It occurred to me that after I told Henry the truth, his feelings for me could change. He could resent me. Hate me. This moment could be the last time I'd be with him like this, and I decided I'd make the most of it. Through my touch, I'd show him how I felt, how much I admired and loved him.

My fingers tangled in his thick silver hair, pulling him closer, wanting to meld into him.

"God, Samantha . . . you have no idea what you do to me."

"Show me." I pulled him closer, needing to feel the raw connection as deeply as possible.

His hands roamed over my body, leaving trails of heat in their wake. It was as if he knew every inch of me, every secret desire that lay hidden beneath the surface.

"I need to be inside you—"

"Yes." I opened for him, inviting him to take what he wanted. He started to roll away, and I groaned in frustration.

"Condom," he said by way of explanation.

"It's okay." I reached for him. "I'm on the pill." In the back of my mind, I knew this was a risk. The pill had failed me before, but at this moment, all I could think about was being a part of Henry without barriers, physically or emotionally.

"Are you sure?" His blue eyes were intense as he looked at me. "I thought you said—"

"If you're worried—"

"I'm not worried." He positioned his body against mine. Did that mean he was okay if the pill failed? Guilt tried to overtake the love and desire I was feeling. I desperately pushed it away.

His gaze held mine as he slowly pressed inside me. Emotion flooded my chest as inch by inch, he filled me. It was more than his body I felt inside me. The barrier between us dissolved, and for a brief moment, we were one.

Once he was seeped deep in my body, he dipped his head and kissed me. Slowly, tenderly, until I wondered if he was feeling the same emotions I was. Tears pricked my eyes at the unfairness that we could love each other and yet not be together. Not if Henry wanted to keep me a secret from Victoria and his business. But clearly, he did, as he was clear that this affair would only be while we were away from New York.

"Samantha." His whisper of my name drew me back to the present where I let go of the past and worries to focus on this moment. He moved and I responded, our bodies moving like a dance in perfect harmony. Each time he sank into me and our eyes met, it was as if another layer of our souls were connecting, joining.

Soon, need ramped up and the slow lovemaking turned desperate as we each sought pleasure. The tension built to a crescendo, reaching the edge where I teetered in that moment of torturous anticipation. Henry drove in again and sent me soaring. I cried out, arching into him, clutching him close, never wanting this moment to end.

As we lay entwined, our breathing ragged and hearts pounding, the ache in my chest built. Why did it have to be like this?

I started to move, but Henry tugged me close. "Stay for a minute," he murmured, his voice heavy with exhaustion.

I gave in again, nestling in beside him. I closed my eyes, savoring his scent and sound of his heart.

I WOKE UP WITH A START, disoriented as to where I was. Warm breath teased my ear. I was with Henry in his bed. I panicked that I might have stayed the night. Looking at the nightstand, I saw that it was just after midnight.

I turned to Henry and for a moment, let myself take him in. His chest rose and fell gently, the rhythm of his breaths soothing yet heart-wrenching. I was torturing myself, so I untangled myself from his strong embrace.

I found my clothes, and once dressed, I hesitated at the door, glancing back at the peaceful scene one last time. A tear trickled down my cheek, but I quickly wiped it away. I left the sanctuary of

Henry's room, feeling a cold emptiness.

IN THE QUIET of my own suite, I found Pax sleeping soundly, blissfully unaware of the turmoil that filled my heart. I reached down and brushed a lock of blond hair from his forehead. Pax was the embodiment of everything pure and good in my life. It was hard to believe I could feel more guilt, but I did as I realized that it wasn't just Henry who deserved to know about Pax, but Pax also deserved to know about Henry, to have a father like Henry.

I headed to bed, unable to stop thinking about the passion and tenderness Henry showed me. Our connection was undeniable. I longed to tell him everything, to lay my soul bare and hope that he would understand, but acknowledging the truth could destroy us as well.

THE MORNING ARRIVED FASTER than expected. I had breakfast with Pax and Marie, who planned to go to the zoo today. After eating, I met Henry in the hallway. He leaned in, giving me a kiss on the temple, a gesture I hadn't expected. It made my heart ache even more.

"I'm sorry I fell asleep on you."

"I fell asleep too."

In the elevator, his smile was sheepish. "Will you come over again tonight?"

Heat tinged my cheeks. "Do you want me to?"

He snorted. "I think you know the answer to that."

Once in the car, the gestures and innuendo ceased. It was a harsh reminder that I was once again Henry's dirty little secret. I wanted to be angry at him, but it was my own fault. I'd agreed to it. I'd also decided to tell him about Pax.

As we pulled into the parking lot, I hesitated, my lips parting to confess, but the words died in my throat. This wasn't the right time or place. I needed to tell him later when we were alone and in a place where we could hash out the next steps.

. . .

IN THE SAFETY of my makeshift office, I threw myself into work, pushing away the turmoil and instead relishing in the sense of accomplishment. It was the one area of my life where I was in control, and for a while, it dulled the relentless ache of guilt.

I'd just finished reviewing the latest content ideas from the team when Henry showed up in my doorway.

"Hey." He stepped in, closing the door behind him.

"Hey. Everything okay?"

His expression was apologetic. "A business issue in New York has come up, and I need to head back today." He sighed, running a hand through his hair. "I know you have a few days left, so I've arranged flights for you and Pax and Marie when you're finished here."

"Thank you." I guess that meant no late-night rendezvous. Then again, once I told him the truth, he might not want anything to do with me. Since he was leaving, perhaps I needed to tell him now. But at work, when his mind was preoccupied with a problem in New York, it didn't seem like the right time. At least that was what I told myself.

"Believe me, I'd hoped for more time together." The vulnerability in his eyes tugged at my heartstrings.

"Me too."

He stepped over to me, holding his hands out. I took his hands and let him pull me up from my chair. He released my hand to cup my cheek. "A kiss for the road?"

Our lips met in a sweet yet desperate kiss. He groaned, pressing his length against my belly. "See what you do to me?"

I cupped his dick, rubbing it. "Poor Henry."

He moaned and laughed at the same time. "You're teasing."

I don't know what came over me. "No." I undid his buckle. "I'm going to take care of you."

His blue eyes turned feral. "Let me fuck you, Samantha." His hands slid up my thighs, lifting my skirt to my waist. "I like a good blowjob, but I much prefer to be inside you."

My entire body nearly went up in flames at the wild need in his voice. He turned me around and stepped behind me.

I rested my hands on my desk for stability as my legs wobbled with need. He pulled down my panties, and I stepped out of them. His hands rubbed my ass cheeks and he pressed a soft kiss on my neck.

"Hold on, Samantha, I'm about to give the fuck of a lifetime."

I moaned, and my pussy felt like it dripped with arousal. He rubbed his dick between my legs, through my folds.

I wasn't sure if he'd locked the door, and the idea that at any moment someone could walk in and find Henry fucking me terrified me even as it heightened the excitement.

He gripped my hips and thrust. I let out a grunt as his dick filled me, hard and fast.

"Fuck, I love your pussy." He rocked in and out of me, fast, furious.

I was gasping for breath as I held on to the desk.

"Are you there?" he panted.

"Almost."

"Touch yourself, baby. Make yourself come and take me with you."

I reached between my legs, rubbing a finger over my clit just as Henry drove into me.

I bit back a cry as my release blasted through me.

"Yes," Henry said against my shoulder. He moved in and out, drawing out the pleasure as his release filled my body.

My legs shook as he stepped back. He turned me, leaning me against the desk and kissing me. There was a desperation to it, like he expected this to be the last kiss. I suppose it was since he was going back to New York.

He pulled back, looking at me. I expected him to say something, but no words came. I couldn't think of anything to say, either.

He fastened his pants and bent down to pick up my panties. "Can I keep these?"

"I don't have an extra pair here."

"God, the idea of your working without panties makes me want to fuck you again." He started to hand them back.

"You keep them." I didn't know why, but I wanted him to have something of me, of mine, even if it was a sexual object.

"Are you sure?"

I nodded.

He kissed me again and exited my office with my panties in his coat pocket.

The click of the door shutting behind Henry echoed through my office, leaving me feeling empty and alone. My sexy time with Henry was over. Whatever happened next after telling him about Pax, I'd at least have memories of the man I'd come to love again.

I cleaned myself up with a tissue and then pushed everything away to focus on work. My fingers began to move over the keys, typing out emails and reports as if nothing had happened. But every so often, my mind would drift to Henry. His hands on my skin and the taste of his lips against mine. How wonderful he was with Pax. Would Henry still want me once he knew the truth about Pax? Would he ever be able to forgive me?

Time crawled by as I forced myself to focus on work. Just before lunch, my phone rang. I wondered if it was Henry but determined he was somewhere over the United States heading east to New York.

Checking the caller ID, my heart stopped to see my father's name. What did he want?

"Hello?"

"Stop your investigation, Samantha." My father's tone was cold, almost deadly.

"EXCUSE ME?" I tried to keep my voice steady even as fear threatened.

"Drop it, Samantha. This is your only warning."

"Or what? What could you possibly do to me that you haven't done already?"

"Trust me, there are far worse things than being cut off financially.

For example, imagine if certain news were to come to light. Secrets that could ruin you and Henry Banion."

My blood ran cold. Could he know the truth about Pax? But how?

I tried to act like I didn't know what he was talking about. "You're delusional."

"Think of this as a friendly reminder of what's at stake . . . that boy of yours. Be smart, Samantha. Leave it alone."

I swallowed down the panic that he was threatening Pax. "I don't know why you're calling. If you have nothing to hide, then you have nothing to worry about, right?"

"Drop it or face the consequences." There was a pause, and then he hung up, leaving me shaking with a mix of fury and terror. Was he bluffing or did he know something? And what something did he know? It didn't seem possible that he knew about me and Henry or that Pax was Henry's son. Maybe he knew I was staying with Henry and was suggesting we were having an affair, which I suppose we were. Or had been. But it would be easy to explain my staying with Henry since I was Victoria's friend.

No, Dad had to be thinking of something else or just calling to scare me. But even as I tried to reassure myself, the truth loomed over me like a storm cloud, dark and heavy with the potential for destruction.

If Dad found out something, then maybe Alex did too. My hands trembled as I dialed Alex's number.

"Hey, Samantha, what's up?"

"Alex, I . . . I wonder where you are in the investigation of my father."

"It's still in progress. Are you okay?"

I let out a shaking breath, wishing I had some water. "My father called. He threatened me if I don't stop looking into him."

"Threatened how?" His voice turned serious.

"He was vague . . . saying something about ruining me and Henry." Was I saying too much? Would I be exposing me and Henry?

"Sounds like the words of a guilty man."

"Yes, but . . ."

"I don't have the goods on him yet, but we have tracked down that paralegal your lawyer said he sent to see your mom. I've sent someone to interview her. I'd have gone, but with Victoria—"

"Of course, you can't leave her."

There was a pause on the other end of the line. "Do you want to stop the investigation?"

I sort of did. It wasn't like I hadn't considered giving up already.

"Look, Samantha, I know this is difficult for you. But think about what's at stake here. You and Pax are the rightful heirs. Your mother would be sick to know what your father has done. Plus, it just wouldn't be right for your father to get away with this."

"We're not sure he did anything—"

"His call to you is proof he did. He wouldn't care about the investigation if he'd done everything on the up and up."

He was right. I couldn't back down. Regardless of the risk, the truth was worth fighting for.

"I don't want to stop the investigation."

"You don't sound sure."

"I'm just worried about my father. What he might do."

"How about I lay low for a bit and make it look like you've terminated our services? I won't do anything here until I hear back from my guy in South America on what the paralegal has to say."

I let out a breath of relief. "Thank you, Alex."

"Hey, no problem."

"By the way, how's Tori doing?" I felt like a terrible friend for not asking sooner. In fact, I'd been so lost in my own issues, I hadn't been checking in on Victoria.

"Excited for the baby to finally arrive. We're both pretty nervous but also incredibly happy."

I smiled, happy for them both. "I know you'll both be great. Parenthood is an amazing journey."

We chatted for a bit and then ended the call. My father's threat still hung over me, but at least for now, I had a plan. When I returned to New York, I would finally tell Henry the truth, no matter the consequences. If that was what my father had as news, I needed to make sure Henry heard it from me.

22

Henry

I really didn't want to be hurtling across the sky heading east back to New York. Why did I have to leave Samantha now, just when things were starting to go so well between us?

I closed my eyes and let my mind drift back to last night in Samantha's arms. It was like it had been five years ago, only more, somehow. Even in her office having a quick fuck, there was something more. If I wasn't mistaken, I was helplessly, hopelessly in love with Samantha. Resisting her was futile. All the reasons I should resist still existed, but I didn't want to. I wanted her in my life and would figure out how to deal with the issues. I was a clichéd man having an affair with a younger woman who worked for me. News and social media would have a field day with that. My board could force me out. My daughter would probably be upset that I'd fucked her friend. But I was tired of denying myself happiness. The only question was what Samantha felt about me.

As the plane touched down at JFK, I resolved to fight for Samantha, for our future together. I'd convince the board that whatever scandal might arise wasn't worth getting rid of me. Or if that didn't work, maybe I'd retire early and focus on making Samantha and Pax happy.

But I couldn't focus on Samantha at the moment. At the office, I had to deal with the crisis that had brought me home—a potential lawsuit regarding a news story we'd been publishing about a senator.

"Any updates?" I asked one of several lawyers, Jasper, in the conference room, where I, the writers, and fact checkers were gathered.

"We're working on it, Henry."

I glanced around the table. "Were we wrong?"

The writers of the piece shook their heads. "No, sir."

"So, what's the issue?"

"Several other news outlets picked up on something from the piece and have been running with it. The senator has been harassed, as has his family," Jasper explained.

"That doesn't make sense."

"He's suing them too, but Banion was the source of the original story—"

"But we never reported what the other news outlets are reporting," another writer said.

I stared at them all, wondering what I was missing.

"The other outlets took something we reported and extrapolated it to mean something more," Jasper said.

"I'm not liable for other news outlets."

"No sir, and that's what we're putting together in response to the lawsuit," another attorney said.

"Good." I worked with them to make sure my company was in the clear.

Later in the evening, when I returned home, I headed to my home office to check on other areas of the business.

"Ah, Mr. Banion, you're home." Mrs. Tillis appeared in the doorway.

"Yes. Is Caroline still here? I could use a sandwich."

"I'll check. Will Samantha and Pax be here too?"

"They're in Los Angeles." I began sorting through the papers I'd brought home.

"Will they be returning sometime?"

I looked up at Mrs. Tillis with the urge to tell her I planned for Samantha and Pax to never leave. "They'll be back in a couple of days."

"Good. The house has been too quiet without them. I'll get your sandwich."

I'd only been home for a few minutes, but I agreed. The house was too quiet.

I settled into my chair, switching on my laptop and readying myself for another round of emails and reports.

A bit later, Mrs. Tillis returned with a sandwich and I hunkered down to work. I took a break to call Victoria and check in with her. I figured I'd have heard if the baby were coming, but still, it had been a few days since I heard from her.

"Did you hear the news about Senator Kipson?" she asked, amusement in her voice.

"I know you're smart enough not to take a news item and embellish it."

"Damn right, I'm smart enough. What were those numb nuts thinking, publishing that garbage?"

"The senator is including us in a lawsuit."

"Yeah, well, I know you'll get out of it. Nothing you published was wrong. How was your trip?"

I thought of Samantha and Pax. At some point, I needed to tell Victoria about my feelings for them but decided over the phone wasn't the way to do it. "I had to cut it short because of this lawsuit. I took Samantha and Pax to the Tar Pits."

"Oh, my God, with the dinosaurs?"

I was pleased she remembered. "Yes."

"I bet Pax loved it."

She and I chatted a bit more, and when we hung up, I worked some more.

Just after midnight, I called it a day and headed up to my room.

With nothing to distract me, my mind was back on Samantha and Pax. Should I call her? I wanted to, but maybe now that I was here, our moment away from the issues was past. Except I didn't want it to pass. I should call to keep our connection strong.

I checked my watch again, noting it was only just after nine in the evening in California. Surely, that wasn't too late to call.

I took off my clothes, finding Samantha's panties in my coat pocket. I brought them up, inhaling the scent of her sex. God, I wished she were here.

I changed into lounge pants and didn't bother with a shirt as I lay on my bed with her panties and dialed her number.

"Henry?"

"Hey. How are you?"

"Fine." Her voice, usually so full of life, came across strained and tired.

"Is everything okay? You sound . . . off."

"Long day, that's all."

"Is Pax okay?" I wished I were there to take him to all the other fun things in Southern California.

"He zonked out about a half-hour ago. What about you? Is everything okay?"

"Yes. Or it will be. I just wanted to hear your voice before I went to bed."

"Really?" She sounded surprised.

"Yes, really." I wanted to tell her more, but I didn't want to do it on the phone.

She sighed. "My dad called me today."

"What?" That motherfucker. "What did he want?"

"It's not important."

"Of course it's important." I wanted her to feel like she could talk to me. I wanted to be her champion, her protector.

"He just wants me to stop contesting the will. Alex sounds like he has a lead, though."

"Is there something I can do?"

"No. I do want to talk to you when I get back, though."

"About?" My heart thundered in my chest wondering if she wanted to confess her love. I laughed inwardly. She probably wanted to talk about her business. Or, heaven forbid, moving on. Well, I wouldn't let that happen. Or I'd try to stop it. I needed to come up with a big way to show her how much I felt for her, how much I wanted her and Pax in my life. Perhaps I could take them on a trip. Somewhere warm like the Caribbean. I could picture Samantha in her bikini and Pax making sandcastles in the sand.

"It can wait. Have you heard from Tori?"

I didn't want to wait, but knew I had no choice. "I spoke on the phone with her. She sounded tired but good."

"Alex says she's ready to not be pregnant anymore. God, I remember that feeling."

I imagined Samantha round with child. I envied the man who'd created Pax with her. "Do you want more children?" I asked before thinking.

"Ah . . . yeah . . . maybe. How about you?"

I laughed. "I was thinking I was past my prime."

"I think you're prime."

I grinned. "Do you? Did you get that impression last night or in your office this morning?"

"Both."

I could picture her cheeks pink from sexual innuendo. "Guess what I found in my pocket tonight?"

"I can't imagine."

"Really. I was thinking you must have had a draft under your dress today."

She laughed. "What are you doing with them?"

"Do you really want to know?" I wasn't doing anything at the moment, but I was thinking about wrapping them around my dick and wanking one off.

"Yes." There was a breathlessness to her voice that told me she was turned on. It made me wish I'd left something of mine.

Not wanting to be a liar, I pushed my lounge pants down, freeing my erection. "I'm hard as a rock and am thinking of using your panties to take care of it."

Her breath hitched.

"Does that turn you on?"

"Yes."

"Will you touch yourself?"

She was quiet, and I wondered if that was too weird for her. "I've never had phone sex."

"I have no doubt that you'll be good at it. Talk dirty to me, Samantha, while I stroke my dick with your panties."

"I wish I could see it."

I'd learned a long time ago that sex and photos or video from phones could be a potential problem, but that didn't stop me from hitting the video call button and turning my phone so she could see my dick.

"How's that?"

"Sexy."

"It would help if you showed me your body."

She turned on her camera. Her green eyes were dilated with passion. "This is crazy."

"Show me your tits and talk dirty to me."

She pushed the straps of her pajamas down. "What do you want me to say?"

I wanted to lick her hard nipple. "Tell me what you want me to do to you."

"You mean like fill me with that massive cock of yours?"

"Fuck . . . yes." I stroked harder, faster. "I wish you were here. I want to come on your tits."

"Here they are." She held her phone closer to them.

"Yes . . ." I closed my eyes, trying to keep the phone steady on my dick as I stroked, fast, fast, fast and then slow as I tried to draw out the pleasure. "I'm close . . . can you see . . ."

"Yes," she moaned. "I wish I were there."

"I wish you were too . . ."

"I'd lick and suck . . ."

"Oh, fuck!" Cum shot from my dick, landing on the phone and my stomach. I let the camera linger on my belly, rubbing the gooey mess with my free hand. "Look what you did." I brought the phone to my face and I grinned. "Now it's your turn."

"I don't know."

"I'd like to watch you touch yourself. Watch you come."

She bit her lip but then moved. She adjusted the phone and showed me how she was rubbing her clit.

"Can you feel me sucking your clit?"

"Oh . . ."

"You taste delicious, Samantha. I want you to fill my mouth with your juices."

She cried out, arching as her pink pussy contracted and her juices covered her hand.

"Fuck, you're sexy."

"I can't believe I did that."

I smiled at her, hoping she didn't feel self-conscious. "I'm glad you did." I wanted to promise her lots more orgasms. Lots more happiness. Lots more children . . . but I held my tongue.

"Get some sleep. I'll see you in a few days."

"Goodnight, Henry."

"Goodnight." My love.

As the call ended, I couldn't help but smile. Our conversation had given me a glimmer of hope. The thought of being with Samantha and Pax filled me with a sense of purpose beyond work.

I lay in the quiet dark, my heart filled with joy and love. I could imagine Samantha lying beside me, her body pressed close, her gentle breaths whispering against my skin. I allowed my thoughts to drift toward that dream, envisioning a life focused on family again. I could see us walking hand in hand through Central Park, our fingers intertwined. Or lazy Sunday mornings spent tangled in each other's arms.

As sleep finally began to claim me, I clung to that hope that Samantha felt the same for me.

23

Samantha

Three days later, I stepped off the plane in New York, holding Pax's hand as Marie followed closely behind us. We got into the car with Knightly. I wished Henry had been here to greet us, but we'd see him at home.

As the car drove through the city, my gut twisted into knots. Tonight, I'd tell Henry that he was Pax's father. And hopefully, when I told him that I loved him, he wouldn't be too angry about Pax to see what we could have together.

My father's threats loomed over me, and I hoped that once Henry knew the truth, those threats would be nullified. I prayed that Alex would uncover something to help my case, or at the very least, I'd be able to handle whatever my father threw my way.

We drove into Henry's garage. "I'll take your bags up," Knightly said, pulling into an area by the elevator.

"Is Mr. Banion home?" I asked.

"He's at his corporate offices." Knightly helped us out of the car. "He's expected home by dinner."

Though part of me breathed a sigh of relief. Another part wished Henry was home so I could get this conversation over with.

Once on the third floor, Marie and I worked to get resettled into our space. For a moment, I wondered if Henry would ask me to stay when he learned how I felt and that Pax was his child. Maybe he'd move me into his room.

I shook my head and warned myself not to get ahead of myself. It was quite possible that my heart would be broken.

I'd just finished getting Pax's books and toys unpacked when Knightly appeared again. "Mr. Layton is here to see you."

My father? "What?"

"He's in the living room."

My chest tightened. This was the worst possible timing. "Marie, can you watch Pax while I deal with this?"

"Of course."

As I walked toward the living room, I prayed that I could get the conversation done and send my father away before Henry arrived home.

"Didn't expect to see me, did you?" The venom in my father's voice sent chills down my spine.

"What do you want?"

"You know what I want. Drop your investigation," he growled at me.

Alex told me he was going to lay low. Did that mean my father was in touch with the paralegal, or maybe someone told him about the paralegal? But who? I thought back to Marie and my fleeting suspicion of her, but she'd been with me in Los Angeles. I'd been at the office when I'd talked to Alex, and I hadn't said anything to anyone.

"If you didn't do anything wrong, what does it matter?" I challenged him.

His eyes narrowed into small slits. "You'll find out how much it matters if you keep this up." As if he caught himself, he made an attempt to calm down and smile. "I tell you what. I'll give you one hundred thousand dollars and promise to get rid of the dirt about you and Henry if you let this go."

Dirt on me and Henry? How could he have dirt?

"That's a generous offer, Samantha. It's better than you deserve."

Should I take it? No. Whatever dirt he had, it couldn't be much. It would be nothing once I told Henry the truth.

"You stole—"

"I stole nothing. It was mine. Your mother was mine. Her assets are mine!" He poked himself in the chest, accentuating the word "mine" each time he spoke it.

"*Was* is the operative word. She wasn't your wife anymore, nor were you her beneficiary."

"You like playing with fire, don't you?" he snarled at me.

I didn't. Not at all. But I didn't know what else to do. "Get out! You have no right to be here!"

"Or what? You'll call the police? I'm not afraid of them. But you should be afraid of what I know. I know about Pax and Henry."

My heart raced, pounding in my chest like a jackhammer as I forced a laugh. "You're insane. What are you even talking about?"

He sucked in a breath and tried to look sorry for me. "Did you know your mother kept a diary? Oh, boy, was she worried about you. Pages and pages of concerns that you were in a relationship with a married man during your internship. You were so secretive. And then you turned up pregnant when you moved west."

Stop. He had to stop. I knew Mom had worried and even wondered about a relationship during my internship. The fact that she thought it was a married man was helpful. It would take suspicion away from Henry who'd never been married.

I waved his accusation away. "Ridiculous. You're grasping at straws. Besides, that has nothing to do with Henry."

He laughed. "Keep lying to yourself, sweetheart. Remember, the truth always comes out."

"Right, like how you've illegally stolen my inheritance?" My hands shook, betraying my fear. I clenched them into fists, desperate to maintain control.

"Don't test me, girl. This is no bluff."

"Really, Dad? This is what you're resorting to? Baseless accusations?" I tried to force a laugh, but it came out strained and unconvincing.

"Baseless? Here's what your mother never considered. You weren't fucking a married man. You were fucking Henry Banion, your best friend's father and your internship supervisor."

My mouth went dry.

My father shuddered in disgust. "It's sick. He's fucking a woman who is like a daughter to him."

"You have no proof of that."

"I have the fact that you were sleeping with someone during your internship and got pregnant by him. Your mom was sure of that. And now, look at you, living with Henry, your old internship supervisor."

Surely, I could still pass that off as coincidence. "That doesn't prove anything."

"I'll admit, I doubted my logic. I mean, Henry Banion is a saint among saints. He wouldn't abandon a woman he impregnated."

"Right . . . so you have nothing. You need to leave."

"Not so fast, sweetheart." He paused, sitting on the couch as if he planned to stay for a while. "I realized that for this theory to work, Henry couldn't know about the boy." My father raised an eyebrow, his expression a mixture of smugness and disgust. "I bet he doesn't."

"There's nothing to know." I glanced at my watch, wondering how long I had before Henry returned.

"Tell me, Samantha. Did you seduce him, or did he take advantage of you? Which one was it? It feels like you had to seduce him, Henry being such an upstanding guy. But then again, he was your supervisor. He's old enough to be your father. I wonder what the world will think of him when it gets out that he fucked his intern." My father's words felt like daggers, slicing through my life, turning it into something sordid when it wasn't. Complicated and sad, yes, but my time with Henry wasn't sordid.

"You've said what you came to say. Just go."

"I'm right, aren't I? I'm finally exposing the truth you've been hiding from everyone, including Henry. Face it, Samantha. Your lies are catching up to you."

My father's words echoed in my ears as I struggled to breathe. "Get out. Just get out."

"What's going on here?"

I whirled around to find Henry standing at the entry of the living room. No, no, no. I studied him, wondering what he'd heard.

"I'm just having a chat with my daughter." My father's words were nonchalant as he rose from the couch.

"You're not welcome here, Carl," Henry said.

"Really? Is that true, Samantha?" My father gave me a humorless smile. "I need your decision now."

"About what?" Henry demanded, glancing at me before glaring at my father.

"It's a little business deal."

Henry shook his head. "Business? Is this about duping your ex-wife into giving you all her assets?"

My father blustered. "You're not the man people think you are, Henry Banion. You're no saint. You're as corrupt as everyone else. At least my corruption doesn't involve my dick."

"Get the fuck out of my house before I throw you out." Henry grabbed my father and shoved him toward the door.

"Fine, fine." My father held his hands up in surrender. "Last chance, Sam. Next stop is *TMZ* or some similar gossip rag."

Henry stepped into my father's face. "If my or Samantha's name shows up in gossip and I find it's from you, I will make sure you never do business in this town again . . . in the world. Even if my reputation is ruined, I have the money and stamina to make sure your life is a living hell, and I will use it."

My father recoiled and then looked at me in disgust. Henry grabbed him and pulled him out to the foyer and out the door.

I had only a moment to compose myself before facing Henry.

Henry returned to the living room, his eyes piercing as they looked at me. "Is it true? Am I Pax's father?"

I froze, shock rendering me speechless. I wanted Henry to know the truth, but not like this.

"Is he?" Henry bellowed.

I flinched. "Y–yes."

"And you were never going to tell me. Turns out you're more like your father than your mother, after all."

And with those words, the fragile hope that had been growing inside me shattered, leaving only the bitter taste of regret and the knowledge that I might have lost Henry forever.

24

Henry

I was a fool. A world-class idiot.

I had nearly sprinted out of my office to return home, knowing Samantha and Pax would be there. After a few days apart, I was ready to bare my soul to them. I had the courage to let Victoria know the truth about me and Samantha and faith that she would support us. I was willing to risk the scandal in my business, all for a chance at happiness that I had let slip away five years ago.

When I arrived home and heard Samantha's father threatening her, I nearly went to kick the shit out of him. And then he said the words that stopped me in my tracks.

I realized that for this theory to work, Henry can't know about the boy.

Could it be true? Could I be Pax's father?

Initially, Samantha's reaction to her father's accusations had me dismissing the idea. Surely, she would have told me if Pax was my child.

But it wasn't Samantha's father's words that made me believe what he was saying. It was Samantha's mother, Gwen. While Gwen's diary didn't appear to name me, it was clear she believed that the father of Samantha's baby had been during her internship here in New York, not someone she had met in Seattle.

Gwen and Samantha had been close, so the fact that Samantha didn't tell her who the father of her baby was had to mean it was someone Samantha wanted to keep a secret. Someone like me.

I quickly did the mental math. Based on Pax's age, I believed that Samantha had met someone soon after arriving in Seattle, but it seemed quite possible that she could have already been pregnant when she moved west.

A tug of war raged inside me. *Could Pax be my son? Is it possible Samantha never said a word?*

I finally got my legs moving, entering the living room and demanding that Carl leave the premises. The fucker didn't know when to stop so I had to physically push him out.

Once he was gone, I reentered the living room and one look at Samantha was all I needed to know the truth. Even so, I asked. "Is Pax my son?"

"And you were never going to tell me. Turns out you're more like your father than your mother, after all." My blood pounded in my brain, making it impossible to hear what she was saying. It was clear she was desperate for me to understand something, but what was there to understand?

"How could you?"

She stopped and looked at me, her expression filled with regret. "I didn't find out I was pregnant until I was in Seattle, and you made it clear that you and I were never to see each other again."

I needed a drink. I made my way to the bar, pulling out the first bottle my fingers wrapped around the neck of and poured myself a glass.

"You were so worried about Tori finding out about us and the scandal it could cause, and—"

"I know what I was worried about," I snapped. I downed the contents of my drink, wishing it would burn away the pain. Had I really brought this on myself? She was right that I'd wanted to keep us a secret, and Pax would end that. But Jesus, did she really think that was more important than knowing my child? Or was this punishment for what I did to her five years ago?

I looked over at Samantha standing in the middle of the living room with tears streaming down her face.

"Assuming that I could accept that you didn't tell me you were pregnant five years ago, why didn't you tell me now?"

"I was going to tell you. I was going to tell you tonight."

Rage and pain consumed me. I picked up the glass, hurtling into the wall behind me. "Bullshit. You were never going to tell me."

She didn't seem fazed by my outburst. "Initially, I didn't say anything because nothing had changed. You said so yourself. If you accepted Pax as your son, it would be admitting to Tori and everyone else that you'd had an affair with your intern."

Technically, she wasn't wrong, but I still didn't buy it. "Don't you think that was for me to decide?"

She let out a long sigh. "You didn't want me back then, Henry, and you don't want me now. Why would I think you'd want Pax?"

She could have jabbed a dagger straight into my heart and her words wouldn't have hurt me more.

I let out a humorless laugh. "So much you know. All I've thought about the last couple of days was being with you. Jesus fucking Christ, I was thinking about adopting Pax."

Her eyes widened in surprise.

"And for the record, you're the one who kept saying that the things between us hadn't changed. You're the one who would run off and ask me to pretend like nothing had happened." It wasn't that I didn't recognize that I had a part to play in the misery I was feeling at the moment, but it didn't eliminate Samantha's culpability. "You came and lived in my house, watched me grow attached to Pax, and not once . . ." Emotion threatened to bring me to my knees. I sucked in a breath to pull myself together. "And not once did you tell me the truth about him."

"I'm sorry, Henry. I really am. All my reasonings made sense in that time, but I knew that the time had come to tell you the truth, and I was going to. Tonight. I swear to God."

Looking at her filled me with anguish and anger that was difficult to manage. "Well, I guess I'll never know, will I?" I made a beeline to exit the living room, unable to look at her a second longer. I stopped when I reached the threshold and turned to look back at her. "I'm going to be in his life, Samantha. Nothing you can do will stop that." I turned to leave the room.

"What are you going to do, Henry?" Terror filled her voice, telling me she worried I would take Pax away from her. The fact that she would believe I was capable of that pissed me off even more. I wouldn't fight to get custody of Pax away from her. I had the clout and resources to do so, but I wasn't that evil. It wasn't because I didn't want to hurt her, because a part of me did. But I wouldn't do it to Pax who clearly adored his mother.

"I'm going to meet with my lawyer and make sure that my rights are protected. And only because of Pax, I'm going to keep my word to you. You can stay here and work for me as long as you need. In return, you're going to give me unfettered access to the boy and you're going to sign whatever document needs to be signed that says he's my son."

Her eyes were round and dazed, the epitome of a deer's eyes caught in the headlights.

"I don't know what plans you have for when you move out of here, but if they involve leaving New York City, I will demand that Pax stays here with me. I've already lost four years. I'm not going to lose any more."

Her breath hitched. Her lips quivered. I turned away, stomping on the minuscule part of my heart that wanted to feel bad for her. She had brought this on herself.

I reached the stairs before I realized the most important question hadn't been answered yet. I turned again. "Does he know?"

She shook her head. "I thought we would tell him together."

I needed to get my shit together. I couldn't meet Pax as his father with all this anger toward Samantha raging through me.

"Meet me in Pax's room in ten minutes."

She nodded. I headed up the stairs, taking them two-by-two to release the explosive energy raging through me. I made it to my room, shutting the door and leaning against it.

I had a son.

A son that I potentially would have never, ever met. If Gwen hadn't died, causing Samantha to return to New York, she'd still be in Seattle and I'd still be unaware. If Samantha's father wasn't such an asshole and hadn't taken Samantha and Pax's inheritance away, I wouldn't have given her a job and she wouldn't have been in my house, and I would've never known Pax was my son. The idea that only through a set of very specific circumstances did I know about Pax was devastating to me. I never would've believed Samantha was capable of such cruelty, not just toward me but toward Pax as well. What had she told him about his father? What was she planning to tell him as he got older and asked questions about his father?

I went into my bathroom, splashing cold water on my face and studying myself in the mirror. I had to stop thinking about Samantha's betrayal and focus on Pax being my son. This sweet, smart child was my son. My heart filled with love.

Feeling more in control, I exited my room and took the stairs up to the third floor. When I reached the doorway, I looked in and saw Samantha sitting at the child-size table.

Pax was standing next to her, his head cocked to the side and his hands pressed against her cheeks. "Are you sad, Mommy?"

"Yes, I am."

"How come?"

She wiped tears with a tissue. "Because I kept a secret that I shouldn't have. And I hurt Henry."

"Why don't you say you're sorry?"

She gave him a soft smile. "I did. But some things are hard to forgive."

She took both his hands in hers and cradled them close to her chest. "When Henry gets here, I'll tell you what the secret is, and I hope that you'll be able to forgive me too."

"I'll forgive you, Mommy." Pax looked up at her with pure love. Would he look at me the same way?

"I hope so."

"And if Henry doesn't, I'll punch him."

"Oh, no, sweetheart. We don't hurt people for being upset at us."

I hated that I was coming out of this looking like an asshole. Pax was only four years old and probably wouldn't completely understand the full ramifications of Samantha's deception. But as he grew older, he would. Would he harbor any resentment when that time came?

I stepped into the room, and Pax and Samantha looked up at me.

Pax took a step in front of his mother, his eyes narrowing at me. "When someone says they're sorry, you're supposed to say that's okay."

My heart ached that even now, my own son was chastising me. My resentment toward Samantha grew that she would set me up like this.

Samantha tugged Pax back to her. "Remember how sometimes you get angry at me? And that doesn't just go away. I hurt Henry. He has a right to be upset."

I pulled out the chair from the small table and sat, hoping it would hold my weight.

"I want to tell you the secret, okay?" Samantha said.

"Okay."

Samantha took a deep breath while mine stalled in my chest, wondering what Pax was going to think. Would he be happy that I was his father? Would he still be mad at me for being pissed at his mother?

"Pax, sweetie, remember how sometimes you ask about your dad?"

Pax nodded.

"Well, the truth is that Henry is your dad."

Pax's brows furrowed into confusion as he looked from Samantha to me and then back to Samantha. "You mean now he's my dad?"

"He's always been your dad."

Pax continued to look confused. "But he hasn't lived with us. Mommies and daddies live together."

I looked at Samantha, wondering how she was going to explain this to him, hoping against all hope that I didn't come out looking like the bad guy for not being in the family.

"That was the secret, sweetie. I didn't tell Henry and I didn't tell you."

"Why not?"

Samantha's expression was full of regret, but I refused to be swayed by it. "It's a long story. The important thing is that you know the truth now. Henry is your daddy."

Again, Pax continued to consider everything he'd been told. Finally, he walked over to me, and I leaned closer, holding my hands out and putting a smile on my face, hoping he couldn't see the rage burning inside toward Samantha.

"Are you glad that you're my daddy?"

My heart squeezed tight and then thumped hard. Unable to help myself, I reached out and took the boy's hands in mine. "I am over the moon with joy and happiness to know that you're my son, Pax. I hope you're not disappointed."

Pax shrugged as if he were indifferent, and I tried not to take it personally.

"I wish I'd known about you before now, but now that I do, I plan to be in your life. How do you feel about that?"

Pax stepped closer, in between my legs as he nestled into my body. Emotion welled in my chest, bringing tears to my eyes.

"I'm glad. I think you're going to be a good dad."

I let out a laugh as I wrapped my arms around him and gave him a hug.

"Does that mean we're going to stay here and be a family?" he asked.

My entire body tensed as I looked over at Samantha. I would continue to help and support her, and even allow her to stay in my house as long as she needed. But all thoughts of our being a family died when I learned of her betrayal.

25

Samantha

"Does that mean we're going to stay here and be a family?" Pax's innocent question hung heavily in the air, and I felt my heart shatter into a thousand pieces because one glance at Henry and I knew the answer was no.

"Sweetheart . . . it's not that simple." I struggled to find the words, swallowing hard against the lump in my throat. "Not all families live together."

Pax turned to Henry. "Don't you want us?"

I saw a flash of anger in Henry's eyes directed at me. I couldn't blame him. He was looking like the bad guy when I was the one who ruined everything.

"I want you," Henry said carefully to Pax.

"Pax, you'll be able to spend lots of time with your dad. We'll both love you no matter what."

Pax didn't look reassured.

"How about I leave you two to start spending time now?" I rose from the tiny chair.

"Are you leaving?" Pax reached out and took my hand, his eyes looking a little nervous.

"Just the room. I'll be in my room, okay?"

"Okay."

"Why don't you show Hen—your dad the train track you made?"

Pax looked over at Henry. "Do you want to see my train?"

"More than anything." Henry stood.

Pax pointed toward the other side of the room. "It's over there. Come on."

I moved to leave but lingered by the door and looked in as Henry lowered to the floor to play trains with Pax. I'd totally messed everything up. If I'd hoped for a chance at a life with Henry, it was gone now. Despite what he'd said earlier, suggesting he wanted to adopt Pax, I wasn't sure what he felt about me. The memory of how coolly he'd sent me away five years ago still lived in my heart. I had no reason to think he wouldn't have done the same now.

Even so, I should have told him about Pax. The pain on Henry's face was difficult to bear.

I retreated to my room, collapsing onto the bed in a fit of silent sobs. My mother was gone, Henry's anger at me was palpable, and Victoria would surely side with him. I had never felt more alone in my life.

"Is something wrong?" Marie's voice came from my doorway.

I sniffled and worked to pull myself together as I sat up. The news of Pax being Henry's son was going to get out soon, and I could use a friend, but while I liked Marie, it didn't feel right to burden her with my problems.

"Just missing my mom."

She nodded. "Gwen was a lovely woman. She loved you and Pax so much. Can I get you some tea or something?"

I shook my head. "No, thank you, Marie."

She left me to my wallowing. I buried my face in the pillows, willing myself to accept the consequences of my actions. It was clear that I needed to speed up my plans for finding a new place and career. I couldn't remain in this house with Henry, constantly reminded of his anger and disappointment. It wasn't fair to Pax, either.

I don't know what plans you have for when you move out of here. But if they involve leaving New York City, I will demand that Pax stays here with me.

Henry's words returned, sending a chill down my spine. He wasn't planning on taking Pax away at this time, but he could. I'd thought about leaving New York, but even without Henry's ominous threat, I wouldn't now. I wanted Pax to have his father. I wanted Henry to have Pax.

I needed a new place to live, somewhere I wouldn't be haunted by Henry's hatred of me. A fresh start for Pax and me. And I needed to deal with work. At this time, I'd continue to do my job since Henry wasn't firing me, but I definitely needed to get started on my business. Or maybe I should just find a new job.

THE EARLY MORNING light streamed through the windows, casting a warm glow over the bustling kitchen. Even so, I felt cold, empty. I filled my coffee mug and brought milk and cereal up to my room for Pax. It was early, so early that I was the only one up. But that was what I wanted. I wanted to get me and Pax up and out of the house before everyone else. I didn't want to see Henry's despising glares, an attitude that would likely be shared once Knightly, Mrs. Tillis, and Caroline discovered the truth about Pax.

Back up in my room, Pax burst in. "Mommy, look at my drawing." I was thankful he'd done as I'd asked when I woke him. He got dressed and played in his room.

"Let me see." I examined his colorful masterpiece, my heart breaking even more at the three figures that no doubt were Pax, Henry, and Me. "Wow, it's beautiful. You're quite the artist!"

"Can I show it to Hen—my daddy?"

That wasn't part of my plan, but I couldn't very well deny Pax and Henry any more time together than I already stole.

"Sure. Maybe we can—"

"I know where to go." Pax was out of the room before I could finish. I sighed.

"You two are up early," Marie said from my doorway.

"I have a lot to do. I thought I'd take Pax to preschool."

"Oh . . . well . . . okay. I was thinking I'd go see my sister when I dropped him off."

"Absolutely, Marie. Take the whole day off. You deserve it."

I finished getting myself ready, and when Pax returned, he sported a grin and a happy attitude, telling me Henry had responded to his picture in the positive. Of course he would. Deep down, Henry was a good man.

It occurred to me that Pax would likely tell his friends or teachers about Henry being his father. I knew the news would be out eventually, but I had a feeling Henry would want to control the narrative.

"Pax, honey, eat your cereal. I'll be right back." I got him situated at the little window table in my room.

"Where are you going?"

"I need to talk to Henry for a minute." I made my way down a flight of stairs to check Henry's room.

I knocked on his door and opened it when he called out. I entered but stayed near the door. The room was how I'd remembered it from five years ago. I'd been an idiot back then to dream of being with him in this room as his wife. I'd been an idiot to entertain it now.

"Is something wrong?" Henry's voice was cool, distant.

"Pax is likely to tell people about your being his father."

Henry's eyes narrowed. "Do you have a problem with that? You don't want people knowing the truth about how you cruelly kept him from me?"

I understood his rage, but my own anger bloomed as well. "You were the one who didn't want anyone to know about me, your dirty little secret," I spat. "You were so ashamed of me that you sent me away. 'We can't ever see each other again.' That's what you told me, Henry. You're the one so worried about his precious reputation." The pain seared into my chest. "I'd been a fool to fall in love with you back then, a bigger fool to do it now."

I turned to leave his room.

"Samantha." His tone wasn't as harsh, but I was done. Done loving a man who put everyone and everything first except me. I continued back upstairs, finished getting Pax ready, and then I left the house, taking him to preschool.

THE REST of the morning passed in a blur. I was going through the motions but didn't feel present in my life. My mind was preoccupied with rehashing my poor decisions, wishing Henry would understand and forgive me and then chastising myself for needing Henry's love.

I stared at my computer screen, unable to focus on the reports I was supposed to be reviewing. My phone rang, startling me. Checking the caller ID, I saw it was Alex. Did he know? Had Henry spoken to him and Victoria? Was he calling to fire me as a client for betraying his friend and wife?

"Hello?"

"Hey, Samantha. I have some news. Can you meet me for coffee again?" He didn't sound upset at me.

"Ah . . . yeah." I wasn't getting anything done, anyway.

"Same place as before? Thirty minutes?"

"I'll be there."

Thirty minutes later, I walked into the restaurant I'd met Alex in a week before.

His head cocked to the side as he saw me. "Are you okay?"

Clearly, he didn't know anything yet. Should I tell him? No. I decided it was Henry's place to tell him.

"Just a busy day. What's up?"

He smiled. "You'll be glad to hear that we found the paralegal."

"Oh?" That did cheer me up, although with my luck, she wouldn't be any help. "Did she shed any light on my case?"

"Boy, did she ever." Alex slid a piece of paper over to me. "This is a copy of her statement and affidavit."

I started to read as a server showed up and took our coffee orders. When she left, Alex said, "It basically confirms that Lucas

Thompson asked her to visit your mother regarding the will but that Mr. Thompson gave her the papers to sign."

My head snapped up from reading the papers. "What?"

He nodded. "It appears that your lawyer was working with your father to change your mother's will. Mr. Thompson likes to play it fast and loose with the law and gambling, making him a prime target for someone like your father."

My gut roiled. My mother had trusted Lucas. So had I. I thought back to our conversations. "No wonder he kept saying everything looked legal and that he couldn't find anything suspicious."

"Yep."

I sat with this knowledge. "I'm not sure what to do now." My brain was scattered, unable to focus. Maybe the coffee the server brought would help.

"Well, I suggest you get a new lawyer and file those papers contesting the will. In the meantime, we've contacted law enforcement, and as of seven this morning, your father and Lucas were being arrested for felony will and trust beneficiary fraud. They're looking at stiff fines and some jail time."

For the first time since last night, my heart felt light. "Really? What does that mean for me and Pax?"

"We've contacted Lucas's law firm and obtained the original will and documents for your mother's estate. They've offered to help with this pro bono, but you still might want to find another lawyer."

I nodded as I tried to figure out what this meant for me in the near future. I knew estates could take time to settle, but if my father and Lucas were in jail, did that mean their illegal papers were now null and void?

"Do you think I can go back to my mother's house?" I asked.

"I'd check with a lawyer, but I don't see why not. The thing is, your father and Mr. Thompson will likely post bond, so they'll be free. You might be safer at Henry's."

"I really need to find my own place."

"If that's the case, I can arrange to have a couple of men watch the house to make sure your father doesn't harass you. In the meantime, here are all the documents you need. I've included the name of the investigator who will likely be in touch. There are a few lawyer referrals as well. Plus, the papers you need to prove your case."

"Alex, I don't know how to thank you." I wondered what the bill would be. If I received my inheritance, I wouldn't need to worry, but the legal process moved slowly and I imagined my father would still fight me.

"I was happy to help. You're like family."

Family. The word sent a sharp pain through my heart. I wasn't family. Not really.

"I appreciate it, Alex."

I sat for a moment after Alex left. With my father detained and proof of my right to the house and my mother's assets, I could move back into my mother's home. Although the pain around Henry still crushed my chest like an anvil, I did have a small sense of relief. Moving back to my mother's home meant a fresh start, a chance to rebuild my life.

I left the café and returned to Henry's house, deciding now was the best time to pack up and leave. I'd let Marie know we were returning to my mother's house, but she didn't need to leave her visit with her sister. I decided Henry would let her into the house to pack her things later tonight or tomorrow. But me? I had to leave now. I couldn't breathe in that house.

When I arrived, Knightly met me with a warm smile. Clearly, he didn't know the truth either.

"It looks like my father has been arrested and I can return to my mother's home," I told him.

"That's good news, although I'll admit, you and young Paxton will be missed." Yeah, right. Pax would be missed, but not me when they learned the truth. "Do you need help with your things?"

I shook my head. We hadn't arrived with much and wouldn't leave with anything more. "No thank you, Knightly."

I headed up to the third floor. I started by packing up Pax's things, but then it occurred to me that this would still be a home for him. I decided to leave a few clothing items behind for when he came to visit. I packed up all the toys we'd brought. Henry had plenty of toys here already.

With Pax packed, I went to my room and gathered my things, tossing them in my bags. When I finished, I stood in the room, several bags at my feet, ready to leave. Remembering Henry's words threatening me if I left, I knew I needed to leave him a note. Or maybe I could just rely on Knightly to tell him where I went. I hoped Henry didn't think I was trying to abscond with Pax. A chill ran up my spine thinking about a custody battle with Henry. With my mother's inheritance, I'd be well off, but Henry was beyond rich. He was the one percent of the one percent. He was prominent. Respected. I couldn't fight that.

"Done packing?" Knightly's voice startled me as he appeared in the doorway.

"Yes." I forced a smile, unwilling to let him see how much the situation pained me.

"You won't be waiting for Mr. Banion?"

I waved my hand nonchalantly. "I'm sure Henry will be glad to have his home back," I said lightly.

"Shall I drive you?"

"I can't ask you to do that. I'll order a car. Thank you for everything, Knightly. You and Mrs. Tillis and Caroline have been so wonderful to me and Pax."

"It was no hardship. We'll miss having you here. You lit up the house and Mr. Banion."

My heart rolled in my chest at the idea that Henry had been happy with us here. Of course, that was all changed now.

"Thank you again for everything."

"Of course. Let me at least help you get these bags down to the car."

I nodded and thanked him again. Moments later, it seemed, I was in a car, pulling away from Henry's house. My heart was heavy as I looked out the back window. I tore my gaze away, turning in the seat to look forward. That was my new plan. Look forward in life. I wanted Henry to understand and forgive me, but I couldn't live any longer with silly hopes and dreams. Fairy tales weren't true. It was time, past time, I let Henry go.

26

Henry

The memory of the night before woke me with a start. At first, I was filled with rage at Samantha's betrayal. But then I remembered the wooden train whizzing along the tracks as I guided it through miniature tunnels and over bridges while playing with Pax. His bright blue eyes sparkled with excitement, his laughter filling the room like sunshine. This was my son. My heart swelled until I wasn't sure how my chest could contain it.

"Look out, Daddy, there's a cow on the tracks."

Daddy. Jesus. I hadn't realized how much I wanted more kids until now.

"That's what cow catchers are for," I said.

He laughed and then was quiet.

"Everything okay, Son?"

"Are you mad at my mommy?"

Fuck. I couldn't lie to him, otherwise he'd think we could live as a big, happy family, and that train had left the station, so to speak. "I'm hurt."

"She said she was sorry."

"Sometimes, hurts take awhile to heal." Although, as I woke this morning with anger toward her, I couldn't deny that part of it was resentment because I still loved her. The real tragedy, I decided as I dressed that morning, was that I'd probably always love her. Perhaps that was my punishment too for what I'd done to her five years ago. But not knowing my son seemed like too great a penalty for my crime.

A knock on the door pulled me from my reverie. "Come in."

I turned to see Samantha standing in the doorway. My heart thumped hard in my chest at all I'd lost. I blamed her for it. Maybe if I did, I'd stop hurting so much.

"Is something wrong?" I worked to keep my voice flat.

"Pax is likely to tell people about your being his father."

What did that mean? Was she trying to protect her image as a woman who'd steal a man's child? "Do you have a problem with that? You don't want people knowing the truth about how you cruelly kept him from me?"

She surprised me by tensing with anger. "You were the one who didn't want anyone to know about me, your dirty little secret. You were so ashamed of me that you sent me away. 'We can't ever see each other again.' That's what you told me, Henry. You're the one so worried about his precious reputation."

I flinched at her words. The truth of them stabbed me like tiny daggers.

"I'd been a fool to fall in love with you back then, a bigger fool to do so now." She turned to leave my room.

"Samantha." I called after her more out of instinct. I had no idea what to say. She loved me? She didn't stop, and that was just as well because I realized if she could lie about Pax, she could lie about anything, including having loved me.

But she wasn't wrong. Pax would likely say something about meeting his father, and when it came out the father was me, it would be news. Or at least gossip. I had to talk to Victoria first, before anyone else.

I skipped breakfast and had Knightly drive me over to Victoria's. I probably should have called first, but I was grappling with how she was going to react when I told her about Pax. About having slept with her friend.

When I arrived at Victoria and Alex's building, the doorman let me in. One of the perks of being well-known.

"Will you let Victoria know I'm on my way up?" I asked the woman in the lobby.

"Yes, sir, Mr. Banion."

I rode up the elevator to the penthouse apartment. The door opened before I reached it.

"Dad. Is everything Okay?" Victoria looked like she hadn't been out of bed very long. Or maybe it was the fatigue of being so pregnant.

"Everything is fine. Great, even. I just need to talk with you."

"Of course. Come in." She held the door open. "I can make you coffee."

"Actually, water would be nice."

"Coming up." She went to the kitchen while I walked over to the large windows overlooking Central Park. The cool winter morning made me think of the upcoming holidays. Would Pax be able to spend them with me?

"Is Alex here?" I called out.

"No. He's at the office. He wouldn't give me the deets, but it looks like things are about to turn around for Samantha and Pax." She returned with a glass of water, which I downed. She cocked her head to the side. "Are you sure you're okay?"

"Mostly, yes."

"What does that mean?"

"Honey, sit down."

"Oh, God. Are you sick?"

"No . . . God, no. I just have something to tell you, and I'm not sure how you're going to take it, so I'm nervous."

She sat on the couch, looking up at me with concern in her eyes. "I love you, Dad. You know that."

"I do. And I love you too, honey." I went to sit, but nervous energy kept me upright, pacing.

"Whenever you're ready," she prompted.

I stopped, took a breath, and faced her. "Do you remember five years ago when Samantha was my intern?"

"Yes. You helped her get that job in Seattle too. I was mad about that, by the way. But I can see it was a good job for her."

Inwardly, I winced.

"Dad?" Victoria prodded.

Fuck. Just say it. "The thing is, Tori .. .ah, fuck . . ."

Victoria studied me. "What?"

"Tori, I . . ."

Her brow arched.

I blew out a breath. "I had an affair with Samantha."

For a moment, her face didn't show any reaction. Then both her brows lifted and her mouth gaped. "You son of a bitch."

I squeezed my eyes shut, ready for the onslaught. Ready for her to call me a pervy old man. Ready for her to feel betrayed by me and Samantha.

"You got your boxers all in a bunch over my being with Alex, and all this time, you'd slept with my best friend?"

I stopped short. I hadn't expected that. "Ah . . . yes . . ."

"And this was five years ago?"

I nodded. It felt like our roles had changed. She was now the parent reprimanding me.

"And less than a year ago, when it came out about me and Alex, your head exploded."

I sighed. "It's very difficult to think about my college buddy sleeping with my daughter."

"And my best friend sleeping with my dad is no big deal?" She huffed out a breath. "If I could get up and smack you, I would. Lucky for you, I'm too big."

"Tori, five years ago, I was afraid I'd lose you if you knew. I was afraid if anyone knew . . . Jesus, I was a forty-something old man fucking his intern—"

Her brows lifted again. "Fucking. That's all it was?" I heard disapproval in her voice.

"No. It was more than that, but—"

"Oh, wait." Victoria shifted on the couch. "Is she the woman? The one you said you couldn't be with but have clearly been pining for?"

I closed my eyes. "All that doesn't matter now—"

"Of course it does—"

"It doesn't!"

Victoria recoiled.

"I'm sorry for snapping like that, Tori, but there's more you need to know."

"Okay."

It seemed like I got the worst part out of the way, and yet, I struggled with the next. "It's about Pax."

She nodded as she waited for me to continue, but then realization came to her expression. "Oh, God . . . he's your son?"

I nodded.

She continued to study me, and I waited to find out what her reaction would be. "I don't get it. Is that why you found her a job so far away? You didn't want anyone to know?"

"What? No. Jesus." It occurred to me that was what Samantha had thought too. "I had no idea, Tori. I didn't know she was pregnant. I didn't know she had a baby. Hell, I didn't know he was mine even while he was living under my roof. I don't think she ever planned to tell me."

"What?"

I nodded. "I found out by accident. She only confessed it when cornered about it."

Victoria's expression turned indignant. "I never thought she'd do something like that. God, she took four years from you and Pax."

Finally, she understood. I was pleased to see her anger toward Samantha on my behalf. "She won't take any more, though. I'm going to be in his life, and I'd like it if you'd be too. He's your brother, Tori."

Her smile was sweet as she heaved herself off the couch. "Of course." She hugged me. "I can't believe she didn't tell you. That's just . . . it's so wrong."

I nodded.

"So, what are you going to do about Samantha? I mean, if she's the one you've been—"

"She betrayed me."

"Me too." She arched a brow. "You betrayed me. I can't believe you slept with my friend."

Heat flushed my cheeks. "I'd say I'm sorry, but—"

"Yeah, I don't want the details. Except you owe me and Alex an apology."

I laughed. "You're right. I'm sorry."

"Does anyone else know about Pax?"

I shook my head. "I wanted you to know first. It will get out, and I suppose it will be a scandal. Clichéd older man sleeping with his intern and now his employee."

"Wait? What? You're still sleeping with her?"

Fuck. I hadn't meant to admit that. "Not anymore."

"But you were?"

I scraped my hand over my face. "For a moment, Tori, I thought . . . well . . ." I couldn't say the words.

Victoria's expression softened. "For a moment, you thought you might have what you lost, but then you found out about Pax?"

I nodded.

"You can't forgive her?"

I stared at her helplessly. "I don't know how. I look at her and all I see is what she stole from me." That and the remnant of a dream lost.

"Forgiveness is hard, but maybe what she did has an explanation. Maybe she wasn't as selfish as we think."

"What possible forgivable excuse could there be for keeping my son from me?"

She shrugged. "Maybe none. But love isn't always rational. Sometimes, people make mistakes because they're scared or overwhelmed. No one is perfect, not even you."

I remembered how Samantha yelled at me that I'd been ashamed of her and sent her away. I wasn't ashamed of her. I was ashamed of myself. Of my weakness for her. Of the rules I broke to be with her. Of the cliché I'd become.

"So you're okay with what she did? Do you forgive her?"

"I'm upset that she kept Pax from you . . . and from me too. I don't know if I forgive her since I don't know why she did it."

"So you do think there is a good reason to keep me from Pax?"

She stared at me for a long moment. "No. No, there isn't. Not you. You're the greatest father ever." She hugged me. "Pax is lucky to have you in his life now."

With my feelings validated, I hugged her back. "The gossip will be ugly, probably. She still works for me. I told her she could stay at the house. I'm pissed, but I won't toss her to the sidewalk."

"Maybe you could find her another place. You don't want Pax in an environment where his father can't stand his mother." She was right.

"I'll talk to her tonight about it. Thank you for being so understanding and supportive."

"I love you, Dad."

"I love you too, baby." I let out a breath. "I'm heading home. I think I'll work there today and figure out how to get ahead of this. Do you need anything?"

"Nope. Well, it would be nice if baby Hank decided to make an appearance, but other than that, I'm good." She rubbed her belly.

"Alex makes you happy."

Her smile was radiant. "The happiest."

"Then I'm happy for you both."

"Finally!" She hugged me again. With a laugh, I said my goodbye and returned home.

The moment I stepped through the door, Knightly was waiting for me. "You missed Ms. Layton." He took my coat.

"What do you mean? She's at work, isn't she?"

"Apparently, her case against her father is resolved. She's moved back to her mother's home."

Panic burned in my gut. She was gone?

"It seems her father was arrested. Along with her lawyer, or at least that's what we've been able to glean from the Internet news."

"Arrested?" I asked.

"Fraud of some sort."

"Is that so? Well, it doesn't concern us, does it?" I started to go to my office, not wanting to care so much that Samantha was out of my house.

"No, sir. I just thought you might like to know."

"It will be nice to have the house quiet," I said, feeling like an asshole for saying it.

I stood in my office, my heart pounding in my chest. If Samantha had left in such a hurry, how could I be sure she wouldn't try to keep Pax from me? Had she planned to leave today and it was her good luck that her father was arrested? The idea of that grew my feelings of anger and betrayal until they threatened to consume me.

"Yes, sir. Are you okay?"

I realized my staff didn't know the situation. "Did she say anything else?"

"No. Only that she'll be staying at her mother's place with Marie and Pax." Knightly furrowed his brows, clearly taken aback by my clipped tone.

"Thank you, Knightly." My gratitude was genuine, despite my irritation. He nodded, concern etched on his face, before returning to his duties.

I closed my office door, determining I'd tell them later about Pax. Or maybe they'd find out online. I let out a growl. They deserved to hear it from me, but I wasn't in the mood to talk with anyone right now.

Even so, the news about Pax was going to get out. Fucking hell. If only Samantha hadn't lied, we could've been together, and the relationship wouldn't seem so sordid. Now, I was going to come out looking like a dirty old man who knocked up his intern and abandoned her. It gave me one more thing to resent Samantha for.

27

Samantha

I was surprised that the news of my past affair with Henry and having his son wasn't sweeping the Internet by the end of that first day. Granted, Henry owned a big bulk of media, but not all of it. Certainly not the gossip sites.

But the next day, Henry had released a statement, and that was when social media lit up like the Christmas tree in Rockefeller Center. Once the news was out, my life grew smaller than it already was. I couldn't escape the judgmental whispers that seemed to follow me everywhere I went. The weight of those stares and murmurs bore down on me, making it difficult to breathe.

When the news first broke, I called Victoria. I'd so desperately wanted to talk to her but had put it off knowing that Henry was the one who needed to talk with her first.

"I can't believe you did that," was how she answered the phone.

Did what? Slept with her father or not tell him about Pax? Both, maybe. "I'm sorry—"

"You know what, Samantha? It's cringy that you slept with my father, but I could deal with that. I mean, I can't talk can I? I'm married to his friend. But what I can't get past, what I find it hard to forgive, is your keeping Pax from him. Keeping him from me. He's my brother! How could you?"

"At the time—"

"My father is a wonderful man. He's a great father—"

"I know."

"No. I don't think you do because if you did, you'd have told him you were pregnant—"

"He told me he never wanted to see me—"

"You'd have come home and done right for Pax." Clearly, she hadn't heard what I'd said. "You know what, I can't talk about this now. I've got to go."

The line went dead. I sucked in a breath and tried to keep the tears at bay.

Work wasn't any better. "I was so right about you." Alan sneered at me. I had no response because technically, he was right.

The only sympathy I seemed to be getting was from Marie. She'd been shocked but then see-sawed her head. "Your mother thought something was up. She never guessed it was Mr. Banion, but she used to worry so much about you and about Pax's not having a father."

"I'm surprised she worried about Pax's father considering mine is such a jerk."

Marie looked at me with sympathy. "She hoped you'd find love and family. It's what all moms want for their kids."

I had that. It was there for the taking, and I let it slip away out of fear.

But her statement made me think. "Did you know Mom kept a diary?"

Marie nodded. "Yes. For many years."

"I never saw her write in it. I didn't find anything like that when I went through her things after her death." Once again, I wondered if Marie had been helping my father too.

"I believe she kept it under her mattress." Marie laughed. "Like a teenage girl."

"I didn't know that." How much more did she know than I did about my mom?

"Well, I only knew because I changed the sheets."

That made sense. "Would my dad have known?"

She shrugged. "Maybe. Why?"

"Because he apparently found it. That's how everything blew up in my face before I had the chance to come clean to Henry."

She made a face of disgust. "Your father is a vile man. I'm glad he's in jail. I hope he rots there for what he did to your mother and you."

I nodded.

"Now, I know you're looking forward, and part of that is starting a business. I'm here to help. What can I do?"

I felt guilty for suspecting Marie of anything but being loyal to my mom and me. "I'm having a hard time coming up with a business name."

"I can make a list. But first, I'll take Pax to preschool." She stopped, giving me a sympathetic smile. "And I'll bring him over to Mr. Banion's house after school."

I nodded. Victoria wasn't the only one who couldn't seem to talk to me. Henry called the night I moved back to my mother's place and reminded me again that he wouldn't allow me to keep Pax from him. I assured him that I wouldn't. After that, he texted me to let me know he wanted to see Pax. To make it easier on all of us, I decided to have Marie deliver him.

"Thank you, Marie."

Interesting, for all the worry Henry had gone through five years ago about what would happen if our affair got out, now that it was out, no one cared. Oh, sure, there were a few jokes about his being an older man or the clichéd boss fucking his secretary, but for the most part, no one cared. Not Victoria. Not his company. Not even the media except to offer support over having a son.

TWO DAYS IN, I decided I'd work from home to avoid Alan and others who snickered when they saw me. I'd made attempts to contact Larry in Los Angeles regarding the plans we'd put in place and hopefully remind him of my talent so I could get referrals once my business was started, but he'd been avoiding my calls. Was it out of loyalty to Henry?

Late afternoon, Marie returned home and reported that she'd safely gotten Pax off to Henry's. I thanked her and returned to work.

Since Pax was with Henry tonight, I had dinner alone. Afterward, I started to make a cup of tea but then switched to wine and plopped down in a chair, planning to read. I figured reading about someone else's problems would distract me from my own. After several chapters in, my phone rang.

I wasn't in the mood to talk to anyone, but on the off chance it was Henry needing something or maybe Victoria, ready to talk, I picked it up.

"Hello?"

"You think you won, don't you?"

My blood ran cold. I rose and went to the window, wanting to make sure the men Alex had sent were there.

"What do you want?"

"Simple. Drop the charges against me."

"Why would I do that? Henry already knows about Pax."

"Simple." He sounded so sure of himself. "You tell the cops and the court that this is all a misunderstanding, or blame Lucas or whatever as long as I go free, or I'll make sure Henry Banion gets custody of his bastard son."

My knees threatened to buckle. "You're an evil man."

"Regardless, I need you to drop this."

I couldn't imagine how my father could help Henry. Henry wouldn't need help if he wanted to take Pax from me.

"It's not in my hands."

"Bullshit. Don't underestimate me, Samantha. I'll tell everyone how you seduced Henry and took his child. I'll tell them what a terrible mother you are."

"I'm not—" I couldn't think straight with the roar of terror rumbling through my brain.

"You stole his child."

"Please don't do this. Pax is all I have left."

"Your choice, Samantha. Do as I say or lose him forever." The line went dead.

The sound of laughter and the creaking front door snapped me back to the present. I forced a smile as Pax bounded into the living room, his blue eyes shining with excitement.

I stood, pulling myself together.

"Mommy! We had so much fun!" Pax hugged my legs, nearly knocking me off balance.

I smiled. "Really? Tell me all about it."

Henry entered the living room, and my heart ached at the sight of him. He didn't look like he was barely containing his rage as he had the other night, but his indifference was just as difficult to accept.

"We went to the park, and Daddy pushed me on the swings really high!"

"Wow, that sounds like fun." How was I going to protect him from the storm brewing around us?

"Then we got ice cream! I had chocolate, and Daddy had vanilla."

"Did you save some for me?" I teased.

Pax's enthusiasm dropped. "No." He turned to Henry. "I told you she—"

"Pax, I was kidding," I said. "Ice cream would have melted before you got it to me."

"Okay." Pax yawned.

"It looks like someone is ready for bed. Run up and get your PJs on."

He made a face but acquiesced. "Bye, Daddy."

Henry squatted down and gave Pax a hug. "Goodnight, Son."

I shifted uncomfortably when Pax ran out of the room, leaving me alone with Henry.

"Drinking alone?" Henry nodded toward my wine glass.

I remembered my father's words of how he'd tell everyone I was a bad mother. Henry's comment made me think he thought that too. Would they tell the judge I drank too much?

"I'm a good mother," I said in desperation.

Henry flinched. "I know that."

I turned away, wondering why he didn't just leave.

"Is everything okay, Samantha? You seem . . . distracted."

"Me? No, I'm fine. Just tired, I guess." No way was I going to share my father's plan with him. I didn't want to give Henry any ideas about taking Pax from me.

He was silent for a moment. "I know it's a shitshow out there now with the news."

I scoffed.

"What?" he asked defensively.

"The whole time we were together, you worried about your reputation if it got out about us. Now it's out, and everyone is feeling sorry for you and thinking how wonderful you are—"

"You kept him from me."

"You sent me away. You fucked me, made me think you loved me, and tossed me across the country like I was nothing!" God. Now I was being hysterical. Another thing that could be used against me.

He stared at me for a long moment. "We need to find a way to work together for Pax's sake."

"Right. Sure. Okay."

"I'm not the bad guy here."

"No. You're Saint Henry Banion. I'm nobody. I'm just the intern."

"Samantha—"

"No . . . I'm sorry. It's all good, Henry. I want what's best for Pax too. I'm so glad you two had a good time tonight. But it is a school night, so I need to get him tucked in."

Thankfully, Henry took the hint. "I'll call tomorrow. I'd like to make plans for the holidays. Thanksgiving is only a few weeks away."

I was sure I wouldn't be invited to the family gathering. God, I was becoming so maudlin. "Of course."

He left, closing the door behind him, and I sank onto the couch, burying my face in my hands. Why did life have to be so complicated? I wished my mother were here. I'm not sure she'd have any advice, but she'd make me feel less alone.

Pulling myself together, I headed upstairs to put Pax to bed.

"Can we read the pirate book?" Pax asked.

"Arrrr! I'm the tickle pirate." I tickled him and then picked up the book.

"Mommieeee!" He giggled.

Once we'd read and I tucked him in, I headed down to the kitchen. Marie was cleaning a teacup, which made me think of my wine, Henry's comment, and my father's call.

"Marie, do you think I'm a good mom?"

She looked at me with concern. "Yes. You're a great mom. What brought this on?"

"Do you think Henry would try to take Pax away from me?"

"What? Did he say that?"

I shook my head. "No, but—"

"He wouldn't do that, Sam. He loves you both, and he knows how important you are to Pax."

"He doesn't love me."

She arched a brow. "I think he does. I think that's why this situation is so hard for him."

"Well, if he did, which I don't think, he doesn't now."

She patted my arm. "Either way, he won't take Pax. At the very least, he wouldn't do it because it would hurt Pax."

"Promise me you'll help me fight for Pax, no matter what happens."

She sighed. "Of course, but it won't come to that."

As I lay in bed that night, I hoped she was right. I couldn't stop the legal system from going after my father, and so I needed to prepare for whatever he might say or do to get back at me. At least I had a home, and hopefully before long, access to my inheritance so I could fight back. I might be alone, but I was strong and now I had resources. I would do whatever it took to protect Pax.

28

Henry

I arrived home after my outing with Pax, heading to my office to work. I'd enjoyed my time with him except for the fact that keeping up with a four-year-old was going to require my developing more stamina. I smiled as I remembered Pax's laughter and smile as I pushed him on the swing.

It had been difficult to bring him to Samantha's house as I wanted to keep him with me. She and I still needed to figure out how the custody and visitation would work. I thought back to this evening at her house.

The whole time we were together, you worried about your reputation if it got out about us. Now it's out, and everyone is feeling sorry for you and thinking how wonderful you are—

Was she really going to blame me for the bad press after what she'd done?

You sent me away. You fucked me, made me think you loved me, and tossed me across the country like I was nothing!

Her words were like sledgehammers into my chest because she

wasn't wrong. Well, she was wrong about treating her like she was nothing. I'd tried to look out for her.

No. You're Saint Henry Banion. I'm nobody. I'm just the intern.

That statement hit me hard as well. I couldn't say why. We were in this situation because she'd lied to me about Pax. But the look in her green eyes . . . like she was lost and alone and . . . nothing . . . it was haunting me.

"Mr. Banion, Mr. Layton is here to see you," Knightly said with a look of distaste in his expression.

"What? Carl Layton?" I checked my watch. It was after nine. What the fuck was he doing here? Especially since I'd heard he was in jail. "I thought he was arrested?"

Knightly shrugged. "I suppose he posted bond."

I wanted to tell the fucker to leave but I told Knightly to send him in.

"Is there a reason you're here unannounced?" I demanded when he entered my office.

"It's about my grandson."

I scoffed. "You don't give a shit about your grandson."

"Wrong, Mr. Banion. He's my blood, which means he's very much my concern. I know he's yours as well, and I can help you."

"I doubt it."

"I understand your skepticism. My daughter lied to you about something sacred. She's lied about me as well."

I rolled my eyes. "You're no victim, Layton. Say what you came to say."

"Samantha is unstable, and young Pax needs stability, which I know you can provide. Everyone can see what a successful woman your daughter has become."

"Not long ago, you were calling me corrupt, and now you're blowing smoke up my ass."

"Now I'm offering to help you gain full custody of Pax."

What the fuck? "How could you possibly help me with that?"

"I know things. Things that could be used in court to support your claim that you're the better parent. All you have to do is get

Samantha to drop her vendetta against me. I did nothing wrong—"

"The cops seem to think differently."

"That's all on Thompson. The man actually tried to extort me."

"Sort of like how you're bribing me now?"

"It's a business deal. A good one. You know Samantha is a terrible person. Pax shouldn't be raised around that."

"Enough!" My voice boomed, filling the room with the echo of my rage. Samantha made a grave error in judgment, but she didn't deserve to lose her son. And even if she did, Pax adored her. The kid talked about her nonstop. I wouldn't do that to him.

"Your proposal is outrageous. What makes you think I'd ever entertain such an idea? My priority is Pax's well-being, and keeping him from his mother is not in his best interest. I cannot fathom how you could possibly believe that ripping a child away from his mother would achieve either of those things."

"Sometimes, sacrifices must be made, Henry. Sometimes, tough decisions are required to secure the future of those we care about." Carl spoke as if his proposal was the most normal thing.

"Are you saying you're willing to sacrifice your daughter's happiness just so you can get rid of her? That's monstrous."

Carl shrugged. "Samantha is a grown woman who has to suffer the consequences of her actions."

"By what means? Bribing a judge? Threatening Samantha? Forging documents? What lengths will you go to save your own ass? You'd probably sell Pax's soul if you thought it would get you out of the hot water you're in."

"Ah, the great Henry Banion, always playing the moral card. How nice it must be to sit on your high horse."

"Get out of my house now, or I will call the police." I stepped toward him, ready to manhandle him out the door again.

"Fine, I'll leave. But remember this, Henry. If you don't take my offer, you might regret it someday."

"Your threats don't scare me. In fact, let me warn you. You stay away from me, Samantha, and Pax, or you're the one who'll regret it."

"Good luck with that. You'll need it." He sneered as he stepped back toward the exit.

My phone buzzed on my desk with Victoria's ringtone. I grabbed it, poking the answer button.

"Tori? Is everything okay?"

"The baby is coming."

Holy shit. My baby was having a baby.

"The doctor says there's still time, but I wanted to let you know. Alex and I are at the hospital now."

"I'm on my way."

"You don't have to come now—"

"Are you kidding me? I wouldn't miss little Hank's arrival for anything."

"Okay—" Her voice drifted into a moan that had to have been a contraction.

"Take care, Tori. Love you. See you soon."

The call ended, leaving me with only thoughts of Victoria and Alex, knowing that their lives were about to change forever. My little girl would be a mother, and that thought filled me with a mixture of pride. What would Pax think about being an uncle at only four years old?

"I take it you're about to be a grandad too. Then you know my concern for my grandson."

Jesus fuck, was he still here? "Get this through your head. Stay away from me, Samantha, and Pax or I'll make you wish you had." My voice was cold and steady as I locked eyes with Samantha's father. His face twisted with anger.

"Now get the fuck out of my house before I toss you out."

"This isn't over, Banion."

"If you're smart, it is."

With a final lethal glare, he stormed out of my office.

Unease settled in my chest as he disappeared from my office. What dark secrets were buried beneath his deceptive surface? Did Samantha have more secrets?

I shook my head of those thoughts and instead rushed out to get my coat. "I'm going to the hospital. Tori's in labor."

"Oh, how wonderful," Mrs. Tillis said, carrying a tray of cookies she'd apparently been bringing to me.

"I'll get the car," Knightly said, hurrying to the elevator to go down to the garage.

Traffic wasn't too bad for the city that never sleeps. I arrived at the hospital, hurrying to the labor and delivery floor.

"Henry!" Alex rushed to me, looking dazed.

"Alex, is everything okay?"

"Victoria is fucking amazing. I'm a fucking mess. Jesus . . . I'm going to be a father."

I laughed. "You can do this. Did you trudge through jungles hunting mafia types as a mercenary?"

"That was so much less scary."

"You're going to be fine." I thought back to the other day when I finally let go of my resentment toward Alex in favor of supporting Victoria and her love for him. I hadn't spoken to him yet about it. "Listen, I know I've been an asshole about your sleeping with my daughter and knocking her up."

Alex sighed. "Henry, I love—"

"I know. I get it now."

He arched a brow. "You mean now that it's out that you slept with and knocked up her friend."

"Touché, but yes. Well, not just that. She's happy, Alex, and that's all I want. As long as she's happy with you, then we're good."

"Thank you, Henry. I can't tell you how much it means to me."

I gave him a hug. "Now go see your wife. I want to meet my grandson."

He saluted me and entered the room.

I found a seat in the waiting room wondering if I'd hear Hank's cry of life when he came into the world. I thought of Samantha and Pax. I'd missed his birth. Anger gnawed at me. But then I wondered who'd been there with her? Had her mother flown out to Seattle? Or had she been alone?

I'm nobody. I'm just the intern.

I wondered about the last five years. Had Samantha done all of it on her own? Surely, Gwen was a source of support. Samantha had Victoria, except she didn't. I remembered Victoria being angry at me that Samantha was so far away and stopped communicating with her. Was that my fault? Had Samantha cut herself off from Victoria because of my actions? Who did she have now?

No one. Not unless Marie counted. I counted on Knightly and Mrs. Tillis for quite a bit, but they weren't emotional support.

"Mr. Banion?"

I looked up at the nurse standing in front of me.

"Yes."

"Your daughter wants to introduce her son to you."

What? I glanced at my watch. I'd been ruminating about my life and Samantha for four hours.

I jumped up. "I can't wait to meet him." I started to the room, then cursed at myself for not getting a present for them. Oh, well. I'd do it later.

I stepped into the room to find Victoria cooing over a tiny baby and Alex teary as he looked down on them. I couldn't blame him. Tears came to my eyes.

"Hey, Grandpa," Victoria said, her smile lighting up the room. "Come meet Henry Banion Sterling."

I laughed. "You gave him two of my names? I already forgave you, Alex." I reached my hand to shake it. "Congratulations."

"Thank you, Henry. Isn't he the most beautiful thing you've ever seen?" Alex stepped away so I could stand next to Victoria.

The baby was perfect. "He's nearly as beautiful as Tori was at birth." I remembered this moment after she was born. I'd been in awe and terrified I'd fuck it up, and at the same time, sure that I'd made the right choice. Her mother had been ready to leave the hospital. To leave our child. To this day, I never understood that.

"Do you want to hold him?" Victoria held him to me. I looked to Alex, who I felt was the person who should be holding his son.

He nodded. "Enjoy it now because you may never get another chance."

My hands trembled as I cradled my grandson, his delicate features so perfectly formed. "He's absolutely perfect . . ." My breath caught as the joy of this moment mixed with the grief and regret about Pax.

"You okay, Dad?"

I sniffed. "Yeah. Just thinking about when I first saw you . . . and how I missed this with Pax."

Her expression shone with sympathy. "I'm sorry that happened. I'm still in shock about it."

"Maybe that says something," Alex commented.

Both Victoria and I looked at him.

"What do you mean?" she asked.

"I mean you're in shock because you thought she was a different sort of person."

"Right."

"After all the time you and Samantha were friends, one situation has you tossing all that out and thinking she's actually a terrible person."

I felt my defenses rising. "It's not like she lied about something little. I lost four years, Alex. I didn't have this moment."

Alex nodded. "I know. But just because she did that shouldn't discount everything else, should it? Not if there's a good reason."

"How could there be a good reason?" Victoria asked.

"Maybe now isn't the time. We're here to celebrate this wonderful life."

"Actually, Henry, it's the perfect time. You're both here, celebrating new life, and yet you're still clinging to old grudges."

"You don't think it's justified," I snapped.

"Would I be justified in not forgiving you for thinking I'd murder you? You both thought that."

Victoria shook her head in shame. "I'm sorry—"

"Right. And I forgave you even though it tore me in two to think my best friend and the woman I loved thought I'd take money to kill you."

It wasn't the same, I tried to tell myself, although I was failing at seeing the difference. Even so, I said, "It's not that simple. Samantha lied to us. She kept my son from me and she betrayed our trust."

"I wonder why? Do you know? Is she a callous bitch and you were wrong to be her friend?"

"Alex." Victoria put her hand on his. "Let's not do this—"

"Do you know that Gwen Layton kept a diary?" Alex ignored his wife.

I remembered Carl mentioning it to Samantha the night I learned I was Pax's father.

"Carl had it. I had a chance to look at it before it went into evidence."

I shifted, not sure I wanted to know what it said.

"You went through her diary?" Victoria asked, horrified.

"I did." Alex didn't seem sorry about it. I suppose in his job, he had to weed through people's privacy. "Gwen spends a lot of time worrying about Samantha in it. She was convinced that Samantha's secrecy around seeing a man was that he was married."

I cleared my throat. "What's this have to do with anything?"

"Gwen outlines the call she received after Samantha moved to Seattle. Samantha told her she was pregnant. Gwen told her to come home. But Samantha told her she couldn't." Alex's eyes bore into mine, and I wondered why he was pushing this moment when there was much to celebrate.

"Why couldn't she? Her job?" Victoria asked.

Inwardly, I winced even though I wasn't sure what Gwen had written. I knew the truth was that I was why Samantha didn't come home.

"No. It took a visit to Seattle before Gwen learned the truth."

I held my breath.

Alex let out a humorless laugh. "Gwen wanted to meet with you, Henry, did you know that? She wanted you to ferret out who in Samantha's internship had gotten her pregnant and make him do the right thing."

"She should have." What would I have done if she had?

"Really? According to Gwen's notes, the baby's father made her go away. Told her they couldn't ever see each other again."

It took a moment, but then Victoria's head swiveled to me. "Dad. You did that?"

I hated how this was making me sound. I handed the baby back to her. "Why don't you two enjoy this moment?"

"Why would you do that?" Victoria pressed me.

I shrugged. How could I respond?

"I bet I know."

"You've done enough, Alex." I was ready to go back to resenting him.

"You didn't want Victoria to know you were sleeping with her friend. Your dad was still alive, and you probably thought he'd disown you."

I stared at Alex, his words cutting through me like a razor blade.

"You did it because of me and the business?" Victoria asked. It wasn't a good feeling to have your daughter look at you with disappointment.

"He did it to protect himself and didn't care about Samantha."

"I did care for her. I gave her money. I got her job." God, I was a fucking asshole. "Jesus, Alex. You just had a baby—"

Alex's expression softened. "Look, Henry, I'm not saying what she did was right. But in her situation, what could she do?"

I saw like I hadn't seen before that Samantha didn't feel she had an option to tell me about Pax five years ago. Still. "She could have told me while she was under my roof."

"Why? Had things changed?" Alex asked.

Had they? Not soon enough.

"People make mistakes. You both know that. I forgave you both because I love you both. Don't you have any forgiveness in you to give to Samantha?"

"Even if I do that, how can I trust her?"

"How can she trust you after what you did? Trust is earned, not given."

"Is that true, Dad? You made her leave?" Victoria's eyes searched mine for confirmation, betrayal and disappointment mingling with the vulnerability beneath her usual assertiveness.

"I thought it was best."

"For whom? You said she was the one woman you'd loved, and you sent her away like she meant nothing to you."

Her words stung, the painful truth. "Victoria, I . . ." The knot in my throat tightened.

"Maybe things won't work out, but Alex is right. You have a part to play, and you have to forgive her and then ask for her forgiveness too."

She was right, of course.

"I'm ruining this lovely moment," I said, feeling defeated.

"Dad, I want you to be happy." She took my hand. "Did she make you happy?"

I gave in. "Yes." My feelings had come full circle. I'd been horrendous to her, and the chances of her forgiving me had to be little to none.

"Then you need to talk to her like I'm going to do once I get some rest. God, I was really rude to her."

Alex bent over and kissed her temple.

"Let's hope she's as forgiving as you are," Victoria said to him.

A mishmash of feelings flooded me, culminating in an overwhelming need to see Samantha. I turned to leave.

"Where are you going?" Victoria asked.

"I'm going to see Samantha."

"It's three in the morning," Alex said.

"I've waited five years. I don't want to wait another moment."

"Good luck," I heard Victoria call as I headed out the door.

Knightly was resting in the car as I climbed in. "Take me to the Layton house."

"Now?"

"Now."

As Knightly drove through the city, I felt like a veil had been lifted and I didn't like what it revealed about me. Both Carl and Samantha had called me a saint, but I was nowhere near that. I'd had something dear and precious, and I'd cavalierly given it away out of my own pride and fear. Not once, but twice. It would be a fucking miracle if Samantha forgave me and was willing to take a chance on me.

29

Samantha

The soundness of my sleep was interrupted by my phone ringing. I looked at the clock beside my bed. Nearly four in the morning. Who was calling so early? I checked the caller ID. Henry.

"Hello?"

"Samantha. It's Henry. I . . . I need to talk to you."

I sat up, trying to dislodge the fog of sleep. "Is something wrong?"

"Can we speak in person? I'm actually right outside your door."

What? "Outside my door? What's going on, Henry? It's the middle of the night."

"I know. I'm sorry. This can't wait."

I sighed. "Okay, give me a minute." I trudged out of bed and put on my robe, wrapping it tightly around me. I headed downstairs to the front door, opening it a crack. Henry stood on the stoop, blowing air on his exposed hands. Why hadn't he worn gloves? For a moment, I wondered if maybe he'd been drinking.

"Hi."

I stared at him, wondering what the heck was going on. The chill of the night hit me and I stepped back. "Come in quickly, it's freezing out there."

"Thank you." He entered.

"Is Victoria okay?" I couldn't think of a reason Henry would be here so late . . . or early . . . unless something was wrong.

"Victoria and Hank are both fine." His face turned dreamy. "He's beautiful, Samantha."

"Oh. He's here. Congratulations." My happiness for Henry and Victoria was genuine, as was my sadness that I wouldn't be able to celebrate motherhood with her.

"I just . . . seeing him today, it reminded me of when Victoria was born. And how I missed Pax's birth."

I recoiled from him. "Is that why you're here? You felt the need to remind me again of what an awful person I am? It couldn't wait until the sun was up?"

He shook his head. "No. Not at all. In fact, I'm here to grovel. I'm the one who is awful." He closed his eyes like he was searching for words.

"Do you want to come and sit down? I can get you something to drink if you'd like."

He took a step closer to me, but not so close that he was in my personal space. "I just want to tell you that I'm sorry. I'm a selfish man and I made you feel like nothing, like nobody, and I don't know that I'll ever be able to make that up to you."

I studied him, wondering about the change in attitude.

"I knew I hurt you when I sent you away five years ago. I didn't want to, and I thought by finding you a great job that I made up for that. But that was just my justifying what I did."

I crossed my arms over my chest to protect myself because his words were warming my heart and I couldn't afford to let him in again.

"I did worry about Victoria and the business, but the truth was, you weren't nothing, you were everything and it scared me to death.

I'd never been in love. I'd never felt helpless against my emotions. You changed all that, and instead of grabbing hold of you, I sent you away. I'm so sorry, Samantha."

Pax once said that when someone said they were sorry, the proper response was "that's okay," but it didn't feel okay. "I understand."

He blew out a breath, and I figured this was where he'd say, "But . . ."

"I know why you didn't tell me you were pregnant. God . . . I brought this on myself." He cocked his head to the side, looking at me with anguish in his eyes. "Did you consider it?"

I nodded.

"But you didn't because I told you we couldn't see each other."

I nodded again.

"And this time we've been together, you didn't say anything because you thought I wanted to still keep us a secret."

"You said as much. But I meant it when I said I was going to tell you."

"Fucking hell." He ran his hands through his hair. "Were you going to tell me more?"

I acted like I didn't know what he was asking even though I suspected he wanted to know if I was going to tell him how I felt.

"I was going to tell you more."

That stopped me.

"I rushed home that night to tell you I loved you. That I'd always loved you."

My breath hitched and my arms uncrossed.

"Then I heard your father and . . . well . . . you know what happened." He stared at me for a long moment. "Did you . . . did you feel the same?"

"I did."

"I fucked it all up, didn't I?"

"Why are you here?" I couldn't figure out if he was simply apologizing or wanting something more. And if he wanted more, was I willing to risk my heart yet again?

He laughed. "I'm still selfish, aren't I? I rushed over here from the hospital after realizing what a prick I am so that I could put things right with you, and after five years of loving you, I didn't want to wait a second more."

"Love, Henry? How can you say you love me after everything?"

"I know. I don't blame you for being skeptical. But even when I was angry and hurt, my love for you was still there. God, Samantha, you're the only woman I've ever truly loved. The only woman I'll ever love."

My heart wanted to embrace his words, embrace him, but my fear kept me rooted in my spot.

"I know I've messed up and I've probably killed every good feeling you had toward me, but I love you and I want to earn your love again."

"How would things be different?"

"Because I've seen what life looks like without you, and it's unbearable. I may have been able to fool myself into thinking I could live without you, but I was only lying to myself. And it is different because Victoria knows and she thinks I'm an asshole for how I treated you, but she supports us, if you'd give me a chance."

"What about the business? What about your reputation?" It was a dumb question because the truth was out, but that didn't mean something else couldn't pop up that would have him pushing me away.

"Fuck 'em. I didn't know how empty my life was after I sent you away. Victoria kept telling me I worked too much, but what the hell was there to do otherwise? Only with you in my life was there joy and fun and excitement and something other than work." He let out a breath. "Look, I know that I don't deserve a third chance, but if you could let me prove it to you, you won't go through a single day without knowing how much I truly love you and Pax."

While his words impacted me, it was the emotion on his face, the truth of his words showing in his eyes that had me wanting to give in.

"What about what I did?"

"You did it because I was an asshole. A selfish, scared asshole. I understand—"

"But do you forgive me? Could you trust me?"

"Yes." He said it without hesitation. "And I'll earn your trust, Samantha. You'll see."

I stood quiet as a tug-of-war played between my heart and my head. Finally, I said, "I don't know . . . I just—"

"I get it. I've shown up in the middle of the night like a crazy man. You need to think about it. I'll leave you now."

I nodded, thinking that was the safest, smartest route. "Thank you, Henry."

"Okay, then. Goodnight, Samantha." He turned and walked toward the door. As he did, unease settled in my gut.

He opened the door, and the unease filtered up to my heart. Was I really going to let him go? He'd hurt me, but I'd hurt him too. He'd hid his feelings from me, but so I had I from him. Tonight, he laid his heart bare, but I was still hiding in fear.

"Wait, Henry."

He looked over his shoulder. "Is something wrong?"

Could I do this? If I did, would it be different? Could we finally have the love I'd yearned for since the moment I fell for him five years ago?

My love for him overpowered my fear. I rushed to him, throwing my arms around him.

His arms banded around me. "Please tell me this means you forgive me. That you're going to give me another chance."

She sniffled as she pulled her head back to look at me. "I forgive you, but I don't want this to be a chance. We do it or we don't."

He smiled. "We do it." He leaned in, his lips covering mine in the sweetest, tenderest kiss I'd ever had.

I remembered I hadn't told him my feelings. "I love you, Henry."

"I hope that's true."

"It is. I've always loved you."

He brushed my tears away. "I was such an idiot. A coward. But no more. I promise."

He kissed me again, and as he did, the past pain crumbled away, leaving the sweetness of love and hope for a future.

"I'd do anything to make love to you. Is it too soon?" he asked.

I laughed. "No. It's not too soon." I took his hand and led him upstairs and to my room. I closed and locked the door, and then Henry pulled me into his arms and kissed me. His hands caressed my body, but he wasn't in a hurry as the remnants of our clothing fell to the floor.

He stood back, his gaze running the length of my body. "You're so fucking beautiful, Samantha. You take my breath."

I pressed my palm to his cheek. "You make me feel beautiful. I love the way you look at me."

He kissed my palm. "Let me make love to you." He led me to the bed, and as his hands worshiped my body again, I realized that this time, we were truly making love. Sure, I'd loved him before and he'd apparently loved me, but it hadn't been out in the open. Our hearts hadn't been exposed.

I wondered if he felt the same as his fingers danced across my skin, exploring every inch of my body. His lips followed until I was a quivering mass of need.

"I need you." I reached for him.

"I'm right here, baby." He covered my body with his. He took my hand, lacing our fingers as he pulled them overhead. "Samantha."

I opened my eyes to find his filled with passion and love staring down on me.

"I love you." He pressed inside me, slowly, deliberately, until he was fully a part of me. Joined as one, the piece of my heart finally fused back together, the boundaries between us dissolved. He kissed me, and I felt like our souls had merged. Finally.

He withdrew, slid in, and the moment was perfection.

"Feel how much I love you," he murmured against my neck as he trailed kisses.

"Never let me go." I gripped his hands, vowing to never let him go. "Never."

As our bodies moved in perfect harmony, I felt like we were reclaiming a stolen part of ourselves. The faster he moved, the more whole I started to feel.

"Come for me, Samantha. Take me with you into heaven." He

picked up the pace. I moved with him. There'd always been a harmony to sex with us, but now we moved as one, chasing pleasure together.

30

Henry

There had been moments in the past when everything in the world felt right. Nearly all of them were with Samantha. But as I joined with her, a sense of perfection came over me. Like all the pieces of my life finally fell into place.

I closed my eyes, savoring the feel of her pulsing around my dick, her breath against my face, her ... all of her ... making me whole.

I didn't deserve her. I knew that now. If I was honest with myself, I knew it five years ago. Perhaps that was why I'd pushed her away. All I knew was that I was terrified of my own feelings, of how much power this woman had over me.

Today, I was smarter. I was ready to hand over all that I was to this woman. I wanted to commit my life to hers forever. I was lucky to have her forgiveness, but I hadn't earned her trust, and until then, I couldn't ask for forever.

I moved inside her, wanting to make love the entire night, but my body had other ideas. Together, she and I moved, faster, harder, reaching the pinnacle together, our breaths holding, our bodies going taut, until a final plunge and we soared.

Pleasure swept through me, sweet and pure.

"Henry."

Hearing my name on her lips sealed the deal. My heart was now full. "I love you."

I held her, intending to never let her go. I only moved to shift my weight off her. At her side, I pulled her close and kissed her temple. I wanted to stay the night. To wake up by her side. But again, that might be too much, too soon. And maybe she wouldn't want Pax to find us together.

"Do I need to go?"

She looked up at me, and I hated the way her breath hitched and her eyes turned wary.

"I don't want to go," I said quickly.

She relaxed in my arms. "No, you don't have to go. But I should unlock the door and we should get dressed. I don't want Pax to worry if he can't get to me."

She started to move, but I held her in place. "I'll do it." I rolled from bed, unlocking the bedroom door. I grabbed my boxer briefs, sliding them on. Then I picked up Samantha's pajamas and gave them to her.

When she dressed, I lay next to her again, holding her close. As I drifted to sleep, I vowed to never let her go.

MORNING LIGHT STREAMED through the curtains, casting a golden glow on Samantha's skin. I'd woken twenty minutes ago and simply lay, watching her, worried it was a dream, hoping it was real. Next to me, Samantha slept, looking like an angel, peaceful and beautiful. I gently brushed a strand of her blonde hair from her cheek, not wanting to disturb her.

"Are you living with us now?"

My head jerked to the side of the bed to find Pax looking at me. How long had he been there?

"Hey, Son." My heart swelled at the knowledge that we were a family—or would be as soon as I had Samantha's trust. "Hold on, okay?"

He nodded.

I slipped from bed, glad that Samantha was smart enough to suggest I cover up. I put on my slacks and shirt.

"Let's let your mom sleep, okay?" I took Pax's hand and led him out of the room. "Is Marie up?"

"She's making breakfast. Mommy usually helps me get dressed."

"I can help you."

I put the toothpaste on his toothbrush and counted, as he'd instructed me to do, to make sure he cleaned all his teeth. He combed his hair, missing the cowlick, but I decided it was okay. He was able to get into his clothes himself but needed help tying his shoes.

As we walked downstairs to breakfast, I sent a silent prayer that we'd have this nice, domestic life in the near future.

Marie did a double-take when I entered the kitchen. "Ah . . . welcome, Mr. Banion."

"Please, call me Henry."

"Okay, Henry. Will you be having eggs and toast too?"

"That would be lovely."

She had a sly smile on her face as she turned back to the stove. I took that to mean that she was on board with my being a part of Samantha and Pax's life.

THE WEEK that followed was a whirlwind of emotions and new experiences. Each day, I'd find myself at Samantha's mother's house in the evening, feeling more at home than ever before. The smell of fresh-baked cookies or a simmering pot of spaghetti sauce would greet me at the door, thanks to Marie. Pax would greet me by running into my arms and asking me to play. Since Samantha and I rode to and from work together, I spent the entire ride holding her, kissing her, and feeling like the luckiest man in the world.

One of my favorite parts of the day, besides lying next to Samantha, was dinner. When Victoria was young and my parents were alive, we had dinner together, but it always felt like an event. With Samantha and Pax and Marie, it was lively, full of laughter and warmth.

At work, Samantha continued to assess and offer feedback on my various news platforms. I had to threaten to fire Alan once when I walked in and found him disrespecting Samantha. She didn't like it but was enduring it until she could get her business off the ground. Once she told me that, I dedicated my time to helping her achieve that.

We also visited Victoria, Alex, and baby Hank one evening. Victoria nearly groveled as much as I had asking for Samantha's forgiveness at cutting her off. Samantha, of course, was gracious and apologized too for not telling the truth about Pax. Pax was confused about how Victoria was his sister, but he was tickled to know he was an uncle to little Hank.

As far as Samantha's father went, he was facing jail time and he had no leverage to get out of it. I hired Saint Security to make sure her father stayed away from us. As far as I was concerned, he was out of our lives forever.

The next week continued in much the same way—work, family dinners, and quiet moments with Samantha. Each morning, I would help Pax get ready for school, enjoying our newfound routine and the connection it brought. My world shifted, priorities rearranging themselves. Work was no longer the commanding force it once was. Instead, Samantha and Pax filled my thoughts and dreams. Each morning, I woke with the desire to be beside them, to hold them close and share our lives as a family. As I tied his shoes or zipped up his jacket, I daydreamed about a future with them, a life filled with love, laughter, and togetherness.

I did go to my house a few times to check in. While Knightly and Mrs. Tillis felt useless without me there, they were happy for me. I was happy too, except for one thing. I needed Samantha and Pax permanently with me. I couldn't be sure she fully trusted me, but I'd become impatient. I wanted it all.

I met with her in her office, reviewing her business model.

"This is good, but I wonder if you've considered offering a subscription plan. Regular audits, so to speak."

She considered it. "That's not a bad idea. Keep them coming back."

"Right. You generate a steadier income and potentially more referrals since people are getting regular input."

"Thank you. You know, if this billionaire publishing empire doesn't work, I could use someone like you."

Not caring that we were at work, I leaned over to her. "You can use me all you want."

"Why do I think we're not talking about business anymore?"

"Why Samantha, do you think I'm suggesting something untoward?"

She smirked. "Aren't you?"

I laughed. "What can I say? I can't stop wanting you."

Her smile was radiant. It told me that now was the time to make her mine forever. "How about we go to my place?"

"What about Pax?"

"How about you go and pick him up and meet me at my place? I have a surprise for you."

"I like surprises." Her hand slid down my thigh.

"Stop it, woman, you know I'm incapable of resisting you."

She laughed, and after a kiss, we left the office together.

When I arrived home, I headed straight to my office. "Is everything ready?"

"Of course," Knightly said.

"Good. Samantha and Pax should be here soon."

"Oh, I'll be so happy to see them again," Mrs. Tillis said.

And if I had my way, we'd see Samantha and Pax every day from now on.

I was waiting like a lovesick puppy for them to arrive. When they did, I muscled around Knightly to answer the door.

"Hi, Daddy." Pax rushed into my arms. I held him close, feeling grateful to have him in my life.

"Hi, Daddy," Samantha cooed in a way that made my dick twitch.

I arched a brow. "Not in front of the boy . . . you know that. I don't want to have to explain the bulge in my pants." I took her hand and led her to my office. "Come see your surprise."

"What are you up to?"

"Can I see too, Daddy?"

"Absolutely." I opened my office door and motioned for Samantha to go in.

She stood inside and looked around. "Have you been remodeling?"

"A little." I hadn't made too many changes over the last week. Only enough to make the space inviting and functional for Samantha. I took her hand again, turning her to me. "Victoria used to say I worked too much, and maybe I did, but what else was there to do? Now I know what else there is to do with you and Pax in my life."

Her eyes softened sweetly.

"So I don't need this space anymore. I was thinking it could be your space to run your business."

Her brows lifted. "What?"

I wasn't sure if her expression and comment were just surprise or perhaps disinterest. I shifted uncomfortably. "This could be your base of operations. It would save you on office space. You could work from home."

"Home?"

I still couldn't read her expression. Fear niggled in my gut. The urge to retreat grew. But I fought it. That instinct had done me wrong five years ago and recently. I wouldn't let it derail my happiness again.

I sucked in a breath. "I want you to move in with me . . . no . . . that's not right."

She cocked her head to the side in confusion.

I pulled the ring I'd bought from my pocket and dropped to one knee.

"What are you doing, Daddy?" Pax moved to me, looking at the ring.

"I'm trying to ask your mom to marry me. I'm a little nervous." I gave her a sheepish smile.

Her breath hitched.

"I'll ask." Pax looked up at Samantha. "Will you marry Daddy?"

She sniffed back tears as she nodded. "Yes. Yes, I'll marry Daddy."

Relief flooded through me like a tidal wave.

"What's marry?" Pax asked.

"It's when we become a family," I said, slipping the ring on her finger as I stood.

She didn't look at it. Instead, she pulled me to her in a hard hug.

"I love you, Samantha."

"I love you too."

"Can I hug too?"

I lifted Pax up and we all held each other.

"Aren't they lovely?" Mrs. Tillis said.

"Yes. I've brought the champagne," Knightly said.

"You planned all this?" Samantha asked.

I nodded. "Since the night you gave me another chance . . . well, not a chance. We do it or we don't. So we're doing it, right?"

"Yes. We're doing it."

I popped the cork on the champagne and served us all, Samantha, me, Knightly, Mrs. Tillis, and Caroline a glass. Pax got apple juice. We celebrated becoming a family. My house was finally going to be a home. It hadn't felt like home since Victoria moved out when she went to college.

We had dinner together, and for the first time, dining at home felt like a family affair, not a state dinner. So many firsts in my life. I hated that I'd wasted so much time.

After dinner, Samantha and I played with Pax until it was time for bed.

"Aw, but I don't wanna go to bed yet," Pax whined around a yawn.

"We have a busy day tomorrow moving you back into your room and planning the wedding," I said, carrying him to bed. "Do you like your room? Because we can change it."

"Can we have dinosaurs?" he asked as I helped him put his pajamas on.

"Yep. Whatever you want." Once his pajamas were on and his teeth were brushed, we both tucked Pax into bed.

"I thought you said sometimes mommies and daddies don't live together?" Pax asked as I pulled his blankets up.

"Sometimes they don't," Samantha said.

"But we do. Goodnight, Son."

"Goodnight, Daddy. Goodnight, Mommy."

"Goodnight, Pax." With a final kiss on his forehead, she met me at the door of Pax's room, closing it behind her.

Unable to wait, I pulled her close. "Tell me you're happy."

She looped her arms around me. "The happiest ever."

I brushed her hair back from her face. "I was such a coward to have pushed you away. I hate that I hurt you. I plan to spend my life making it up to you."

"How will you do that?" she teased.

"Whatever you want, it's yours."

"All I want is you, Henry. You and Pax. It was all I ever wanted."

Guilt burned deep in my gut. "You thought when I invited you to the Hamptons five years ago that I was going to say something different, didn't you?"

She nodded. "I was young and in love and naïve."

I shook my head. "I did love you then. I wanted all this even then. I just—"

"That was then. This is now. Now, we're together. Pax is here. Victoria and Alex are happy, and Hank is healthy. That's what you should focus on."

I took her hand, leading her to my room . . . our room. "Hank is a beautiful baby."

"He is."

"Do you want more kids?" I asked as I shut the door to my bedroom behind us.

"Do you?"

I arched a brow as I took her in my arms again. "Do you think I'm too old?"

"I don't. But you might not want the late-night feedings and—"

"I want all of it. I've always wanted all of it with you."

"Well, then . . ." She started to undress. "Do you want to start now?"

My dick was practically bursting through my slacks. The idea of implanting my seed, making life in her, was way more erotic than I'd have thought. Still.

"We can wait, if you'd like. You can get your business running."

She finished undressing, standing before me, one sexy curve after another. Her long, blonde hair hung full and wavy around her shoulders. "Didn't you hear? I can work from home."

"Still—"

"Didn't you just say that you found something to do besides work all the time? I have too, Henry. Does that mean I want to give up the idea of the business? No. But I think I can do both. I have done both . . . working and raising a child alone. Now I have help. There's Knightly and Mrs. Tillis and Caroline, and I'd like to keep Marie with us too."

"Absolutely. Whatever you want. It's yours."

"Then get undressed and make love to me, Henry."

She didn't have to tell me twice.

EPILOGUE

Samantha - One Year Later

"Happy birthday, Hank!"

The family stood around the table at Victoria and Alex's home as Victoria set a cake in front of a one-year-old Hank. He reached out to grab the cake.

"We need to blow the candle out first, sweetie." Victoria took his hand, and then she and Alex leaned over and blew out the single candle shaped into a number one. "Okay." She released Hank's hand, and he immediately grabbed a piece of cake.

"You're not supposed to do that," Pax said as he sat next to me.

"He's just a baby. And it's his first birthday, so he gets a little leeway."

What a difference a year made. On this day last year, I was at my lowest, and then everything turned around when Henry showed up in the middle of the night. He'd let go of all his hang-ups and fears, loving me and Pax full-throttle from that moment on.

Admittedly, I was nervous about allowing him into my life again, but as I watched him love us so fully, I couldn't help but do the same. A few weeks after he'd shown up on my doorstep, we were engaged. Having waited five years for an HEA, we married quickly and started working on giving Victoria and Pax another sibling right away. A month after we married, I learned I was pregnant again.

Henry was overjoyed to learn we were having a baby. "This is the first time I got someone pregnant on purpose."

I hadn't thought of that, but both Victoria and Pax hadn't been planned. "You're just too virile for your own good."

"You think so?" He waggled his brows.

"I know so." I gave him a sexy smile.

I left Henry's employment soon after, starting my own business run from my new office in Henry's—our—home. I had a client from day one. Granted, it was Henry. Not long after, Victoria hired me. Today, I had several clients, but not so many that I couldn't enjoy my family.

Life with Henry was beyond what I ever could have imagined. We laughed and loved all the time. He was engaged in raising Pax, so much so that Marie often felt like she had nothing to do. So, I moved her into being my assistant in the business.

My father tried a couple more attempts to screw with us, but Henry made sure once and for all that he'd leave us alone. With Alex's help, my father was buried in legal hassles that went well beyond his attempt to defraud me of my inheritance.

Two months ago, in the middle of the night, I poked Henry, lying next to me. "It's time."

He grunted. "Again?" He rolled over and reached for me. "Not that I'm complaining. I can get hard anytime you need."

I laughed. "Not sex, Henry. The baby."

I never saw a man move so fast. He was out of bed, slipping on his shoes and pants he'd left next to it like a fireman.

"Well . . . why are you still lying there?" he asked, his eyes a little crazed.

"I just need a minute." I rubbed my belly and breathed through the next contraction.

"Please don't have this baby here, Samantha."

When the cramping subsided, I rolled out of bed. "I won't. We have time."

Ten hours later, Gwendolyn Banion arrived in the world, pink and perfect. I wished my mother could have been here so baby Gwennie could know her namesake.

Speaking of which, as Victoria handed out pieces of cake, Gwennie let out a cry that had my milk filling my breasts.

"Looks like someone's hungry," Henry said, bringing her to me.

"Can she have cake?" Pax asked as I rose from my seat and took the baby.

"Not yet."

"You can have her piece," Victoria said, sliding a plate over toward Pax.

I shot her a look. "Are you going to hype your brother up on sugar?"

She grinned. "Isn't that what big sisters do?"

From the outside, our family probably seemed strange. I was married to my best friend's father and she was the sister of my children. Then there was the fact that she was married to Henry's best friend. But for us, we couldn't be happier.

"So, when are you having another one?" Henry asked Alex. "I sort of like being a grandfather."

Victoria arched a brow. "Hey. If you're ready for more babies, knock up your wife."

Henry winked at me. I was sure there was another child, maybe two, in our future. But not right now.

"I wouldn't mind having another," Alex said. "Should we get started?"

Henry winced, as I was sure Alex knew he would. It was one thing to talk about grandchildren. It was another for Henry's friend to talk about having sex with Henry's daughter.

AFTER THE PARTY, we headed home. Pax, as expected, was hyped up on sugar, so Henry roughhoused with him to burn off the energy.

Watching them together, laughing and playing, always filled my heart with awe. I was so grateful that we had finally found our place together.

I fed and put Gwennie down and then took a shower to rinse off the day. Not long after I'd stepped into the hot spray of water, Henry joined me.

"Pax is conked out," he said as he stepped behind me, running his hands up my abs and up to my breasts.

"You wore him out."

"He wore me out too." He pressed a kiss on my neck, his body against mine.

"You don't feel worn out." I rubbed my ass over his growing erection.

He laughed. "I've got one last hurrah in me for the night." He turned me in his arms and kissed me. "Tell me you're happy."

Every now and then, he'd say that, like he needed reassurance that he was doing what he'd vowed to do.

"The happiest. And you?"

"I couldn't be happier if I tried." His blue eyes studied me. "Sometimes, I have dreams that this isn't real."

"That sounds like a nightmare." I looped my arms around his neck and kissed his chest. "Does this feel real?"

He let out a soft groan. "As real as it gets."

I pressed my hand to his cheek. "I love you, Henry Banion. You have a wife who adores you, a son who thinks you make the sun rise, and a beautiful daughter."

He grinned. "I have it all. I don't deserve it—"

"You do. We all do."

"Sometimes, I still beat myself up about five years ago."

"Well, knock it off." I wrapped my hand around his dick, wanting to distract him. "There's no sense in doing that. Plus, who knows if we'd be here now if you'd done anything different? I don't know about you, but I feel like now is perfect."

He nodded. "Now is perfect. Or almost perfect."

I arched a brow. "Almost?"

He pressed me against the warm, wet tiles of the shower and lifted my leg over his hip. He settled his dick between my thighs and pressed in. Our moans of pleasure filled the bathroom. "Now is perfect," he murmured against my neck.

"Perfect," I agreed.

I hope you enjoyed Silver Fox's Secret Baby. And now... **you should definitely read Alex and Victoria's story.**

"Have you joined the Mile High club yet?"
"No..."
"Do you want to?"
I shouldn't have said yes... but I did.

Alex Sterling. My father's best friend... and my mile-high lover.

My father thinks I'm in danger and Alex is the best man to protect me. Maybe we'd both do a better job of staying out of harm's way... if we could keep our hands off each other.

But when our steamy encounters result in a baby bump, I know I have to hide the truth from my father... as well as his enemies who are still out to hurt me.

Except now it's not just me.
Get Mile High Baby here.

SEAL DADDIES NEXT DOOR (PREVIEW)

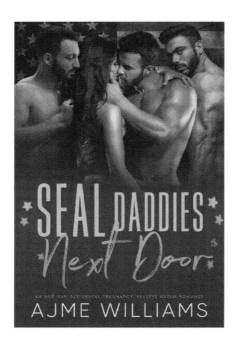

DESCRIPTION

**Becoming rich overnight led to a series of nightmares.
But the three *much* older Navy SEALs that entered my life as a
result were more like a fantasy come true.**

The electricity I feel with them makes me forget that the man who
surprisingly left me an inheritance has been murdered... *and I'm the
prime suspect.*

Reed, a protective single dad, has a rugged charm that could steal any
woman's heart.
Asher could cut glass with his razor-sharp features. Yes, he's
exceptionally strong but what draws me to him is his heart of gold.
Miguel has Spanish blood in him. His temper is unmatched, but
you'd never guess that when he cracks dad jokes.

These men fill my heart with joy... and my bed with heat.
My soul belongs to them, but do I even know who they really are?

Their traumatic past won't let them get too close to me, even though
the two pink lines on the stick bind us together.

I may not know who the dad is, but I'm taking a leap of faith.

They say I'm too innocent for my own good.

Am I naïve to think that I can trust them with my life, and with my baby?
Our baby?

1

_____

Juniper

2 *021*

Item one: go on a date before Mama chews my ears off.

Item two: don't say anything stupid on the date.

Item three: don't run away if he calls you sugar.

Item four: okay, maybe run away, but tell Mama you ran because you got a case of the collywobbles. Do not, I repeat, do not tell her the date went to pot.

I'd had it up to here with my mama telling me I was gonna die a "lil' ole spinster." It used to be cute about five years ago.

But now, at the tail-end of twenty-nine, it was like I had this massive time-bomb strapped to my chest, and it'd explode any second.

I could almost hear her southern drawl in the back of my ears. For context, most of our conversations flowed along the same pattern these days.

"Well, sugar, I was just wondering if you'd met any nice fellas lately."

"Oh, Lord. Here we go again."

"Now, don't you go getting all huffy on me, Juniper. I just want you to be happy."

"I'm perfectly happy, Mama. I don't need no man to make me happy."

"Now, that's just plain silly. Everybody needs somebody."

"I've got plenty of somebodies in my life, Mama. I've got my friends, my books, and that dratted cat who visits me now and then. I think he likes me more than he does his folks."

"I don't know about that. That cat's not gonna take you out to dinner or dance with you under the stars."

"I can take myself out to dinner, Mama. And as for dancing under the stars, well, I'll ask the cat. Who knows, maybe I could bribe him into it."

"Hey, Ms. Davis?"

I looked up, pen in my mouth, at the little kid standing in front of me.

"What is it, Janie?" I smiled at her. Cute kid.

"Well, ma'am, I was just wonderin' if it'd be alright if I kept holdin' onto that *Faraway Tree* book for a spell longer."

"I know I missed the due date and all, but it's just so dang good, and I got a heap of homework that's been eating up my time somethin' fierce.

"Could I maybe bring it back in four days or so, pretty please?"

Janie's tongue grew sweeter than the tea in front of me with each word she uttered.

Her eyes enlarged in a dual attempt to convince me she was an adorable little Dachshund and that I had to excuse the late return.

It never failed.

I covered my lips with my hand in a poor attempt to conceal my grin.

"Okay, Janie, but this is the last time. Do you promise to read to the younger kids next week in return?"

She bobbed her head of golden hair enthusiastically. "I do!"

"Good girl. Off you go."

It was an unseasonably warm day here in the heart of Oakmont, Georgia, but I wasn't complaining.

I sat behind the circulation desk of The Quill and Hearth Library, a place as whimsical as its name. We actually allowed patrons to sip on sweet tea while they read their books.

I enjoyed the slow heat and the bird-like chattering of children. I loved the lower level for this very reason. It was a wonderland for the little 'uns.

We had a storytime event later that day. I could count on the little regulars to show up and demand a new fairytale. I'd been studying up for it too.

Maybe I could just talk about how Rapunzel should have gone renegade and used her hair to whip the shit outta that evil woman who'd caged her.

Or maybe I was just mad because I'd had a pretty sour conversation with Mama not ten minutes ago.

Funny thing about people who adored you—they knew your cues.

They didn't need to say much, but oh, when they were positioning to attack you, and I mean verbally decimate your soul, all they needed was one word.

Or a line. Or a few of them. You get what I mean.

"You're about to hit the big three-o and still ain't got yourself a man. What the hell are you waiting for?"

"When you gonna find a beau who's worth his weight in grits?"

Ugh. She didn't need to tell me I was old and single. In fact, no one did. I could feel the life force between my legs drying up.

I tried to focus on the pretty little place that gave me so much joy.

Big windows let in buttery-yellow sunshine, and every nook and corner had a cozy reading space.

There were rows and rows of books, neatly arranged by subject and author and utterly orgasmic for my OCD-fueled mind. Hey, I was a girl who loved her lists and her shelves.

You wanted fun? You had to have a method to it.

I let out a satisfied sigh as a ray of light fell most becomingly over the dark wooden shelves. They looked lush as a lover's embrace, a comfortable in-between of secrets and safety.

My job was to make sure this place remained as calm as it looked.

Easier said than done when I was always around kids.

I couldn't help chuckling as I heard a "'squee'" from their section. Some newbies had to have found a new adventure. That's why we turn to books anyway, right?

We couldn't physically be everywhere all at once. But in the library, you could train your mind to take you wherever you wanted to go.

You could even get married to the fanciest Prince Charming. Not that it would ease my mama's heart.

Life was good in Oakmont, though, all things considered. As they said around here, "If you don't like the weather, just wait five minutes."

And I didn't mind sticking around longer. Better than going home to nothing. I could call Sadie or one of the girls.

I just didn't want another pity party today. Hell, I'd get enough of it in a week when I actually hit the big three-o.

Bam!

I jumped up from my desk to investigate the source of the loud crash. On crossing two rows, I found a group of kids who'd built a fort out of picture books.

They were all hooting and hollering, running around as if they were facing down an army of monsters.

I could hear one of them, a scrappy little boy with a missing tooth, shouting, "Y'all ain't gonna beat us! We got the strongest fort in all of Oakmont!"

Another little girl, a bandana wrapped around her head like a pirate, squealed in her tiny voice, "We'll see about that! We're gonna knock that fort down and take all your treasure!"

The boy with the missing tooth turned to me with a big smile and said, "Hey, Junie. Wanna join our army and help us beat the bad guys?"

I bit back a laugh and replied, "Well, I don't know if I have what it takes to be a soldier, but I sure can cheer you on!"

The kids all laughed and kept on battling, and I stood there a little while, basking in the warmth of their innocence.

They'd gone and made a whole little world inside the library. Anything was possible, and the only limit was their imagination.

Suddenly, my eye fell on a dark-haired boy standing some rows away and eyeing the tyrant group with sad, dog-like adoration.

I walked over to him and knelt down. "Hey there, what's your name? Are you new here?"

He shot me a furtive look before nodding. "Yep. I'm Billy. I came to get an action book."

I looked him up and down, and my gut instinct kicked in.

"How'd you like something with more adventure and magic? We're doing a reading of *The Hobbit* soon. Wanna stick around for that?"

He blushed. "Ah . . . I don't think I can."

"Why not?"

He shuffled his feet and looked down at the floor. "I . . . my dad says magic is for little sissy girls, and I need to be a man."

Ah. Of course his dad said that.

I pursed my lips together and thought for a second before replying.

"Well, little Billy, what do you want to read?"

His face was immediately lit by hope. He looked like a sunny day. You know, the kind where trees sway gently in the breeze and leaves rustle softly in the wind. You look overhead and see a brilliant shade of blue, with just a few straggly clouds drifting lazily. It's everything you hope for, especially if it's hurricane season and you don't know what the next moment holds.

"I'd love to read magic books," Billy mumbled, "but I know my dad won't be happy about that."

"Where's your dad right now?"

"He's at work. He said my nanny will come pick me up after one."

"What if we make ourselves a little secret? You stick around for *The Hobbit* readin', and I'll treat you to a good ol' fashioned fairy tale 'bout a Wishing Chair that can take you anywhere you want to go.

Why don't you give it a try and see how it makes you feel? Don't let your dad be the one callin' the shots all the time, now."

The hope that burst across that little face made my heart churn. Man, I was sure his dad loved him, but fathers could be assholes sometimes.

But then again, at least his one stuck around. Mine wasn't even there to see me get born.

"You won't tell on me?"

I made a three-finger salute. "Scout's honor."

After Billy pottered away to join the other kids, I made my way to the history section. I was doing a bit of reading about the Ku Klux Klan, and it caught my interest.

This fascination had begun the very night I finished my tenth re-read of *Gone With The Wind.* Say what you would, but I'd never get enough of O'Hara and her damned gumption.

I was neck-deep in the Civil War era when I felt a gentle tap on my shoulder. Turning, I smiled. "Hey, Harold. Here for some history?"

"No, I just came to meet you. And I saw you getting that young'un into trouble!"

Harold Montgomery, sixty-something, missing two teeth (one he'd retouched in gold), and as eccentric as a pink-haired lady driving a blue Cadillac.

He'd become my friend over the last six months. I'd met him when he was scouring through the Civil War section, looking for titles on ancestry.

We got on like a house on fire, so to speak. It was actually funny, the things we had in common.

I squared my shoulders defensively. "Ain't no one telling a kid that they can't have their fairy tales. The world will mess 'em up soon enough. Let 'em be young while they can."

Harold chuckled. "Young lady, I have no complaints. In fact, I think you did the right thing. The father deserves a sentence for trying to deprive his son!"

I relaxed. "Maybe I could go all Avenger on him."

He walked with me to the counter. "What are you doing tonight?"

Nothing. I was just gonna go home and sit on the back patio in a pair of pajamas with my mama's quilted throw over me. I'd probably bury my face in a tub of bourbon pecan ice cream straight from the tub with extra bourbon and maybe a drizzle of dark chocolate.

A perfect dinner for a single lady on the verge of discovering her first gray hairs.

In all fairness, this dinner would pass muster with my mama.

She approved of a lot about me, even some parts that could make others run the instant I opened my mouth.

Harold probably surmised the extent of my evening adventures from the dreamy look on my face.

"I can see you're getting distracted, so I'll be quick. I'm hosting a dinner at my mansion. I want you there."

My eyes bulged. No way.

Nestled amid old oaks and magnolias in the very heart of Oakmont's historic district, the Montgomery mansion had become the stuff of local legend.

The house itself was a masterpiece of Antebellum architecture with its grand columns and sweeping porches, but it was the rumors that made me uneasy.

It was common hearsay that Harold's ancestors were all members of the Klan, and they'd even used the house as a meeting place during the Civil War.

Some even whispered that the hidden rooms and secret tunnels beneath the mansion housed the Klan's loot.

But despite what I'd heard, I believed my heart more.

Harold was a gentle soul, always ready with a smile and a kind word for his neighbors.

Sadie used to tell me it'd take him a lifetime to undo the reputation of his ancestors, but you had to give a man props for trying.

He continued surveying my face like I was some fascinating archaeological artifact. Or a gecko.

"So, what's it gonna be?"

I smiled. "Will you have bourbon pecan ice cream for dessert?"

Why did he look so relieved, like he *needed* me to be there?

His Southern drawl came through immediately, although he'd spent almost his entire life out of the country and in London.

Harold wasn't one for convention—it seemed to hurt his soul.

But in moments like these, he was as Southern as the rest of us.

"Bless your heart for sayin' yes. I reckon this shindig is gonna open doors for you. It's gonna be like a lit matchstick, sparkin' up a whole new flame in your life."

Well, bless his heart too. What in tarnation did that mean?

2

Juniper

I unlocked the door to my lonely, single life.

Okay, I totally did not mean to sound that bitter. At least I had my own little space in Oakmont's central precinct.

Magnolia Street was home to my quaint apartment, filled with charming brick buildings and old-world trees.

I stepped in through the front door and immediately found myself surrounded by the warm glow of the setting sun. It cast a soft halo of light across my living room.

The neighborhood cat, Bumbles, was already snoozing out on the balcony, his furry body stretched out on the cushion I'd left for him.

This was the fourth night he'd stayed with me. I knew the neighbors were gonna say I'd kept him high on catnip.

From my window, I could see a pair of graceful egrets flying toward a nearby marsh.

A group of chatty cardinals hopped along the branches of my old friend, the oak I'd named, well, Mr. Oakwood Hardy.

Yes, not all was bitter about this place. It was small, and there were days I wished I could open the door and shout, "What's for dinner?" but . . . it was okay.

I was okay.

Sighing, I made myself more sweet tea and settled down on the sofa with a new list. The sound of a distant train whistle floated through the open window.

My phone drawled out a lazy tune. I looked at the name on the screen and groaned.

"Hey, Mama."

"June bug! How about you come on back to the nest and let Mama feed ya? I'm fixin' to fry up some chicken."

My mouth watered at the words. No one could make fried chicken like my mama. Juicy and tender, it exemplified Sunday meals with her.

She did mashed potatoes and gravy, collard greens and corn-bread . . . the whole nine yards.

I loved to soak up the gravy and potatoes in the bread and do a perfect bite with a bit of everything.

But again, after I moved out, my mama's invitations to dinner became more and more of a call to an unavoidable war.

She'd feed me and bombard me with questions I had no clear answers to.

Some of them weren't all that bad—like what kids I'd met at the library or what Sadie's husband was doing.

The moment she moved to Sadie's husband, she'd redirect to ask me when I'd catch my own.

Like this was an unavoidable bout of a new strain of COVID that I just had to have.

I sighed and shook my head, almost picturing her crestfallen face.

"Mama, I'd love to, but I can't tonight."

"Oh?"

It was plain as day that her curiosity had been piqued by my words, as I could hear the telltale lilt in her voice.

Lord have mercy. I reckoned I could've phrased that a mite bit better.

No doubt she'd be fixing to inquire about my plans and whether there were any fine gentlemen involved in them.

"You headed out with a good-lookin' fella tonight?"

Talk about hitting the nail straight on my own fuckin' head.

"No, Mama. No date. I just got an invite to this fancy dinner."

"Where?"

I hesitated for a second. My mama, like all the old-timers in this city, did not trust men with a tarnished reputation—even if this reputation had nothing to do with them, per se.

They could be golden, but if there was one black sheep in the family, it meant they had a little devil in them.

Plus, my mama hated Harold Montgomery.

I honestly had no idea why. It began the day he met me in the library and insisted on dropping me home. In his Aston Martin DB11.

At the time, I was still living with Mama. I'd only moved to this place about twenty days ago, mostly because I wanted to be able to walk to work. And I felt like I was getting too old to share space with someone I loved but who also drove me nuts.

Mama took one look at him and told me never to see him again.

I didn't push it then, and I didn't want to push it now. But I was never good at one thing when it came to her. I didn't lie to her. I couldn't.

Not when that's what she'd known the entirety of her life before I came along. That's all she had from the one other person she loved—the one who got away.

"Harold Montgomery's party, Mama."

She sounded like she'd choked on a peach.

"Hell no, Junie! You're not going to that man's house! You know what they say about that place and the secrets? You know his ancestors used to torture others to get money and loot their jewels, right? Why do you want to associate yourself with that?"

Why did I, actually? Apart from the obvious curiosity I had about the house, there was just something so affable about Harold.

He was old and weathered and sweet. He talked to me like he really cared and wanted to be part of my life, even if it was just a sliver.

That meant something.

"Mama." I spoke sotto voce. "Harold's tried to undo all that his entire life. Maybe we could just give him a chance."

"Child, I ain't givin' no man like that the time of day, and neither should you. Don't you remember what I done told you about your daddy? You gotta be strong, just like your Mama. You hear me?"

Okay. Not the way I'd hoped this would go. Against my better judgment, a swell of bitterness rose inside me.

"Mama, I don't want to have this conversation. Not when I've asked you about Dad so many times and got nothing back."

"Honey, you know good and well he was nothin' but pure evil. The second he found out I was carryin' you, he up and left without a second thought."

And you've never let me forget it.

"I'm sorry I'm such an inconvenience." I spoke sharply. "But I'm old enough to make my own decisions. I understand you may not agree with them, but I hope you'll care enough to respect them, anyway."

"Junie, now you listen to me—"

I hung up.

Oh, I'd never hear the end of this. But I'd deal with her temper and tears tomorrow. I knew she meant well.

But even I got tired of being made to feel like I was responsible for her never getting married.

All I ever knew about my dad was that he was super rich, and his folks told him he could either be livin' in the boonies with my mom or he'd have to leave her and return to his roots.

No points for guessing what he chose.

I wanted to make peace with it. But that was damn hard when the topic kept cropping up like an unrelenting tide of heat poking like nails on my skin.

My phone rang again. I just flipped that switch to silent and high-tailed it outta there.

I reckoned I needed to blow off some steam, so I went to dump a bucket of ice-cold water over my head.

By the time I got out, it was already sundown. The buttery glow of the last rays of amber sunlight had melted into soft pinks and purples against a deep blue sky.

My invite said I needed to be at the party by nine, so I took some time to gussy up.

Hell, I'd be a Southern belle ready to stir up some trouble at that party.

I slipped into a ruby red cocktail dress, feeling like a hot tamale in a sea of ice cubes.

The entire next hour saw me hurling a tirade of cuss words as I tried my best to coax my curls into shape. I managed to tease my hair up high and let it fall in loose, beachy waves around my shoulders.

I could have sworn Dolly Parton would be proud of that hairdo.

The figure smiling back from the mirror was all curves, gentle, swaying, and redolent of summer scents. And I loved it.

I loved every stretch mark woven like lightning on my skin, each freckle and meander and wrinkle.

It had taken me years to come to this place where I was learning to fall in love with myself. I'd spent two decades on the other side.

Then, two heartbreaks and a side of controversy later, I realized I could spend all my life at war with myself, but it would never make living any easier.

And I didn't want to remember myself that way. When I turned gray and crocheted my way into retirement, I wanted good memories.

This was me making those happen.

I finished by adding just the right amount of sparkle to make my eyes pop and my lips pout. With that, I strode into the living room and immediately regretted my decision.

You ever been around an introvert?

You know, that special breed of people who get excited to make plans and then immediately run out of social battery the second the plans are about to begin?

Yup, that was me.

Too late to back out. My Uber had already arrived.

I stepped out of my apartment, suddenly feeling like a toad in a dress. Thankfully, my Uber driver, Hank, was an angel.

"Howdy, Ms. Davis. I'll be your Uber driver for the evening. You look pretty as a peach in that red dress!"

I chuckled. "Thank you kindly, Hank. You sure do have a way with words."

As the ride began, I lost myself in the easy ramblings of Hank's thick drawl and the sights I saw on the way.

Old oak trees blurred into a bouquet of brown, green, and yellow draped in a soft evening wind and Spanish moss.

Every brick building here had something that tied it to the remnants of life from the Civil War era.

I leaned back and sighed. "I don't think I'll ever be able to live anywhere else but the South."

Hank cleared his throat. "Well, speakin' of living here. A few years ago, I was driving this very car when all of a sudden, I hit a pothole so deep it swallowed my tire. I was stuck there on the side of the road, wondering what to do. That's when a bunch of good ol' boys in a pickup truck pulled up beside me and asked if I needed help. And you know what they did? They pulled out a rope, tied it around the car, and yanked me outta that pothole like it was nothin'!"

"Only in the South, right?"

Hank grinned. "You got that right, Miss Juniper. We may have our share of potholes, but we sure do know how to help each other out."

Before I knew it, the easy ride brought me to the drop-off leading up to the main door of the Montgomery mansion.

The pathway was lined with lights and an abundance of heady flowers. I followed a trail of guests to the door.

A tall, silver-haired figure stood at the threshold.

He looked like a direct import from England. Like he'd been flown in after a long-standing decade of serving the Queen herself.

"Name, please?"

"Ha!"

Why did I say that? Why was I so awkward? I wished the marble floors would just swallow me whole.

"I mean . . ." I fumbled, trying not to let his hawk-like eyes pierce through me. "I'm Juniper. Juniper Davis."

He took a minute to go over the names on the list he held in his hands. A very agonizing minute.

Maybe this was some joke Harold had played on me?

I nearly turned and pulled a Cinderella before he spoke again, his tone cold as day-old turkey right outta the freezer.

"Welcome to the Riviera party, Ms. Davis. You may go through to the salon."

"Thanks, you too."

Before I could give him the chance to throw me out for the stupidest comeback ever, I ran into the salon.

I was immediately bombarded by an onslaught of people in clothes worth more than my year's salary.

On any other day, I'd curse myself for being a social anomaly, but right now, I was absolutely blown away by the opulence of the interior.

The entire salon could have swallowed my apartment, with ceilings so high they could go on forever. Tall windows, rich, warm walls, and ornate moldings were everywhere.

I meandered through the room, but not before I overheard a conversation between two guests.

"My dear, it comes as no surprise that Mr. Montgomery has spared no expense for this evening's affair."

"I hear he's preparing to make a rather momentous announcement. No doubt, an attempt to conceal the origins of his vast wealth."

"Truly, the Montgomery family has a dubious reputation in certain circles. There are whispers of thievery and deceit."

"I have heard tales of a scandalous affair involving Mr. Montgomery and a woman of questionable reputation in his younger days."

"It is quite clear that he is a man with many secrets."

They turned around and saw me, and one of them—a big ol' fella in a fancy vest, his eye accentuated by a ridiculous monocle, scowled.

I took off running quicker than a spooked hen.

Trying to shake off the heaviness of the air, I approached a group of people near the bar.

"Hey there," I said, raising my voice and giving in to the sudden burst of social energy. "What's everyone drinking?"

One of the men in the group turned to me and grinned. "Whiskey, of course. We're in the south, honey. What else would we be drinking?"

I chuckled and shook my head. "I shoulda known better. Make mine a double."

A few drinks later, my bladder had a mind of its own. I rushed out of the salon and found myself in a maze of a corridor. Where the hell was the washroom?

I was about to give up when one of the doors burst open and Harold stormed out, his face red, angry, and unlike anything I'd ever seen before.

Something made me hide behind the wall opposite the room.

A young man followed him his hands bunched into fists.

"You're gonna regret this. You hear me?"

I realized I knew his face. And it was one of the few things I wanted to forget most in the world.

End of preview. *Get the entire story here.*

ABOUT THE AUTHOR

Ajme Williams writes emotional, angsty contemporary romance. All her books can be enjoyed as full length, standalone romances and are FREE to read in Kindle Unlimited .

Books do not have to be read in order.

Heart of Hope Series
Our Last Chance | An Irish Affair | So Wrong | Imperfect Love | Eight Long Years | Friends to Lovers | The One and Only | Best Friend's Brother | Maybe It's Fate | Gone Too Far | Christmas with Brother's Best Friend | Fighting for US | Against All Odds | Hoping to Score | Thankful for Us | The Vegas Bluff | 365 Days | Meant to Be | Mile High Baby | Silver Fox's Secret Baby

The Why Choose Haremland (Reverse Harem Series - this series)
Protecting Their Princess | Protecting Her Secret | Unwrapping their Christmas Present | Cupid Strikes... 3 Times | Their Easter Bunny | SEAL Daddies Next Door | Naughty Lessons

High Stakes

Bet On It | A Friendly Wager | Triple or Nothing | Press Your Luck

Billionaire Secrets
Twin Secrets | Just A Sham | Let's Start Over | The Baby Contract | Too Complicated

Dominant Bosses
His Rules | His Desires | His Needs | His Punishments | His Secret

Strong Brothers
Say Yes to Love | Giving In to Love | Wrong to Love You | Hate to Love You

Fake Marriage Series
Accidental Love | Accidental Baby | Accidental Affair | Accidental Meeting

Irresistible Billionaires
Admit You Miss Me | Admit You Love Me | Admit You Want Me | Admit You Need Me

Check out Ajme's full Amazon catalogue here.

Join her VIP NL here.

WANT MORE AJME WILLIAMS?

Join my no spam mailing list here.

You'll only be sent emails about my new releases, extended epilogues, deleted scenes and occasional FREE books.

Printed in Great Britain
by Amazon